flying

A Peacock Springs Novel

Jordana Blake

just vibes media, llc

To my fellow late-diagnosed neurodivergent ladies:
Please keep showing up as you are. It would be terribly boring here
without you.

And to Lyle, for loving and liking me and my weird brain.

dear reader

The following story is the product of my undying love for TV and movies of the late 1990s and early 2000s. Lily's story reflects common experiences of late-diagnosed ADHD in women, including my own ADHD that went undetected until my 30s.

When reading from Lily's POV, please keep in mind that she's learning to manage rejection sensitivity dysphoria (RSD) and emotional dysregulation. Detailed information on ADHD in girls and women can be found on my website.

Additionally, the story includes open door sex scenes, reference to marriage immediately after high school that ends in cheating and divorce, toxic family dynamics, minor verbal abuse, and the use of alcohol and cannabis.

Please be kind to your mind.

Love,

Jordana

WELCOME TO
Peacock Springs, New Jersey
Coffee Crumbs
Beagle's Bagels
Salvatore Butchery
Town Hall
Pru's Tarot & Tea
Mechanic
The Stocks
Main Street
Library
Public Square
Rosie's
Pages
Miss Nicole's School of Dance
Bangor Drive
Grant's Condos
Curl Up & Dye
Cottage
Veterinarian
Yale Court
Dragon Fly Lane
Dry Cleaners
The Featherweight
Independence Way
Delaware River

the dicktionary
cum see our (pea)cocks

labor day weekend

one
Lily

"THERE IS nobody I would come back to this stupid fucking state for but Stef. Yes, Delia. I'm on my way."

Pete, my spunky Shiba Inu, is desperately trying to get his snout through the cracked window of my Wrangler.

"Rude," Nessa Rabin shouts in the background of the call.

Stef, Nessa, Delia, and I have been a tight-knit group since middle school, at least in theory. I've been traveling for the last decade, and even thinking about coming home makes anxiety bubble inside me.

"I mean, obviously if it was either of you…" I trail off. I'm overexplaining myself. Again. This is Nessa. She is teasing me. But with so much happening, the instinct is hard to control.

The four of us couldn't be more different now that we're grown, but that doesn't change our history. Today, Stefanie Santos Manolo is bright and sunny, full of love. Delia Shane is always making things more beautiful. Nessa Rabin may be the smartest person in any room, and then there's me.

"Hello, Lily Long, you still here?" Delia asks.

I shake my head, forcing the intrusive thoughts away. "No, no, I'm still here. Sorry. What?"

"Where are you now?" She huffs out the words. I can always count on her not to put up with my deflecting.

"Um, on the way." I attempt to sidestep the question. I want to show up for Stef's birthday-slash-surprise-proposal party, but I'd prefer to avoid my hometown—Peacock Springs, New Jersey—almost as much. It's been nearly a decade since I was briefly married, divorced, and then disowned by my parents. The town is full of ghosts, the whole lot of them causing a tug-of-war inside me. I can't get myself to commit to a plan.

"Yes, you've said that. Let's make this simpler. Are you delaying because you're worried about how you left things at home?" Nessa asks. "Are you afraid that there's not going to be a weird festival every month or town meetings about nonsense?" she teases, trying to disarm me.

I snort. "Festivals? Quirky artists and family values somehow in a blender? Gossip? Weird double standards? It's been ten years, not ten million. I expect it'll be pretty much the same..." I trail off, biting my lip.

"Delia, I'm off the clock," Nessa practically yells. "You can be the therapist for our dear avoidant friend. Maybe you can get her to at least tell us where she was when she left for this road trip home."

"Um." I pet Pete's auburn flank, focusing on the way his fur feels beneath my hand to steady myself. But a horn blares and startles me, and I end up yanking the wheel. My hands are shaking and I can't get enough air into my lungs. I can't multitask right now. Not safely at least. "Holy shit." My rising anxiety over the upcoming weekend has made me too scattered. "Deals, sorry, traffic swerved," I pant.

There are too many tabs open in my brain, as usual. Each demands too much of my attention, though none are as loud or clear as Nessa's voice. "Planning to sleep in the Jeep?" she asks. "I'm going to bed and I'm not letting you in if you don't give me an idea of what time you'll be here. Don't wake me up. Nighty-night."

Delia sighs. "I'll put the key under the mat in case you show up overnight. You still know where, right? My grandma's old place on Dragonfly Lane."

"Thank you. I'll probably get in tomorrow." It's a lie. I'm almost there, but if I tell them that, then change my mind, they'll never let me go. This way, I have the option of faking a flat tire in the middle of Pennsylvania or a dead engine in Virginia. Then *oopsie, sorry*. I love my friends more than words, but my hometown is haunted.

"Listen, gals." There's another big blast of a horn as a clusterfuck of cars merges from the I-95 NJ Turnpike to every connecting highway in Central Jersey. "I don't want to get in an accident, so I need to focus. I'll be there. I swear." I cross my fingers as I talk, as if that means anything as an adult.

We say our goodbyes, and I hang up wondering why I can't just go to their place.

Their house isn't the only option either. I could message Seth Whitter or River Hendrix. Either would probably let me stay, even if Seth would grumble about it and River might worry about our parents' friendship. If they're even still friends. I don't know who my parents are friends with anymore.

With each passing mile, the voices in my head multiply, the busybodies' idle chatter getting louder and louder. With sweat dripping down my back, I peer at myself in the rearview mirror, noting how pink my face has become.

I peel off my sweatshirt in hopes of cooling off. If I don't get my heart rate under control, I'll be in trouble, so it's time to try deep breathing, then maybe move to repeating over and over that I can do anything I set my mind to.

Unfortunately, none of it quells the anxiety growing inside me as I get closer to a place I've actively avoided for a decade. There's a good chance that something or someone will make me snap. Or cry. Or both. So much for being a yogi and master meditator. It is during moments like this that I miss the taste of a cigarette.

If I was into gambling, I would place bets on how quickly the unwanted comments, questions, passive-aggressive compliments, and stares will start. This is a small town, after all. Gossip is a currency.

Once we hit the party, I have to contend with the queen herself: Stef's mom, Susan. I can practically hear her in my head.

Lily, you poor thing. No one serious since the divorce? Have you seen your mom yet? Belinda is so sad that she hasn't heard from you. I hope you will try to make things right with her. You only get one mother, you know. Truly, you should try to make amends with the people you've hurt. At least you had the decency to show up for Stef and Lee. Well, anyway, enjoy the salmon puffs.

All the while, I will bite my tongue and stew, coming up with all the responses I wish I was brave enough to use. I haven't found my voice yet, not when it comes to the adults from my childhood.

A few miles down the road, my phone rings again. This time Stef's photo flashes. It's a favorite of mine. The two of us as fifteen years old, all long limbs with knobby elbows, braces, and matching gym shorts and school mascot T-shirts.

"Hey, I can't talk now. Everything okay?" I blurt out, my voice a little too high.

"Yeah," she replies slowly, drawing out the word like she can sense my anxiety. "Are *you* okay?"

No, I am not okay. No, I cannot lie to you. So, no, I cannot stay on the phone.

"Oh yeah, you know me, always on the move. I'm navigating the Wrangler through unfamiliar territory. Can I call you when I'm parked?" There. That sounded almost believable.

"Duh, you didn't have to pick up. I want to make sure we video chat before the party Lee insisted on having at the Featherweight. It's this weekend." Dropping to a whisper, she adds, "He's being weird, Lil."

In the background, a door closes. Then Lee is calling, "Babe, I'm back with dinner."

Relief engulfs me. Saved by the freaking bell.

"Okay, I gotta go, but we better talk. Soon." She hurries off the call before I can accidentally spill any secrets.

A university bus, empty of the usual caffeine-riddled twenty-somethings, nearly takes off my right side-view mirror.

"Welcome back to Central Jersey, babe," I mutter, causing Pete to tilt his head. "Welcome to you, too, little pup," I add, giving him another pat.

The image of New Jersey most visualize is nothing like the place I am talking about. This isn't the crowded shore houses or the industrial airport. Central Jersey is a unique landscape, made up of farms and sprawling fields of grass. It's close to both New York and Philadelphia, meaning neighbors root for either city's team or argue about whether a local favorite breakfast sandwich is called a Taylor Ham or a pork roll egg and cheese.

Despite the deep anxiety pulsing in my ears, a hint of comfort swirls through me. It's the sensation home always brings with it. All that being said, I've accepted my fate: there is no way I'm entering Peacock Springs as anything but a sweaty, anxious mess.

two
River

AT THAT SAME TIME

"WE'RE ALL SET. Don't stress." I clap Lee's shoulder. The move is meant to reassure him, though I can't imagine anyone not being stressed before proposing. Not that I have ever gotten close. Hell, I haven't dated anyone for half as long as he and Stef have been together.

"Easy for you to say." He shakes out his sandy blond hair. It hangs a bit longer than usual. From his clean-shaven chiseled jawline to the hint of trouble in his bright blue eyes, he looks like the quarterback type. "Once she says yes, George River Hendrix, best bar owner in town, will you serve as co-best man alongside her brother? I'm not sure how often we'll see Mateo before the wedding."

"I'm the only bar owner, but yes. I'd be honored." I smile wide, all the while burying the anxiety that rolls through me. The last time I was the best man at a wedding, I was standing beside my former friend Grant Morgan while he and Lily Long said "I do."

He gives me a man hug, and as if he's reading my thoughts,

says, "Did Delia tell you? I'm at seventy-thirty odds that Lily Long makes her first appearance in Peacock Springs since high school." Grinning, he claps my shoulder and mimics the reassurance I just gave him. "We're all set. Like you said, nothing to stress over."

My stomach somersaults and I step back. Turning away, I take a deep breath, grasping for even a hint of composure, then grab his takeout order from the kitchen window. I shove the bag into Lee's hands. "Go home and feed Stef. I'll walk you out."

She might come back, my mind shrieks. Those familiar pangs of longing warring with self-loathing flood my system. *I should have stopped the wedding. This is my fault.*

"Go. Get out of here. I need to check that the AC is on." I wave at the door.

He scans the dining area, probably noting the moving fans and blowing vents, but he doesn't call me on the lie.

With a nod, he turns and strides out.

Lily Long could be here, my mind continues to scream as my body burns up.

three
Lily

MY STOMACH IS RUMBLING, and soon the strip malls and diners I'm passing will turn to fields and farms. Pulling off at a twenty-four-hour diner checks two boxes: it delays my arrival and gives me the opportunity to eat. Gosh, I've missed these Jersey staples. I scoop Pete up, then wander to the front door, where a uniformed woman is scowling, as if doing her job and seating me is an inconvenience.

"Do you have pet-friendly seating?" I ask, donning my friendliest smile.

"Back patio. You'll have to walk around," she mutters, not bothering to look at Pete's bright red vest and the emotional support animal patches sewn onto it.

With a nod of thanks, I put Pete on the sidewalk and guide him around the building. He may have the ESA vest, but I'm not sure it was done legally. As a traveling fitness instructor and influencer, I've had the honor of working with many amazing women-owned brands. Unfortunately, I've spent my fair share of time with women like Raven, the spoiled woman who booked a Japan trip for the fashion content and dog photos, then abandoned her pup on the tarmac at LAX. Luckily, we'd gotten close by the end of the trip, probably because I kept sneaking him sushi under the table. I took the lost boy and called him Peter Pan.

Once I'm seated out back, I watch the employees move like they're performing a dance. A server brings me a glass of water as well as a full bowl. Then he tells me he'll be right back. I open the large laminated menu and squint when the pages reflect light from the sun dipping overhead.

When the server returns, I order. "Disco fries, please. And any chance you can grill up a burger patty for the dog?"

With any luck, the greasy fries smothered in gravy and melted cheese will be a balm on my nerves. If not, at least I'll get the hit of nostalgia that comes with scarfing down food I can only get in my home state.

The man jots down my request using fast strokes of a clicky pen. Then with a wink, he promises to let me know if there's any issue getting the food for Pete. After a few minutes, he returns with a steamy plate of fries and a small plate with a single burger patty on it.

"That going to be it tonight, miss?" He's now leaned over the back of an extra chair.

"Probably not, but I can't decide. Can I hold on to this for now?" I hold up the menu.

"This is America. You can do anything you want," he cajoles.

I laugh reflexively.

He has a little bit of a fun uncle vibe, his easiness draining the tension from my shoulders. When he's gone, my mind wanders, imagining the conversations going on at the other tables.

At a nearby table, a pair of high schoolers sits. I'd guess they're discussing the start of their senior year, college applications, and how this is going to be the best year ever. The conversation continues after plates are cleared, and the two of them hold hands across the table while making intense eye contact. They remind me so much of who I was the last time I was home. Back when I was young and in love. Excited about the future my ex-husband and I dreamed up together.

I toss a fry back at the basket, just the thought of Grant Morgan making my blood boil.

Part of me wants to run over and warn the teen girl not to turn out like me. But that would be too impulsive and outgoing, even for me.

Instead, I have the conversation in my head. It's probably safer this way.

What would I do if I was meeting high school Lily? Time-travel movies always warn us not to mess with the future, but I think I would say something to my younger self. *Run, girl. You are in danger. Also, start wearing sunscreen immediately.*

If some woman who looked a lot like me approached like that, would I even have listened?

I hope so, but would I be who I am now if I hadn't gone through the chaotic marriage? If he hadn't cheated? If I hadn't left?

"Oh, Petey, what am I going to do? It's been a decade. These people don't know me anymore." My chest tightens. "Did they ever? Yeah, the girls will be excited to see me. But... they will complain too. They will argue that I'm here now and that it's all ancient history, so I should just come back."

"Sorry, did you ask me to come back?" the server asks, suddenly at my side.

"Thanks, I'll just take the check." The words have barely left my mouth before the black folio is dropped on the table. I double the cost and slip the cash in to ease my guilt. I barely ordered anything, yet I sat here for a long time.

Though it doesn't feel like long enough. Standing, I raise my arms and stretch, forcing my shoulders away from my ears. The tension is back. Exhaling, I will my muscles to relax. It's no use.

Noticing a nearby park, I lead Pete in that direction. Maybe a short stroll will do the trick.

We meander for a bit, always keeping the car in my line of sight so I don't get turned around.

When Pete finds the perfect little patch of grass and does his scratch-and-spin move that tells me that he's ready to do his business, I confirm that I have a biodegradable bag in my pocket, then sigh and look up at the sky. The soft blue shade with sporadic big white fluffy clouds flying overhead is picture perfect. I set up to take a few selfies once he's finished and note the rolling gray-blue clouds behind me. Lowering my phone, I turn and get a good look.

In late summer that can only mean one thing: an early evening thunderstorm to cool off the day.

I use the bag to clean up after Pete, ready to rush back to the car and avoid the weather. Naturally, Pete decides to live up to the mischief his breed is loved for. Playing like he's going to pounce at me, he crouches low, tail wagging, and gives a stubborn smile.

I ask, command, cajole, yank the leash. When I move in to scoop him up, he scoots away. I guess Pete wants to delay things too, but I'd prefer to do it while dry.

A drop of rain lands on my cheek. Another on my arm. I glance back at the storm again. Dammit. Already, it's pouring behind me. Thankfully the loud thunderclap scares Pete into my arms, and I haul ass to the car.

"Yes, we made it in the nick of time," I say as I dive into the driver's seat, as though he understands me. The rain pelts my car seconds later, making it nearly impossible to see out the windshield. The visibility is so bad that I'm not sure I can safely get back on the road. Thank you, Mother Nature.

———

AFTER DOOM-SCROLLING MY SOCIALS, I let all of my nervous thoughts spill to the dog. "I know I was chaos from eighteen to twenty…" I trail off with an exhale.

He does a head tilt. It's typical of the breed, but it makes him appear skeptical.

"Eight. Twenty-eight. Fine. I'm chaos and so are you," I tease, scratching between his ears.

He smiles, panting, his tongue hanging out, his eyes full of unconditional love.

Pete licks a long line up my face, a telltale sign that he's anxious. We're twin statues of fear, rising as the summer thunderstorm swells. The bleak gray clouds and water streaks mirror how I feel: Foggy. Filtered. Inauthentic.

"I don't want to go back to Peacock Springs." I huff. "But I want to support Stef like she supports me. It's the right thing to do." As the rain comes down, my thoughts bounce from my loyalty to Stef and my desire to stay away from my parents and ex-husband and back again. Finally the storm settles inside my mind and outside the windshield.

Looking at the dashboard, I grumble, "Fuck, it's really late, and I don't want to sleep in the car." If I don't get on the road and knock out the last hour of the drive, I won't make it before Nessa is asleep. I fire up the engine and pull out of the parking lot to continue the miserable drive.

four
Lily

THE ROADS to Peacock Springs are winding, and as I pass by the fields where we used to throw parties, memories I haven't thought about in ages pop up.

Grant and I first kissed at one of those parties. Delia was never sure about him, and River, my best friend, pulled away from me, but he did get closer to Grant, so I assumed it was some sort of boy code. Stef and I would giggle while Nessa would ask endless questions about dating and kissing and so much more. Seth would sit off to the side with a book and a beer clearly pilfered from the Featherweight. We were good kids for the most part, but like most teenagers, we liked to let loose now and then.

I cross Independence Way, a busier suburban street, then Dragonfly Lane and Yale Court. The familiar green signs with white letters stand tall and proud on silver poles as I weave my way through the neighborhood and pass the schools. Outside of a once-familiar house on Bangor Drive, I pull to a stop.

Under the cloak of night, I'm shielded from view, but from here, the tiny Tudor seems to be as I left it. Mom's flowerbeds are neat and trim. Dad has kept the lawn meticulous as always. The maroon sedan in the driveway leads me to believe that Mom still gets the garage spot. There are no lights on, which makes sense, given that it's nearing midnight. I sit, staring, unsure of why I'm even here.

Closing my eyes, I envision myself here that last night.

———

TEN YEARS AGO

THE STRONG SCENT of black tea with lemon and honey permeates the air while the mug warms my hands. I'm shivering despite the warm spring evening. The last twenty-four hours have been hellish.

"You'll go back tomorrow and apologize," Mom informs me sternly. "You'll tell him that you forgive the infidelity and that you'll never let his needs go unmet again. Then you'll be sure to show him how sorry you are."

"Are you really suggesting that it's my fault that Grant cheated on me?" I wrap my arms across my body.

"Lily, do not argue with your mother" is all Dad contributes. As usual.

"Daddy? Really?" I'm on the verge of tears as the two people I hoped would take my side poke more holes in this awful situation.

Early one morning, I used his computer to check my email and was greeted by an incoming text message. Landan Sherman, town darling, naked and thanking my husband for the previous night.

"Next, you'll go to James Kelly and create a plan to make things right after disrupting the Fairy Folk Fest," my mom goes on. "You owe it to the town business committee. They've scheduled an emergency meeting tonight," she says primly, ignoring my question.

The committee meets at the Featherweight. Maybe one of my friends is working and can give me the scoop.

I nod along. "I'll consider it, Mom." That's the closest I'll come to agreeing.

With that, I stand and leave. With nowhere else to go, I guess I'll head back to the condo. The place no longer feels like my home, but I don't have a choice. I'm eighteen years old, I've been married for seven months, and I don't have a job. I'm not even going to school.

I'm stuck in an awful condo in need of repairs that Grant's dad gifted us. Grant has been promising to fix it up. Someday. Until then, I'm here playing house while he plays college hockey bro and uses the space for parties. Weekend after weekend, red Solo cups full of cheap alcohol and skunked beers litter every surface. I've gotten one part of the college experience, I guess.

As I leave my parents' house, I text River. With any luck, he worked tonight and overheard something. I'm pulling up to the condo when my phone rings.

"Hey," I answer.

"Hey. Listen," River says, his voice low, "you need to pack your things and head out of town. Just until things get sorted and people cool off."

My stomach sinks. "What do you mean?" I sit back in my seat, staring at the black ring of grass in the front yard from the tiny fire I set this morning. After the sexy text message came through, I snapped, and I set his hockey gear and some signed Wayne Gretzky thing on fire on the lawn.

"Where are you?" he asks, his words quick and anxious.

"Scene of the crime, technically," I answer with a ridiculous giggle.

"Stay put," he orders me. "I'll be right there.

This is the most forceful I've ever heard him, so I do as he says.

A few short minutes later, River jogs over, dressed in his usual jeans and bar tee. He pauses briefly, his attention drifting over me, before pulling me into a firm hug. The kind he hasn't given me since Grant and I started to date.

"Is something wrong?" I ask as he holds me a little too tight, his body trembling.

"Please. You need to pack up and go," he murmurs into my hair. "The town council is going to sentence you to the stocks. I was working, so I don't have all the details, but I do know you'll have to spend a day dressed up in old timey garb with your ankles locked in the stocks." Pulling back, he grasps my arms. "You should go to Nessa's or Stef's dorm. Visit a college. Think about what *you* want for yourself. Give it a week or two, and they'll calm down." His eyes swim with pain as he surveys me like he doesn't quite believe they will.

All I can do is I wrap my arms around his torso, bury my face in his chest, and let my tears fall.

"Thank you, I miss you," I choke out.

TODAY

I **PRESS** my forehead to the steering wheel, missing the closeness I shared with River. Maybe I should have called him on my way. We've reconnected from time to time, usually over a social media chat, only to have things fizzle out. One of us gets busy and can't respond as often. Then days turn into weeks, and they turn into months. Then the cycle starts over again. I care about him, really. He's one of the best friends I've ever had. It's just that when a person is out of my sight, they can fall out of mind too. Unless I'm obsessing. River lives in this comfortable middle ground. He's a consistently inconsistent piece of my life.

As I pull away from the curb in front of my parents' house,

curiosity gets the better of me and I head toward the square. I want to see for myself whether there's any evidence of the fire ten years later. I head toward Main Street and park on the far side, away from those damn stocks, meaning I'm closer to the salon, Curl Up & Dye, and the Featherweight.

Across the square, the glimmering golden peacock statue outside town hall catches my eye. Even in the dark, it's hard to miss. The grassy town center is infamous for the peacock habitat. Thankfully, it looks like the birds are locked in the housing enclosure tonight. For the eighteen years I lived here, they were notorious for breaking out and starting trouble.

Like a peacock's train, there are vibrant pops of color everywhere, the buildings decorated in deep blue, green, and purple with gold accents.

Pete scratches at the door and whines, so I leash him and take him for a walk so he can relieve himself. Like I knew he would, he pulls me toward the vet's office and bird habitat, his sniffer already working overtime.

"Those damn stocks are still up in front of town hall," I grumble as we meander a diagonal path that runs beside the bird enclosure. The flower shop sits on the south side of the square, along with Seth's family's bookstore and the center of town gossip: the salon. Across the way on the north side are the library and a fitness studio where I took dance as a girl. Between the studio and the vet sits the condo. Grant's condo. And the second level of nearly all the businesses are apartments owned by the Morgan family.

The entire west side of the square is taken up by River Hendrix's family. The Featherweight bar & restaurant inside a giant Victorian home that has been home to the town meeting point for more than two hundred years. Along with it is an abandoned back cottage and acreage that leads to the riverbank.

Lost in my own thoughts, wandering aimlessly, I smack into a large solid object and bounce back.

Head tilted up I discover the object is actually a person. Male. Very male. Dressed in a dark T-shirt, a pair of jeans, and well-worn work boots.

He grasps my arms, steadying me, his warm and callused palms sending a zap of electricity through me. Dragging my focus up, I take in the thick dusting of soft dark brown hair along his exposed forearms, then the rougher hair along his chin and cheeks. With the glow of the streetlamp behind him, I can't make out his features.

I glance back down to Pete, who has wound himself around us at the ankles, his leash tethering this mystery man to me.

He smells like pine and leather, his scent purely masculine. He guides me a couple of shuffle steps, careful we don't stumble and fall, toward the lamplight.

Only then do the blue-green eyes register. The lines around them are new, but I'd recognize the shape and color anywhere.

"River?" I ask, the single word barely audible.

five
River

"LILY?" I blink once, then again.

Lily is home, walking a dog in the park, after midnight.

It takes longer than it should for the details to click in my brain, and when they do, I mentally facepalm myself. *This* is what Lee was talking about when he picked up dinner.

Of course. Lily would never miss Lee's proposal. She and Stef have always been close, and their connection only grew when Stef took her in when she left Grant. Lily lived with Stef for a few months before heading to California.

From there, she went off the grid. The rumor was she worked on a pot farm as a trimmer. Months later, she showed up online in full force, decked out in spandex and teaching yoga and fitness classes virtually. She built a following and traveled as a fitness influencer.

The dog is familiar. She documented their trip back from Japan a few years ago.

Though that doesn't temper my excitement at all. *Reel it in, dude.* I need to contain myself. Here I am, almost thirty years old and acting as giddy as I was at fourteen.

"Hi, old friend." I smile down at her. My body is noticing

things before my brain catches up. My hands are still on her, our chests only inches apart, her heat radiating into me. Her breath softly skims my shoulder, that simple act creating far more of a reaction than I could have ever imagined.

In seconds, the restraints around our legs loosen. The dog is still sniffing and walking, and luckily, he is freeing us in the process.

Once we can put some space between us, I release Lily and offer my palm to the dog to sniff. He gives it a quick survey, though he quickly moves on, hooking his front legs around one of mine and humping my calf. The tension that has built over the last sixty seconds ends when Lily breaks into a giant smile followed by an exuberant giggle.

"River," she says, eyes dancing, "meet Peter Pan. It looks like you have an admirer."

"Peter Pan?" I guffaw. "Does that mean he's asking me to be one of his lost boys?"

Shaking my leg gently, I free myself from Peter Pan's clutches. Then I scoop Lily into a hug and lift her off the ground.

For one glorious moment, I think I've saved myself from my semi, but when her soft curves press against me and I inhale the scent of chamomile tea and lavender on her skin, I find myself dangerously close to a full-on boner. She smells heavenly. Fuck, this is too much. Setting her on her feet, I recite the 1990 New York Giants roster hoping thoughts of Lawrence Taylor will kill any boners.

It is probably wishful thinking on my part, but I swear her cheeks go pink as she studies me. Trying to reclaim the days of comfortable companionship, I extend my hand and offer to give her the updated tour.

"Didn't you hear?" I tease as we start down the sidewalk, bumping her shoulder with mine. "Mayor Jim Kelly has asked me to take the midnight shift to protect our town from former residents."

"Mayor Jim Kelly?" she asks, brows in her hairline. "As in…"

"Yep. The same Jim Kelly who told your mom about the party planned for when she was out of town."

"That bastard." she nearly shouts. Eyes widening, she slaps a hand over her mouth, still holding the leather leash.

"James Kelly retired and put his son on the ticket. Your former high school nemesis is the town vet and mayor. You may want to play nice for Pete's sake."

She groans, and every one of my senses tingles.

"For *Pete's sake?*" I tease. "Come on, you have to admit that was funny."

I guide her toward the Featherweight and stop at the front gate. The original iron fencing and archway greet us.

"Welcome to the Featherweight," I say. "Owned and operated by yours truly for two years now." My chest swells with pride as I sweep my arm out, gesturing her for to follow me.

It's been a lifelong dream to be trusted with my birthright. I'm the oldest son, a George—though I've always gone by my middle name—just like my father and his father before him. Each George has run the family business. I can't mess this up. It's too important. We survived prohibition and have produced whiskey on-site for over a century. If I play my cards right, I'll one day find myself handing the keys over to my own son or daughter.

"I started to dabble with some small batch beer this summer," I ramble as we take the path to the front porch.

"That's exciting. So what's on tap?" she asks.

Everything feels so simple. Easy. Our friendship began the fateful day Miss Sainz paired us up for fourth-grade reading and language arts. From there, Lily became a near permanent fixture in my life. She convinced me to quiet down and listen when necessary, cheered me on, and laughed at my jokes. Our moms became friends too, and that was sort of it. Until Grant.

Ever since Grant, I've had a pit in my stomach. I've been holding on to a secret that eats at me. One I don't want to tell her now, not wanting to ruin the night. *You knew at the bachelor party that he was in love with someone else. You didn't stop the wedding. It's your fault this happened to her.* My brain is lecturing me like it does often, but I stuff the guilt down, hoping to enjoy this moment here. Now.

"As you recall, six generations of men named George Hendrix have been the proprietors of this fine establishment."

As we walk along the pebbled path, I point at the enormous Queen Anne Victorian estate, using my best tour guide voice.

"In typical fashion for the era, there's a series of hedges lining the wrought iron fencing. The archway we passed through is covered with climbing rose bushes, still in bloom, despite it being the end of the season." I watch her face as we approach the house, giddy to take in her reaction to the transformations. "Here, the newly added entryway is the perfect spot to host your next garden party. Even at night, the place is well lit by Edison bulbs strung between posts." At the end of the path, we near the porch that leads to the biggest renovations.

"The exterior was updated last summer. The wraparound porch has been refurbished to allow the wood grains to show, giving the place authentic charm. The house itself was repainted a crisp white, with each of the intricately carved details along the trim, latticework, and railings boasting the colors of our town's mascot: the peacock. All things in historic Peacock Springs downtown are, of course, a mix of white, gold, emerald green, sapphire blue, and deep amethyst." I tip an imaginary cap at her.

Lily's melodic laughter causes me to smile, childishly gleeful that she's really *here*. Maybe before the weekend is over, I can close the distance in our friendship and regain the right to call her out of the blue. Maybe I can finally tell her about the past.

My gut clenches. *No, that's silly. Telling her will only hurt her.*

"What good would this town be if any of these buildings were decorated with warm colors, or neutrals," she teases back.

"Neutrals? Psha! Look here: a large white porch swing rocks

gently in the breeze, and the espresso-colored wooden ceiling fan moves slowly in tandem." I sway as if I'm illustrating the point.

"You're wild, River." She chuckles.

"Hey, I am extremely proud of the ambiance I've created." My chest tightens. "This place has really become part of the tourist revival around here."

Pausing on the steps, she turns and surveys the grounds, lips parted and eyes filled with awe. I can't wait for her to see it in the daylight. Right now, the darkness is hiding the true splendor of the gardens in front and river views out back.

"I love what I've done with the place. It's nice to show it off." Shrugging, I open the heavy wood door and wave a hand to invite her inside.

six
Lily

RIVER CONTINUES to fill me in on updates, going on a little too much about seamlessly blended floor stain.

I approach the familiar hostess stand and break into a playful grin. "Just the bar today, thanks," I say as if I'm a patron. With a wink at River, I walk with Pete through the space. Halfway to the bar, I call over my shoulder to him. "He's a service dog, I swear."

He ignores that comment, continuing his tour. His lack of response makes my stomach tighten. Dammit, I want this to be easier.

"If you recall, these were once separate rooms, but we hired Tom to open the pace up. And above us," he points, tipping his head back, "there are large beams that connect to all these shelves. Plus, the cutouts allow people to set drinks down during busy nights, and event planners to put out more decor. It's worked out nicely."

He's so excited that his voice speeds up as we walk. His animated tour is adorable. I just need to get out of my head to enjoy it.

"Library still here?" I arch a brow. God, we spent hours eating French fries and working on homework together in there.

He dips his chin. "I kept both of the private rooms," River confirms. "The old study and the library. They work well for dinner parties and small group meetings, which is great for business."

While I belly up to the bar, he rounds it, bringing down an array of items and leafing through the menus. I'm lost in thought, checking out all the newness mixed with the familiar, when he asks me a question I'm not prepared for.

"How are your folks? Are you staying with them this weekend?" His tone is casual, and he's in bartender mode, flipping a white dishrag over his shoulder, a move he must do hundreds of times each day.

My heart slows and I focus on doing one of those grounding exercises I teach to stave off the dizziness taking over.

Name something you can see.

I see a glass of water. He must have set it in front of me while I zoned out.

What is something you feel?

I put a hand on the drink, relishing the coolness of the glass.

What do you hear?

Beside me, Pete shakes his head, making the tags on his collar jingle.

What do you taste?

I sip the cold water, the liquid coating my tongue and throat. It doesn't taste like much, but I'm coming back to the present.

"I'm, uh. I'm not really in touch with them," I say, breaking into a sweat. "I don't—I don't know. Belinda and Neal." I snap my mouth closed. I call my parents by their first names, though I've only done that for the last few years, so he may not know that. "Uh, my folks kind of cut me off when everything went down." Head lowered, I take a deep breath. "You remember how you told me to get out ahead of the whole sitting in the stocks thing?"

River nods, fidgeting with the towel now.

"Actually, how about that drink?" I'm far too anxious to get through this conversation without some liquid courage.

"This is my papa's moonshine, it's strong, so let me mix something up for you," he says.

Before he can, I take the mason jar and gulp a hefty amount down. It burns my throat and makes my eyes water, but I don't mind. It's the shock to my system I need to broach this topic.

"This is so uncomfortable." Avoiding River's gaze, I stare at Pete, who is roaming the floor. "I tried, I swear." Without looking at him, I return the jar to the polished wood bar. "They took Grant's side, and as far as I know, that hasn't changed. About eight years ago I offered to come home for the holidays. Belinda said that I destroyed her family, and if I wasn't willing to right my wrongs, then I wasn't her daughter. Neal…" I pause. I don't even know what to say about him.

Silently, he slides the jar to his side of the bar.

"Eventually, I realized that family isn't all it's cracked up to be. But Stef's more than family, so I'm here. Barkeep." I tap the bar twice with a shaky hand. "Refill please."

"You sure?" he murmurs.

With a nod, I snag the moonshine out of his hand and throw back another gulp. Next time I will wait for him to mix it into something more flavorful.

"Will you be the first to taste test something I've been putting together for the party?" he asks, his head bowed sheepishly, as he plucks a clean jar from the counter behind him.

Quickly, he gets to work, and in less than a minute, he's sliding a new jar my way.

"This is pink. Very pink." I swirl it and bring it to my nose for a sniff.

"I call it the blushing bride. It's made with a bunch of ingredients from local farms. It's a hard cherry-herb lemonade. The moonshine gives it a kick. What do you think?"

"This is amazing," I chirp, unable to keep from grinning.

These bouncing moods are so familiar to me that I don't notice them much anymore, but right now all I am doing is noticing things. I'll tuck that away for later and roll with it.

"What did you include here? Tell me everything," I ask, leaning forward on the bar.

The question moves River off the subject of the Long family drama and allows me to push all of those awful feelings back into the box I locked them in long ago. The issues that come with being in the same zip code as my biological donors are things tomorrow's Lily can tackle.

"Its base is Papa's moonshine, along with cherry lemonade, basil-mint syrup, and a little soda water for bubbles. It felt like Stef. Traditional meets off-beat. The lemon slices reminded me of how sunny her personality is, and the cherries are from Michigan, so they're a little nod to Lee."

"And how they met at school in the Midwest. I love it, she will love it. This is amazing," I say, picking up my glass for another taste.

I finish the drink quickly, and as the buzz kicks in, everything feels a little softer. This town is weird, sure, but most of the time it's the wonderful kind of offbeat that's perfect for inspiring art and food, and it brings people together. The regular town meetings and festivals bring out all kinds of characters, making for great people watching and daydreaming.

Frankly, even sitting in the stocks, like I would have been sentenced to had I stuck around, sounds as hilarious as it is horrible.

Even back then, it wasn't the punishment itself that bothered me; people volunteer to wear historical costumes and serve time for tourists plenty. Shifts are short, the stocks aren't actually locked, and you get to sit on a bench and watch the festival take place.

No, what got to me was that my family believed my reaction to Grant's infidelity was worse than what he did. It was the way that he went right back to Landan. The way no one faulted her for the affair either. It was the realization that I was disposable to everyone I thought loved me.

"Hit me, barkeep." I say.

River winces, the look telling me the words were more of a shout than a request. "Easy there, tiger. This stuff is deceptively strong. You should wait," he says.

Waiting has never been my strength.

I hop off the barstool and walk around the bar to get a refill for myself.

seven
River

I AM MESMERIZED by her curves, the slender muscles she's currently using to fight her way toward the shaker with the rest of the batch of blushing bride. It's half full, since I intended to pour myself. Placing it on a high shelf did nothing to help the situation. Because with Lily on tiptoe, I can't stop myself from taking in the curve of her calves, her lean legs, and that full round ass I can't help but want to grab.

Despite her previous push to avoid the subject of her parents, she's part way through her third drink, and anger is slowly rising behind her somber dark eyes.

"I made it clear that we couldn't keep doing that, and if that's all they could say to me, then I wouldn't come back." She shakes her head, focus fixed on her sandal-clad feet. "I think they were honestly relieved to be done with me. They haven't tried to contact me since."

The rage, sadness, grief, anxiety, and self-loathing that flowed through this confession were hard to watch. I regret asking. I should have known better.

Reaching out, I brush my fingers over her soft wrist. "I'm sorry. I shouldn't have asked."

"Going *all* the way back to your *original* original question," she says, her words slurred, "Delia left the key out. Just need to walk Pete and me, Pete and I? Pete? Over there. I'll crash on the couch." She lists to one side, the words coming out quickly, like her every thought is making its way out of her mouth. "Or... I'll grab my tent and camp? Nessa said if I wake her, she'll do bodily harm, and I don't know that I can be quiet enough... so, yeah, camping it is." She sways and grabs for the leash but misses it completely.

"Absolutely not," I say as she tries to snag it again. "You know as well as I do there's a perfectly good apartment upstairs. You'll stay here. I doubt you can walk to the girls' house like this anyway." It comes out a bit harsher than I intend, but she doesn't seem to notice, or she doesn't seem to mind. Either way, bossing her around like that is strangely satisfying. And it's stirred up feelings that have no business being associated with the difficult topic we've covered this evening. I take the car keys from her hand and make a mental note to grab her things once she's asleep.

She takes a deep breath, inhaling with her mouth but exhaling through her nose quietly. Her cheeks are still dusted with light brown freckles, her face the same heart shape I remember, but the familiar flecks of reddish-brown are gone from her irises. Her pupils are blown out, suggesting she's aroused, drunk, or simply afraid to be back. As her chest heaves with each breath, she rolls her shoulders, causing her long waves of chocolate and caramel hair to shift slightly. She's debating something. It's written all over her face. Then, out of nowhere, she slides past me around to the customer side of the bar, and immediately stumbles over a chair.

"Race ya." She smirks over her shoulder, then darts for the stairs. She slows, however, to run her fingers along the golden fleur-de-lis wallpaper. She's beautiful like this, expression soft as she admires the way the light plays off the gilded design.

Pete passes her and starts up the steps, snagging her attention, and she follows him stride for stride, like this is part of their nightly routine.

Entering the apartment, I find Pete curled up on the couch in a little ball. Lily, on the other hand, has torn her shirt off already. She's wrestling with the crisscross straps of her sports bra, huffing and grunting with each twist.

As much as I'd love to see her naked, this isn't how I plan to go about it. So I turn away, though not before I catch a glimpse of a shadow along her ribs. Does she have a tattoo?

I drag a dresser drawer open and grab an oversized bar T-shirt, then toss it toward her without looking. I refuse to lower myself to crassly taking something not actually given to me.

"You can look." She giggles a moment later.

I turn to find her wearing the shirt like a dress with her pants around her ankles. When she sways, I'm convinced she's going to trip herself, so I stride over and put an arm around her waist. As I guide her toward my bed, her warmth radiates into me.

Eyelids heavy, she says, "I can take the couch. This is your home."

"Nah. Guests get the bed. In you go." I guide her onto the mattress the way I've done for many friends who've found themselves too drunk to drive home over the years.

Once she's safe and lying down, I settle on the couch. On the nights I close, it takes a while to unwind, but tonight, with Lily so close, I'm not sure how I could possibly relax into sleep. Her lavender and chamomile scent lingers around me, and it takes everything in me to fight back a host of inappropriate thoughts about the woman—

She snaps up straight, then scrambles out of bed and rushes by me.

"Wait. Lil, where are you going?" I jog down the steps behind her, careful to close the door to keep Pete inside the apartment.

"I didn't try your beer! I wanted to hear about it. Shit!" She rounds the corner. There's a soft knocking sound, then a few stumbling steps.

Fearing the worst, I pick up the pace, though my muscles relax when I discover her sitting on the barstool from earlier in one piece.

"You need your sleep. Come on," I gently encourage her.

"No sleep. I'm fine. Great. Wonderful." Her reply is husky, thick with sleep. "Fan-fucking-tastic," she whispers, probably thinking I can't hear her, her head lowering toward the bar. "I'm so happy to be home. This is a brilliant idea. I'm not going to regret this." She slumps lower, her cheek now pressed to the lacquered wood, and the grumbling fades into a snore.

I scoop her up—one arm under her knees and another behind her back, then climb the steps up to the apartment. After she's tucked in again, I change into gym shorts and a clean tee. As I'm pulling the shirt over my head, I hear the soft sounds of crying muffled under the comforter.

Lily has been on her own for the last decade, and while her friends love her dearly, her lifestyle has put her on the fringes. I'm not surprised she's home for the proposal, though I hadn't thought about how hard it would be to come back. A failed marriage is one thing, but add in her parents' behavior, and it's a recipe for disaster. I kneel next to her on the bed, close to her curled up form, and run a hand through her hair and down her back.

In a hushed tone, I make a vow. One I wish I'd had the backbone to make at nineteen.

"No matter what, I'll make this okay. I'll catch you if you fall."

A lump forms in my throat, and my eyes heat. "We are so happy you're here. Just wait till you see the girls and Seth tomorrow. We won't let them treat you like that anymore." When her breathing has evened out, I stand and turn for the couch.

She grasps my arm and tugs with more force that she should possess this drunk and half asleep. "Please stay. Just hold me. Please." She sniffles. "Nobody just holds me."

Fuck. My chest aches painfully, those words burning themselves into my brain so I'll never forget them.

With a sigh, I peel back the covers and join her, wrapping my arms tightly around her middle and guiding her to rest her head on my chest.

I am holding Lily. My Lily. In my bed. My head spins a little. The girl I spent hours playing pirate adventures with, who made me actually read our assignments, is here, in my arms. The girl I crushed on through middle and high school. I've always longed to have her here. Mine. In every possible way.

Then the unhappy truth creeps into my thoughts. This is Lily. The woman I allowed to have her heart broken by Grant. I've always loved her from afar, but could she love me back if she knew? Could she forgive me for not stopping the wedding? I don't know that I can forgive myself.

For now, at least I can comfort her. I can hold her without expecting anything more. I can help her. I can protect her tonight.

In the moonlight, with her familiar face smoothed out by sleep like this, she looks peaceful. While I can't see those coffee brown eyes, I know they have a fire behind them, and soft vulnerability too. Every line and divot fascinates me, and her breath ghosting over my chest sends shivers down my spine.

"I want to live in this moment forever," I whisper into the night as I brush a lock of hair from her face.

In return, she sighs and her brow relaxes further. Her arms tighten around me, as if she is agreeing, if only for this night.

eight

Lily

A PAINFULLY BRIGHT streak of light cuts into the room, waking me. I roll over with a groan, smacking into a set of firm abs and a smattering of coarse hair.

Eyes still closed to the brightness, I allow myself to doze, and despite one part of my brain knowing the figure beside me isn't Pete, I find myself lightly stroking the hair, relishing the comfort it brings.

My head is pounding, but the events of last night slowly come back to me: the diner, driving into Peacock Springs, and drinks with River. Right, River.

My eyes pop open, and rather than finding Pete at my side, I'm met with a broad chest. Shit. Turns out I'm not petting my dog. I'm petting River's chest and stomach.

He's dressed in a pair of soft gym shorts. Nothing else. *Fuck, he's so cute... but he's so... this town.*

Snatching my hand away, I squeeze my eyes shut, feigning sleep. But it's futile when I'm a walking, talking wardrobe malfunction. Or maybe it's my body that's malfunctioning. The elastic of my low-impact sports bra cuts into my ribs and my underwear is wedged firmly between my cheeks.

I could crawl out of my skin just thinking about the day ahead. It was going to be hard no matter what, but add in the hangover? *Fuck.* Hoping I can adjust my pants and panties without waking River, I slip my hand around to my back, but rather than finding my flared leggings—yoga pants, whatever they are called today— I'm met with bare skin. *What?*

Cringing, I crack one eye open. Only then do I discover I have an audience for this uncomfortable self-assessment. River is propped against the headboard, displaying his strong chest dusted in a heavy coat of brown hair. His torso and arms look toned, from how physical his job is rather than in a gym-made way. His pointed jawline is covered in a scruffy brown beard that stretches to his wide and defined cheekbones. The body and facial hair, the heavy set of his brow, and the smattering of crow's feet have morphed the boy I once knew into a man. An achingly handsome man.

Sitting up, I pull the large T-shirt to keep my lower half covered and look down. The navy fabric is soft and well worn, with white academic-style letters reading *Featherweight Boxing Club est. 1866.* Below the words is a set of boxing gloves.

"Thank you?" I ask, giving my bedmate an awkward smile.

"You're welcome?" he teases, repeating my tone.

"Um, so about last night." I'm anxious and have no desire to know what a fool I made of myself.

"You were drunk, but you didn't do anything weird. And you didn't get sick," he assures me. "I bring our friends up after a night of drinking pretty regularly. Nothing to stress about. Well, you did drop your pants and throw your arms out and sing *ta-da!* to prove the shirt is a dress," he teases.

Cheeks burning, I grab a pillow and toss it over his face.

I want to be angry, but the most I can manage is mild irritation.

He excuses himself to the bathroom to get cleaned up for the day, and I cover my own face with the pillow and drift back into a light sleep. I don't want more information about how we ended up semi-clothed in his king-size bed together. *At least it was River.* He was my childhood protector.

"That good, huh?" River asks, returning. "Fortunately, I already put in a delivery order with the Bagel Beagle. I hope you still order a pork roll, egg, and one slice of cheddar, with salt, pepper and ketchup on a whole wheat everything bagel."

"Taylor Ham," I firmly correct him.

"It's literally the same, and you know it," he fires back, his eyes lighting up in delight. He always did love this ridiculous argument.

"It's literally the product of John Taylor and was called Taylor's Prepared Ham before people started calling it pork roll," I tell him. The information is useless, but collecting trivia is one of my special skills. "But I'm extremely happy to hear there is a Taylor Ham, egg, and cheese headed my way." Grinning, I kick my feet a little. Maybe breakfast shouldn't excite me this much, but I salivate on command like one of Pavlov's dogs thinking about New Jersey bagels.

"Ooh. Is Benny still doing deliveries with the humans? I haven't seen him in so long." I ask, excitement zipping through me.

Humming, he counters. "Benny will probably be along for the drop, but the Benny you recall has sadly crossed over the rainbow bridge."

I slump, my heart aching for the little guy.

River chuckles. "Seriously, Lil, he was like a million years old when we were kids. You have to be somewhat unsurprised by this news."

Standing at the foot of the bed, he stretches. A familiar mischief twinkles in his eyes as he reaches a long arm overhead. With his other hand, he absentmindedly scratches his abs.

My mouth goes dry. Damn, I want him to do that again too. With a shake of my head to dislodge the thought, I force myself to move. Reminder to self: there's no reason to ruin a friendship. Would he want to hook up? Maybe. He might think this was fun for a bit, but eventually, he'd get fed up with me. With my inability to stay put. With my habit of speaking faster than I can think. I'd cry over a random act of kindness or become so excited by a new song that I have to create a workout for it, only to listen to it nonstop for days on end before moving on. No, River would not want the chaos that comes with all of me. I'm tired of trying to meet a person who will stay, so I accept the temporary offers. But he can't be that for me. It's better to keep the great friends I see periodically who still love me.

"Oh, shut up. I'm going to pee. When I get back, can we make coffee?"

"Wow," he teases. "You're really not with it."

I take a deep breath in and the aroma hits me. A heartbeat later, my face heats, and I turn to hide my embarrassment.

Unaware of my mortification, River wanders to the kitchen. "It's programmed. Otherwise I'd never wake up. How do you take it?"

I peek over my shoulder and watch his backside as he moves around the kitchen. He shifts, pulling mugs from a cabinet, then snags a bowl and fills it with water, then places it on the floor for Pete.

My heart thumps heavily. He's not only taking care of me, but he's got Pete covered too?

I'm going to melt. When was the last time someone wanted to take care of me?

Snatching my pants off the floor, I call, "A fuck ton of sugar, one ice cube—"

"No milk, right?" he says

My breath catches. I haven't seen this man in a decade, and he remembers that detail? No one has ever remembered that. *Then again*, a little voice in the back of my mind says, *you don't stick around long enough for anyone to learn that kind of thing.*

I push that thought down too. The New Jersey air is stirring weird feelings inside me.

Pants slung over my arm, I dart for the bathroom while River's back is turned. But just my luck, I stumble over my own feet and land with a thud in the doorway to the bathroom. Flat on my face. A cool breeze moves across my lower body, signaling that my ass is exposed, and my stomach is pressed against cold tile. I scramble up and right River's oversized T-shirt, then slam the door shut.

I've been awake less than ten minutes, and already I'm overwhelmed. By tonight, all of Peacock Springs will know I'm back. The moment I step out of this apartment, there's a chance I'll see Grant, Landan, my mother, or some gossip lover. After all these years, I've regressed to my nineteen-year-old self: the jilted wife and young divorcee. This town only knows the insecure version of me. The angry and explosive young woman who left here. The worst thing is, she's returned.

It's like the decade I spent working, traveling, meeting people, having sex with no strings attached, and falling in and out of lust with other wandering souls never happened.

Assuming that I'll need to sneak across the square, I work on a strategy to tackle my best approximation of a morning routine. I'm cursing myself for being so irresponsible last night and not bringing my things in when I notice my duffel bag sitting on a bench near the sink.

With a relieved sigh, I rifle through my possessions until I find my toothbrush, soap, and hairbrush.

"You are one of the good ones," I shout through the door. "Thanks for grabbing my stuff so I don't have to do the walk of shame through town. Now I can shower and change like a proper person. Towels?"

"The ones on the rack are clean," he confirms.

"Amazing. Be out soon," I promise before turning on the shower.

While the water heats, I relieve myself and take a moment to give a mental peptalk.

"You are twenty-eight," I mutter, head in my hands. "You have a decade of experiences behind you. The Jeep. Air in your lungs. Food and caffeine headed your way. It is not your job to live for someone else's desires or expectations. You can be a badass anywhere, so flush and get up." Sometimes getting things started, even things I love to do, is harder than it should be.

As I step under the spray, the hot water causes my muscles to jolt and flinch, though it only takes a moment for them to adjust and relax. I lather up with lavender soap and brush my skin softly with the pads of my fingers.

Before I can think too much about what I'm doing, my mind drifts to River. To the way my sweet friend grew into a gorgeous man. He still has the charm and smirk, and now he has the muscles, a light beard, and body hair. He's clearly not a boy anymore.

The goose bumps that erupt along my arms are confusing, but they're not as alarming as the ache settling between my thighs. How long has it been since I got laid?

Anxiety and excitement feel the same in the body. I'm taking my anxiety out on today's events sexually.

With that reminder in my head, I work through deep breathing exercises. When they fail to calm me, I move the water first to cool, then to cold, to douse the sensation.

No way this is actually about River Hendrix. Right?

I'm toweling off when the doorbell rings and my heart lurches. River isn't familiar with the way Pete likes to dash off. So I yank out the clothes packed at the top of my bag and throw them on.

In a hot pink tie-dye shirt and cut-off shorts, I rush out of the bathroom.

I'm too late. Pete has already followed River, barking and running down the steps.

I shout, "Pete, stay! River, don't open the—"

Shit. River doesn't hear me over my dog's incessant noise, and the moment the door is cracked open, Pete barrels toward the bagel delivery boy and the beagle lying on an old, rusted Radio Flyer wagon.

The kid, who can't be much older than fifteen, jumps, dropping the bag and backing away.

Naturally, Pete goes straight for my breakfast on the sidewalk. But so does Benny the Beagle. He hops down and tussles with Pete over the bagels. It ends quickly and without any blood, but the skirmish is loud, and I worry it will draw folks from the nearby storefronts out.

Thankfully, the street is mostly empty.

Victorious, Pete makes off with the bag. He lets out a high-pitched whine that tips me off to his plans. He wants to hide treasure. Before I can stop him, he digs at the lattice around the porch and slips under it.

It takes thirty minutes, treats, bribes, and begging before he gets close enough that I can snatch him by the collar and drag him out.

When he's finally securely in River's apartment again, I crate him.

"We need a new breakfast plan," I think out loud, sweat dripping down my back. I could also go for another shower. *Ew.*

"No worries. Coffee Crumbs instead?" River offers.

Swallowing my anxiety, I shrug.

nine
River

"LET me make myself look slightly less messy," Lily says as she pops back into my bathroom and closes the door with a soft click.

I pace across the room. "If you want to stay in, we can do something else. How about leftovers downstairs?" I ask.

She doesn't reply, and I pace back, boldly moving closer to the door.

With my hand in the air, ready to knock, I'm stopped by the sound of her voice.

"I'm not too worse for the wear," she mutters. "Maybe a little sweaty… although Belinda would be mad that my hair is so frizzy." A rustling sound, then a sigh. "Better, but I still need something." More rustling, like bags shifting. "Come on, Lily," she goes on. "Show everyone that you are happy. Shoulders back. Chin up. Confident body language. Confident, not smug. No, that's not confident. Now you're just flirting with yourself. Do not go there, Lily. River may have gotten hot, but he's still completely off-limits. Get in. Get out. Get back to your life anywhere but here."

I should have moved away. I should not be listening to this.

But I'm stuck, hand frozen in midair. Mouth completely dry. She called me *off-limits*. She called me *hot*.

I've barely managed to stumble back a couple of steps by the time the door swings open and Lily emerges with her hair pulled into a big clip. She's wearing a clean shirt made of a soft, silky material and a big fake smile that doesn't reach her eyes.

"Lead the way. It's your town," she teases, gesturing toward the door.

———

WITH COFFEE CRUMBS directly across the square, it is about a ten-minute walk from my apartment. Fifteen if you run into Miss Nicole outside the dance studio. Giving Lily a once-over, I ask, "You ready?"

"Nope, but let's go." She laughs. Stepping outside, she winces against the sunlight and digs into her oversized tote, eventually pulling out a glasses case. Once her sunglasses are securely on her face, she repeats her instructions for me to take the lead.

"Have you told Delia and Nessa that you're here?" I ask, hoping to distract her from worrying.

My phone buzzes in my pocket, and I slip it out, scanning the notification on the screen. Dammit. I knew it wouldn't be long before the gossip started, but this has to be a record.

PEACOCK SPRINGER:

ALERT Lily Long believed to be in town for the first time in ten years. Teal Jeep Wrangler parked near the square and a brunette walking with River Hendrix spotted.

We all pretend that the Peacock Springer isn't run by the Salvatore women, but it's obvious. Curl Up & Dye is the Salvatore family salon and the center of all town gossip. They seem to control the narrative of all rumors unless they include Carmine and Anna Lucia being part of the mafia. Those are typically reserved for hushed whispers far from their matriarch. Her daughter, Ava Marie, and granddaughters Bella, Chiara, Tina, and Sofia work at the salon on and off too. The Springer could be run by any of them, but my guess is that it is all of them.

She winces as we pass the townhouse where she lived with Grant. Following her gaze, I elbow her lightly and tease, "Don't stare so hard. The grass grew back."

"Don't care about the lawn. It's… she's… look up," she stutters.

Jaw clenched, I follow her gaze. Instantly, my heart sinks.

Behind sheer curtains, two figures stand, one distinctly feminine and the other masculine. Guess we're being watched by her ex-husband and his wife. His second wife and high school sweetheart. The one he cheated on Lily with.

My phone buzzes in my hand, and when I read the notification, I scoff.

PEACOCK SPRINGER:

LS: *UPDATE* Lily Long photographed outside ex-husband's home. Stalking? [pic]

PLACING my hand low on her back, I guide Lily toward the corner restaurant. I pick up the pace a bit and lean in to whisper in her ear. "Chin up, shoulders back. The Springer is sending out alerts about you."

"You heard me," she hisses, though the words are followed by laughter. I hope she isn't hiding being mad. I can't tell yet. "Wait." She pulls up short, frowning. "The Springer? Is it not still printed weekly?"

"It was upgraded to text alerts. There have been two about us already. Look," I say and hand over my phone.

She scans the notification, then swipes away to the call screen, dials, and pulls her own phone out of her pocket. She declines the call and hands my device back.

Her phone's screen is cracked, and when she notices me looking, her face flushes an adorable shade of pink.

"It's just the screen protector. I need to get a new one," she blurts as she peels off the broken sticker and brings it to the trash can outside town hall.

As she turns back, her eyes drift to the old stocks. This Revolutionary War relic is mostly a tourist attraction, but for Lily, it's a metaphor. She wanted to be free, and they wanted to lock her away here. The cement bench is flanked by two columns and attached wooden boards with four circular cutouts for four ankles. The boards are held together by an ancient brass lock.

"Forget this is here," I whisper and take her by the elbow next door to the bakery and coffee shop.

"Busy morning," she muses at the door, surveying the handful of regulars.

"No more than usual," I say, craving to touch her, soothe her.

Once we've settled at a table, she picks up the oversized menu, hiding behind it.

A moment later, my phone buzzes, and a new text appears.

NEW GROUP: PS, I'M HOME! [LILY LONG, RIVER HENDRIX, NESSA RABIN, DELIA SHANE, SETH WHITTER, LEE CARTER]
LILY:

I'm back babes! I'm having breakfast at CC with River.

What do we tell the future Mrs. Lee?
SETH:

You really came for the party?

NESSA:

You said came <upside down smiley face emoji>

DELIA:

God, you're all so predictable.

WELCOME HOME, LILY!!!

LILY:

Thank you, Delia. At least I know there is ONE
PERSON happy I'm here.

SETH:

When has anyone called me "happy" about
anything?

LEE:

<pair of eyes emoji> I'm the newest, so someone
tell me. Was there one really great Christmas
where he got a PlayStation or something?

NESSA: REACTED HAHA,
DELIA: REACTED !!
RIVER: REACTED !!
LILY: REACTED HAHA

SETH:

Blow me

LEE:

You're not my type. Speaking of adorable and
feisty Filipina girls, Stef knew you'd *maybe* be
here for her birthday dinner. I'm hoping she's not
suspicious.

River, have you thought of anything you might
need help with on-site before then?

RIVER:

Beyond good to go. Don't lose the ring.

ANOTHER TEXT COMES THROUGH, this time in a thread
between Lee and me only.

I SHAKE MY HEAD. Blaze is a clever nickname, given her history with minor arson.

Plus the whole pot farm thing.

"Psst, Lil," I whisper, leaning around her menu. "I have a few questions. I've wanted to ask you for a while, but over text didn't feel right."

Eyes widening, she taps her fingers on the table.

"The rumor about the pot farm?" I break into a sly smile.

"True. Next rumor?" she snaps.

"Um, are those heiresses paying for you to travel with them?"

"Yes. It's like they want me to be their pseudo-friend, but I'm there to lead workouts and smack treats out of their hands. Ooh, the coffee cake. Is the blueberry coffee cake the same?" She switches topics mid-thought.

"Yep, want a piece?" I offer.

"More coffee too, please. All the coffee," she begs.

Ridiculously, her words make my dick twitch.

As I slide out of my chair, she pulls a well-worn novel out of her bag.

As I head to the counter, my chest aches for the sad little girl who's hiding. She's not like this when she's livestreaming. That woman is passionate about following one's inner voice and building community. I'm starting to feel silly for believing what I saw on social media.

I order, and once I've got our coffees and her cake, I turn back to the table.

She's still tapping her fingers when I return, and there's a hint of moisture behind her eyes. With a frantic whisper she asks, "Is your phone buzzing this much because of me?"

I grab a saltshaker and wave it. "Don't be salty. I have other friends."

She breaks into laughter, her fear vanishing. Damn, I've missed making her laugh. I need this in my life. Forever and always.

I turn on the charm, hoping Lily can see herself through my eyes; that she'll see the mountain of admiration I have for her independence and strength.

Lily thinks she took the fall after that town meeting ten years ago, but fleeing the state with her tail between her legs didn't prevent her ex's toxic behavior from unmasking itself. If anything, he's worse off than she is. How can I get her to see that?

Before I've come up with an answer to that question, Lily flashes puppy dog eyes my way, her bottom lip pushed out as she silently begs for something she's yet to share with me.

I find myself thinking about what it would be like to press my mouth against that pout. Catch her lips with my teeth. Hold tight to her long thick hair as I deepen the kiss. *Shit.*

"What's next?" I inhale, then hold my breath, waiting for a reply.

"Can you walk me to Stef's?"

ten
Lily

I CAN ONLY IMAGINE Belinda's reaction when she discovers I'm in town. And if she hasn't already, she will soon. As I walk back across town toward Stef's house, every person I pass gawks.

Only a few more hours before I return to my life. I only need to survive one more day here. Then I'll head to Manhattan to interview with the streaming home-fitness group. They've been trying to get me to come in for a while, and though I can't imagine myself there, and even though just the thought of being surrounded by the buzz of people in New York City feels like a physical weight on my chest, I'll go. I'll network. It's one meeting. It's one day.

Stef and Lee live in a storybook-esque coastal blue vinyl-sided bungalow with bright white shutters capped by matching flower boxes. Each box is bursting with tiny orange marigolds, lavender, and black-eyed Susans. There is a big birthday sign on the front door in pinks and teals drawn by Lee and his middle school students.

I'm mid-knock when the door flies open and I nearly punch the birthday girl.

"Oh shit. Hi," I exclaim.

She returns the greeting with an ear-piercing scream and a hug so forceful we stumble into the house in a tangle of limbs.

River coughs in a poor attempt to cover a laugh behind me. Lee already has his arms out to stabilize us.

Squealing, Stef scoops me into a second hug that knocks the air out of my lungs. "You are here. In. New. Jersey."

"Babe. Can you at least try to survive until the party? Maybe longer?" Lee teases as he moves her aside with a quick kiss to her temple. This gesture is a simple one, but it sticks with me—the sweetness, the comfort. I can't recall my parents ever showing affection like that, and I certainly didn't receive any during the few months I was married. Maybe it would be nice.

Stef and Lee were partnered on a project during their junior year of college. Her sunny energy and his critical nature made them the perfect team. They got an A+ and celebrated over drinks. One drink led to another, and from that day forward, they were inseparable.

We settle in their living room to chat, and after a few minutes, Stef excuses herself.

Thinking out loud, I mumble, "How has it taken so many years?"

River elbows me, silently hushing me, and I give him a side-eye. *What? Lee knows how long they've been together.*

"Manicures?" Stef asks eyeing me when she returns.

"And cupcakes? In another town?" I ask, hopeful I can avoid the public eye for a bit.

"Definitely cupcakes," she agrees. "It *is* my birthday weekend."

The smile that overtakes me is so big it hurts my face, a sensation I haven't experienced in years.

———

BACK IN THE JEEP, with Stef by my side, I swear I could float away. Being in the presence of one of my closest friends is like walking onto the beach and getting that first big lungful of fresh air. It's peaceful and grounding.

Finally, with the address in my GPS and the town behind me, my nerves dissipate.

Stef is talking about the upcoming school year with a fiery passion. "I've been working on revamping the special education program for the lower grades. Every. Single. Child who comes into my school will be given the tools necessary to succeed instead of being pushed until they break. Did I tell you about the grant I wrote for an AAC device?"

"A what?"

"AAC. Augmentative and alternative communication. It's like a super tablet for folks who can't use their own voice to speak. Too many people confuse someone not using their voice box with having nothing to share." She pauses at a yield and exhales. "Like last year, I met this wonderful first grader who absolutely can talk, but he's struggling in certain situations. When my grant was approved and we received the AAC, it made such a difference. I almost cried when he came into my office and used it to thank me. He was so proud." She beams.

My friend has barely changed in all this time. Long jet-black hair falling around her shoulders, warm olive toned skin she'd called *mestiza*, rounded cheeks always on display because she's always smiling. I have always admired the ease and tact she has in every moment, the ability to bring about changes.

"Getting this out there now so you know," she says, her smile suddenly gone. "I called my mom about this *birthday* dinner. She said the Morgans were never invited. But Belinda and Neal know you are here—"

"La, la, la. If I can't hear you, I don't have to know." I cup my hands over my ears. Is it childish? Yes. But it's necessary.

"Okay, so I'm right. You didn't tell your mom you'd be here directly. No contact at all?" She pins me with her perfect school administrator tone and stare.

"No, Ms. Santos Manolo, my mommy doesn't know," I singsong.

Maintaining her firm disposition, she asks, "And will Lee be proposing before or at the party?"

"Before. What. No. I didn't. He isn't. I'm not," I stutter in time with my racing heart. Shit. I've always struggled to think before I speak.

"Lily," she huffs, "the only other reason you'd be in town is if one of your parents died. Since Belinda and Neal are still breathing, then I must be getting engaged."

My heart is thundering so violently that as I approach the traffic light ahead, I step a little too hard on the brakes and whip my arm out to shove her back into her seat.

Stef lets out a whoosh of air.

I yank my hand back but can't help but deflect. "Damn, nice tits, lady."

This results in a round of giggles and helps me delay the inevitable conversation. Fuck. Deep breath.

Once inside, they seat us at opposite ends of the row. *Score!* Maybe I really can avoid the proposal talk between now and the party.

Truth be told, Lee is perfect for her. His striking resemblance to her childhood crush from *The O.C.* is pure kismet. Stef's older brother, Mateo, used to watch it when he was supposed to be babysitting us. Back then we didn't understand much of what was happening, but we did know the blond guy was trouble and so cute. Lee, who practically lives in paint-stained jeans and T-shirts with Chucks, would make the perfect stand-in for the mysterious member of a late '90s boy band.

Being from Michigan alone makes Lee special around here. It's rare when a person from someplace that isn't New Jersey doesn't mercilessly mock it. He's never complained about this town, probably because his hometown is small too. And weird. This place is so weird.

Best of all for me is that Stef and Lee have sparked a sliver of hope inside me that a couple can be equals. Lee is the sort of man a woman marries. He doesn't simply let her shine; he consistently revels in her successes. Yet when the hard parts of her job and the massive amount of empathy she possesses overwhelm her, he holds her up while she cries and reassures her that she's strong, even while feeling softer emotions.

Even when I dated a woman, I found myself shrinking behind my partner. That relationship taught me that gender roles weren't the issue, but something inside me. When my voice is loud, my feelings larger than life, my excitement like fireworks, or my sadness lingering, I am not who my partner believed me to be in the beginning. However, my constant caretaking, availability, and support taught those partners what they wanted. Just about every person I've dated has gone on to meet their forever partner after they were done practicing with me.

I'm drifting toward those darkest thoughts, the ones that can send me spiraling, when Stef leans over and in the sweetest tone says, "Really? After twenty years, you think that sitting a few seats down will get you out of this chat?"

"Fine." I groan, head dropping back. "What do you want to know?"

Her eyes glimmer with the sort of mischief I haven't seen in ages. "Since I'm getting engaged, which color should I choose?" She opens her hand, showing me two bottles of polish. "Susan will expect something soft, neutral, like this pink. But summer is almost over, so I was thinking brighter one last time. Like this coral. There was also a fuchsia…"

Tension builds inside my chest, and I realize that I'm frowning. Quickly, I slap on a smile and nod toward the brighter color. "Coral. Definitely the coral. It will look beautiful with your skin tone." I focus on my manicurist so I can avoid Stef's attempt at eye contact.

"Come on, Lil. You've avoided the PA side of the river for a decade. You can't tell me you're back so you can sit your time in the stocks at town hall, then have tea and tarot at Prudence's shop with your mom. Oh, maybe you're here so you can go on a double date with Jim, Landan, and Grant."

Busted. I turn, staring at her, jaw slack. What do I do now?

Lightly, Stef uses her finger to push my jaw shut.

Wheeling closer in her chair, she tosses her arms around me in a sisterly embrace.

I whisper sternly, "You better act surprised."

"Thank you." Eyes welling, she squeezes my hand. Then she moves back to where she was asked to sit.

My heart clenches. My friend wins the kindest, most empathetic, human award. Every time.

That's why I'm here. I would be a fool to miss such a happy moment of her life.

———

AFTER OUR NAILS ARE SHAPED, cleaned, and painted, we walk to the shop that makes the best cupcakes in the state.

"How long were you in town before I found out?" Stef presses, either teasing or tense I can't be sure.

"Not a full twelve hours," I admit.

"Uh-huh, and you slept where again?" She arches a brow.

"River's loft."

"Was that the plan before you rolled into town?" she asks, her face brightening. "When did you reconnect with him this time? Oh my god," she shrieks, clearly reading into the situation more than necessary.

Wincing, I reel back, nearly knocking the box of cupcakes she ordered to bring home with her off the table. I take a large bite from the chocolate cake and vanilla buttercream to avoid her questions.

The silence just gives her room to continue asking.

"So you did reconnect before this? He's filled out nicely, right?" She waggles her brows. "Not that he hasn't always been fit, but he's a full-on man now. Did you finally make out with him?" Stef's eyes are as large as dinner plates and her smile is milliseconds from looking absurd. "Would you date him? Do you think you can stay and be my maid of honor? Oh my god, I have so many questions."

I swallow the bite of cupcake, then dryly say, "Clearly you have questions. But I need a minute to think." I take a second bite, collecting my thoughts, then let them out in a stream of consciousness. "Well. Yeah. Obviously, River is fucking hot now. I can't stand it. But I don't think that's how he sees me." My hears sinks a little. "When I changed my number, he didn't ask for the new one. Like, yes. River and I talk over DM from time to time, but I get a lot of messages from men because I make my living wearing spandex on the internet. You don't want to know what some of these guys send me." I shudder.

"If you didn't have his number, how did you end up there and not with Delia and Nessa?" she asks.

I cringe. "Um, honestly?"

"No, lie to me." She nudges me playfully.

"I rolled into town without a plan. I called Nessa and Delia but was dangerously close to having a panic attack over it, so I stopped on Route 1 to eat disco fries and delay. I kept telling myself that despite my urge to turn around and skip this, I'd regret it. So I forced myself back onto the road. I drove by Bangor Drive—"

"You did?" she asks, confusion written all over her face and laced into her tone.

"I didn't knock. I just idled on the street, staring at the place that used to be my home." I shrug, trying to act nonchalant when I am very *chalant* about this. "Eventually, curiosity got the better of me. It was late, and I figured everyone would be in for the night, so I parked the Wrangler downtown so I could take Pete for a walk before using the key Delia left out for me. Instead, he dragged me into the square and straight into River, who wanted to give me a tour of the Featherweight and offered me a drink."

"Then what?" she prods, as if I wasn't going to keep rolling along.

"I got drunk," I say simply, shrugging. "Then River, true to form, put me to bed. Clothed. No, I did not make out with him. He's definitely attractive, but I don't think he sees me that way." I lick my lips, head lowering. "I'm just Lily, the pathetic divorcee. You know how dating goes for me. I meet someone beautiful, and we get along for a few weeks. Months sometimes. Eventually they tell me that I'm not the marrying kind. I get back in my Jeep and head to a new place, and everyone moves on. I mean," I say, my voice dropping to a whisper, "even my parents did."

I swallow to hold back the flood of emotions that well up any time I think about my many broken-hearted moments along the way.

"Anyway," I say, "I knew it wouldn't be long before the whole town knew I was here. The Featherweight is close to the salon, and once a Salvatore women saw me, the news would spread like wildfire. Are they invited tonight?"

"Not sure." She presses her lips together. "There will be absolutely no Morgans. But the Kellys were invited. Jim's not as bad as he used to be. I'd dare say he's even tolerable."

"Oh, tolerable?" I tease. "Goody. What I truly did not anticipate was my dog tackling the breakfast delivery guy and running off with my bagel sandwich. That's how I ended up out in public."

"With River." She smirks.

Resigned, I say, "With River, but I really don't think it is like that."

Yeah, maybe petting his chest and stomach hair this morning when I thought I was reaching for my dog was… it was comforting, but it was the closeness of another person. That's all. It wasn't specifically because the man I was petting was River. I'm probably just horny. I'll fix the problem once I leave town and I bet it won't be a thought again.

"Anyway, I'm not here to discuss my personal life. Let's discuss you, soon-to-be bride-to-be."

"Can you say that again, but faster?"

I roll my eyes, not bothering to acknowledge that I'm back in word-soup territory. "Did you have an inkling this was coming? Have you started to plan? Do you know what kind of ring he'll give you? Have you thought about bridesmaid dresses?"

Her eyes light up, and her face splits in a giddy smile. "I found the ring." The mischievous look is back. It's one she's been making for as long as I can remember. "I was cleaning the bathroom last week and I stumbled on a little green velvet box in one of Lee's drawers. It was right there, in the vanity, where his deodorant usually goes. I was not snooping."

"Sure, whatever you say, babe." I wink.

"It's perfect, Lily. Like I've straight up never seen anything so perfect. So me. Like…"

"Like?" I interrupt her. "Which one of us is the educator and which is the West Coast bohemian?"

"Shut up." she whines, though it quickly turns into a laugh. "Rather than a diamond, he chose an opal." She actually squeals. "I'm hoping it's one from Mom's collection direct from the South Sea." She sighs. Her mother has several Filipino opals, and Stef has always coveted them. "God only knows if Mateo will ever settle down enough to try out a committed relationship. I really want it to be one of hers."

Stef's older brother lives in New York and works in real estate. I don't have a clue what he does exactly, but it's time consuming and pays very well. Beyond that, he's been sort of a mystery to us the last few years.

"I hear he's been trying to get involved in humanitarian-type projects. Maybe I'm wrong, but he's been asking Nessa questions about her work at the hospital."

Nessa, our longtime friend-group therapist turned real psychologist, has been passionate about women's rights and advocacy for as long as I can remember. "It's weird that they're talking, right?"

She hums. "It's even more weird that they still hate each other."

The longer we're together, the harder that tug on my heart becomes. I've missed her. I've missed them all. I don't want to miss things anymore.

———

I GET LOST in my daydreams on the drive home. It happens often; I've always been a little flighty. So when I tune back into what Stef is saying, I realize I've missed half of her story. *Crap.* I side-eye her, noticing tears in her eyes.

My heart lurches. Are they good tears? Bad tears? Crap.

My brain must have *heard* some of this without processing.

"I'm about to get engaged," she blubbers, clueing me into the topic, "and you're still rootless. Floating from gig to gig, without a permanent home. We're your family, you know, even if your parents suck."

"I do have a permanent home." Tapping above my heart, I remind her, "The only place I need to live is in your heart. It's even rent-free. My favorite price."

What she doesn't realize is that if I did come home, her opinion would change. If I lived here and they were around to witness all my fumbling, they'd be annoyed. We'd go out, and I'd do something over-the-top or talk too much, then I'd hide out on my own for days on end. Forgetting to call them back. Forgetting plans.

"Traveling like I do, I tend to find other wandering souls. My friends here are my foundation, yet I can float in and out, making new friends everywhere I go." I'm desperate to mask the exhaustion of fast friends, fast friends-with-benefits, and consistent change with excitement.

Each time I have started to think maybe I do want roots, my partners have not been on the same page. Every time I catch an unreciprocated feeling, the story plays out identically. First we end things, then sometimes we hook up again because it is "easy" —although it isn't. Magically, after the commitment-phobe moves on, they meet someone they want to spend a lifetime with. Like that movie *Good Luck Chuck* with that terribly not funny dude— Dane something—I am the person people fuck before they go out and find true love.

"Stefanie Anne Santos Manolo almost Carter," I say, needing to change the subject to keep the intrusive thoughts at bay. "Do not deflect. This conversation is not about me."

At the same time, she bursts out, "Lily Jayne Long, don't you dare claim you cannot find love again."

eleven
River

"SHE STAYED HERE LAST NIGHT," I tell Delia as we prep the bar for tonight's party.

"We figured that out when you two were spotted together this morning," she says, heaving a dishwasher rack of glasses onto the bar top.

"And?" I nudge. Delia has an opinion on this, I have no doubt, and she will share, so we might as well get it over with.

"And," she hums thoughtfully, "I'm wondering if you think she'll change for you." The confident bite of her words hangs between us.

What is that supposed to mean? Aren't they close? My brain spins, questions popping up at a rapid-fire pace. I raise the empty blue ice buckets and say, "Kitchen." I walk away before I scream or ask too many desperate things or say something I regret.

"Boss." Delia yells, her voice barely audible over the noise as I dip the bucket into the industrial ice maker. The cool air helps to calm my anger and frustration, and the lifting and adjusting allows some of the twitching in my muscles to subside. Once the containers are full, I lug them back to fill behind the bar, working in silence, hoping to move on.

"River," Delia says more gently this time as she takes the bucket from my hands. "I'm sorry. I'm mad at her. I'm so happy she is here, but I'm so sick of this. I'm not sure if calling her on it is even fair, but I hate watching her hold on to something so illogical, even as she pretends to be confident and calm in her meditation streams."

Delia uncorks a bottle of white wine and pours herself a half glass.

I raise an eyebrow before motioning for her to proceed.

"River, come on. You aren't stupid." She sighs.

"Delia, come on. You aren't saying anything," I mimic.

She gulps down the glass, refills, and hands it to me. Waving her hand, she motions for me to drink. While my mouth is full of the dry, tangy, cold liquid, she continues.

"She cares too much about what other people say or do. The only time any of us see her is if we go to her. It's like she thinks that all of Peacock Springs is against Lily Long, when there are only a handful of people who have a negative opinion. The number of people who care about the outdated town rules is shrinking every day. Seth took over the bookstore, you took over here. We're *adults* now, and we have as much of a voice as anyone else. Why doesn't she let us help her? She may put on a good act, but she's not happy. It's why I call so often. It's why Nessa keeps her book club brunches going over Zoom. I wish she could see how much I care. I know very well what it's like not to have a family outside our friend group."

"Fair point. And did you want me to drink this so I'd know how foul it is?" Grimacing, I swallow the last bit of wine, then set the glass down.

"My tips have suffered greatly since you switched to this brand." She huffs. "I'm glad you see the light."

"Hey," I say, softening my tone, "you do have a family in us, though. I hope you know that."

Her eyes shimmer as she blinks back tears and nods. "It's

ridiculous that Landan and Grant were allowed to drive away my sister. It was bad enough when Landan…" She trails off.

"When she what?"

"This is so embarrassing." She drops her head into her hands.

"Probably, but I can't imagine it's nothing another glass of bad wine can't fix," I tease.

"Okay." She blows out a breath. "Landan has always been good at finding that thing you're most insecure about, then dropping it casually at the perfect moment. She did that a lot when we were friends. It took a long time to see how fake that relationship was, and it always hurt."

"You're right, you need the good stuff when dealing with people who manipulate emotions and cut others down like that." With that, I hand her a glass of water. "Unfortunately, we've got more setting up to do. Let's go. Rosie's is delivering the flowers, and I need you to help me make sure the dream Susan had of a ray of sunshine made of flowers comes to life."

twelve
Lily

AT SIX SHARP I descend the steps from River's studio. The Featherweight is jam-packed with Peacock Springs' usual suspects. Prudence reads cards at a table, surrounded by Stef's female cousins. Pippa Whitter, Seth's middle sister and co-owner of Pages, and Albert, the librarian, are engaged in a debate about who is allowed to prominently display which new releases to avoid long holds and low sales.

Carmine Salvatore is in the kitchen chatting with the line cooks. I consider thanking him for his support during the months I tried to learn to cook, though that idea is quashed when his girls swarm around him. No thanks. Not interested in being front and center for the firing squad.

Rosie, the florist, is adjusting a bouquet. She's done an incredible job with the flower arrangements. Yellow blooms decorate every flat surface, creating a burst of sunshine. There are easily over a thousand of them scattered around in every shape and hue. They pay tribute perfectly to Stef's warm demeanor.

Susan outdid herself with planning and decorating. The place is filled with ornate framed photos of Stef and Lee, the two of them growing from infants to adults, including images of family, friends, and milestones. The traditional cap and gown photo with Mom and Dad flanking the graduate stings, though it does lead me directly to a series of gold serving platters holding a variety of appetizers. Their heavenly scent was wafting upstairs as I got ready, making me drool.

My stomach rumbles as I quickly fill a plate and try to make myself blend in. I peer from group to group, assessing who will be respectful enough not to ask a barrage of invasive questions. I'd huddle at River's side, where I know it's safe, but he's behind the bar—despite swearing he'd have someone cover this evening— and the Kelly men are talking to him.

The duo are the rule-loving sticklers who'd likely be happy to march me across the square and plop me down in the stocks just because I'm within town limits, and I'd rather avoid people who don't want me here.

I search for Nessa and Delia, hoping they aren't mad that I haven't connected with them since I arrived. I can explain, if Nessa will allow it.

When I start to sweat, the crowd getting to me, I shuffle for the door to the porch for air, but I'm thwarted by an imposing figure. I send up a silent prayer: please be a cousin or an uncle who won't know me.

But when I breathe in the same scent I woke up surrounded by, my panic abates.

"River," I say, my voice breathy.

He runs his hands down my arms, causing jolts of electricity to dance across my skin. He pulls me in closer, hugging me.

I go willingly, grumbling, "I need a fucking drink."

Unused to causal touch, I linger, letting his sturdiness steady me. I've missed hugs like this. How did he know?

His lips skim my ear. "You've got this, tiger. Drinks we can do, but maybe we'll make them a little weaker tonight."

Entwining our fingers, he leads me through the crowd. I keep my eyes on the floor, ensuring I don't step on anyone while silently reciting a calming phrase. *You do not know them anymore, and they do not know you. You do not owe them anything, and they do not owe you.*

After we duck under the arm of a waitress raising a tray and approach the bar, I snag a bottle of top-shelf tequila.

"Less strong than yesterday, remember?" he teases me. "Have at it."

Grinning, I line up a series of shot glasses.

He huffs, mumbling about my defiance.

Nessa and Delia's voices reach me as I pour the first few shots. I wave them over, and as they approach, Seth rounds the bar and joins us. The men do a manly greeting ritual, starting with high fives with back pats and moving into vocalized adoration, then ending with a hug.

The performance is just over-the-top enough to break my momentary anxiety and cause my heart to overflow. I love these people. I've missed them and I want to be here.

Don't I deserve to be here? The question plants itself in my head, but I squash it quickly.

"We need a toast," Delia chirps.

Seth raises his glass. "To honor."

Delia groans.

His toast is a crude one, from what I'm told. I've never heard the entire thing, and as River claps a hand on the back of Seth's head and he stops, I realize I won't tonight either.

All I know is if he mentions something about coming "on her," and it always brings about ire in Delia and Nessa.

"I can cut you off before you get your first drink," River warns. "Show some respect."

Nessa, always one to swoop in and stir the pot, counters with, "To River. The best *best man* in town."

We all respond with "To River," then toss back the sweet floral añejo.

Tension lines River's face, and as his eyes dart to me, the

reason for his discomfort hits me. This is not the first time he's held the role. He was the best man in my wedding too.

Throughout my childhood, the Hendrix and Long families were close, and since Grant and River played hockey together, it was perfect. His mom, Elizabeth, was often around, since she and my mom would work together on school activities and town events. Hell, it was Elizabeth who found me digging under the sink the day my first period started, reading the boxes of feminine products. She broke down what we learned in health class. She sent me for clean underwear, showed me how to put the pad on, and waited by the door while I changed. When I exited, she pinched my cheeks, then gave me a soft hug, explaining that her mom had done the same. It was a family tradition to bring the blood back to a person's face to ensure rosy cheeks and beauty in womanhood.

River stood up with us on our wedding day, and he planned a boys' night out. It was another typical hockey party at Kirk's mom's house. Yet the tension in his demeanor makes me wonder if there is something more to it. Since he was the best man and my marriage to Grant ended so spectacularly badly, does he believe he's cursed? I've never taken him for a superstitious person. I should take him to Prudence for a reading.

Before I can suggest it, the front doors swing open and the crowd roars, "Congratulations!"

Stef is visibly *not* surprised as she and Lee make the rounds, greeting their families, college friends, sorority sisters, and townsfolk. As they approach the bar, I pray Lee can't tell or doesn't care that she knew about the surprise.

She's blissfully lit from within as she waves her new jewelry around for all to see and the both of them happily partake in another round of tequila shots with us.

Between the drinks, appetizers, and shots, I'm soon desperate for a trip to the ladies' room. It's urgent enough that I step directly into a woman exiting the bathroom.

"I'm so sorry, excuse me." I blurt out before I fully process what's happening.

Belinda is exiting as I rush in, and now my head is spinning. Whether it's because of the cloying scent of her floral perfume or the alcohol I've consumed, I can't tell. The women's room door shuts too quietly for me to gauge how long she stood there before walking out.

Did she care that it was me? Would she want to talk?

My chest aches as my brain comes up with yet another question. One of the hardest. *Does she miss me?* She *is* my mom. Even if Belinda Long is not my favorite person, she's my mom. I can't count the number of times I hovered over her contact card in my phone, thinking that if I called or texted, maybe she would help me. Nothing serious, just advice on adulting.

Why has she never called or written to me?

The world tilts on its axis, my head spinning. I desperately need to leave.

Once I've done my business, I walk to a row of sinks topped by a large mirror. While I wash my hands, I take a self-inventory. Makeup: not running. Hair: a bit frizzy because of the humidity, but not bad. Freckles: those are showing, and she can get over it. I can't help that she hates her own and I inherited them. It's a trait I've learned to love over the last few years. Outfit: feminine and appropriate. My blue dress is a shade between midnight and royal. A soft cotton cut to cover any undergarments, heaven forbid the people around me know I'm wearing a bra with straps. My neckline is modest, and the simple gold chain with the *L* pendant my parents gave me at graduation still skims my throat. I'm wearing peacock feather earrings, dangling and fluttering within my waves. The hemline is respectable, and the metallic gold sandals are tasteful.

All in all, this is a cardigan away from fully Belinda-approved, but it's too hot for the added layer.

As I return to the party, my thoughts continue running away

with themselves. *She did not try to speak to me. I guess she will ignore me. Is that better than making a scene? Probably.*

I'll try to accept it, but the bile in my stomach is creeping toward my throat.

As I return to the spot where I left my friends, I find Jim standing alone. When he sees me, his shoulders climb toward his ears. His tension is palpable, but I'm too frustrated to be passive.

Poor Jim gets all of the wrath meant for Belinda.

"Fuck, Jim, you know where the girls are. Just tell me."

I'm not sure how River tolerates their cordial relationship. His stuffy demeanor makes me boil.

"Could you please just get over whatever caused you to dislike me so much that you'd sabotage the only party I almost hosted in high school?" Snap. "Could you at least act like a human being toward me?"

"Yeah, thanks for the invite, Long," he grumbles, backing away.

Eyes narrowing, I take a step forward. "What was that narc?"

I'm about to pounce when a firm arm bands across my middle and pulls me into a warm chest, then a disembodied hand shoves a s'more into my mouth.

"Easy there, tiger." River nods. "I've got it from here, Jim."

thirteen
River

"LILY JAYNE LONG, you are going to be the goddamn death of me," I huff as I pull her through the crowd.

When we get to the coat closet in the hall near the staircase, I shove her in and shut the door behind us. Immediately, I know I've made a mistake. The space is too cramped for more than one adult. But it's too late to back down now. As I fumble for the light switch, I accidentally graze what I'm certain is the curve of her breast.

All my nerve endings light up, but I fight the sensation.

I've only seen drunk and angry Lily once before, and that girl set her ex-husband's possessions on fire.

Tonight, she's been doing fine. I only lost sight of her for a few minutes, but when I found her again, she was fully engaged in a tantrum.

"Jim's not a narc," I tell her, running a hand through my hair. "He's the mayor and head of the historical society, and I have to keep him happy if I want him to approve proposals and suggested updates. We aren't teens anymore, Lil."

She blinks back tears, refusing to meet my gaze. She didn't

have more than a couple of shots, but suddenly, I'm concerned she's as drunk as she was last night.

She sways into me and—

"Shit," I huff out, catching her. Holding her with one arm, I dig out my phone and shoot off a text.

"MOM, MRS. SANTOS MANOLO," Lee booms from the main bar, "have you had a chance to talk to Nessa tonight? We were thinking that instead of the church wedding, we might ask her to officiate. She had some really interesting ideas to share."

Nessa jumps in. "Of course we'd include facts about God being a woman and a pagan moon ceremony," she says, her voice retreating.

"Come on, sweetheart. Let's get you water and some rest." With Lily's arm draped over my shoulder, I sneak her upstairs.

A tap on her ass meant to be sportsman-like leads to thoughts of spanking her while naked. Great, now my dick is too snug in my pants.

Nope. Not going there. She's leaving and I'm tied to here. I take a few deep breaths, but my dick, the traitorous bastard, is relentlessly trying to convince me otherwise. Lily is maid of honor and you I'm co-best man. She's going to have a bunch of wedding-related reasons to be here over the next year.

Once I've laid her on the mattress, I smooth her skirt down and remove her sandals. Then I coax her up until her head is on the pillow and tuck her in.

All the while, unease swirls inside me. This is off. I swear she didn't have enough alcohol to put her in this state. I want to figure it out. I want to help her. To hold her. But I'm in charge of the logistics for this party, and if I slack, it'll reflect poorly on my business.

"Focus, River," I grumble as I jog back to the party.

As guests dwindle, I send team members home one by one until it's just our tight-knit circle quietly chatting. A creaking sound above causes me to whip around and eye the door leading to the stairway.

Sure enough, a slightly disheveled Lily stands on the stairs.

She's pulled her hair into a ponytail that swishes across her neck. She swapped the dress for the T-shirt from last night and bike shorts, along with a pair of mismatched socks. My heart squeezes at just how at home she looks in my space; the sensation grows to a full ache when she searches the room.

"Belinda left after she saw me, didn't she?" she asks, her voice cracking.

Six sets of eyes land on the woman who's shaking like a cornered animal. The nervous energy in the room is thick, the elongated pause growing more uncomfortable.

"Did I ruin your party?" she asks, her lip wobbling.

Collectively, the women pull her into a group hug.

I wish I was soothing her, and Seth can tell. He elbows Lee, "Congrats, you got River the best gift for your wedding. His dream girl in his bed."

"Oh fuck off," I scoff.

Lee smirks and pumps his eyebrows at Seth.

"Delia, you're my shift lead for breakdown tomorrow. I'm not taking this abuse after I threw an extremely discounted"—I give Lee a pointed look—"party. Do not clean out the bar without a plan for restocking."

I glare at her and Seth, who give me wide-eyed innocent looks.

"Ten-four, boss," she says. "Clean up and restock the bar after Seth and I clean it out. No problem."

I scrub a hand down my face. "Not what I meant, Deals. I hate you all…" Grumbling, I head to for the stairs.

Behind me, a chorus of "We love you too, River" breaks out, echoing off the walls.

Once we're safely in my apartment, I collapse with my face in the pillow and stifle a scream.

When there's a soft knock on the apartment door, I shake myself out of it, then gingerly answer.

Lily stands in the hall, her eyes sad and her mouth still trembling. "I can still stay here, right?"

As if I could say no to her.

Before I can answer verbally, she steps up and wraps her arms around me.

"Please don't make me walk over to Delia and Nessa's. If I do, the Springer will be going wild again."

I pull her into a full embrace. When her body goes slack against mine, my muscles loosen. She sniffles into my shirt, so I drag her to the couch and sit with her tucked into my side. Once sitting, her cries resume and gain strength. Unsure of what to say, I rely on my fingers to convey comfort by running them lightly through her soft waves up her nape.

"I saw Belinda. Almost knocked her over entering the ladies' room. When I came out, she was gone. Didn't say a word. Not even sorry or excuse me. She acted like I was a stranger. Like I was nothing. Air." She lowers her voice. "She's so disappointed in me. She has barely spoken to me since the fire."

Along with pain, there's longing in her tone. A hope that

someone will believe her and maybe even take her side. Ironically, if she asked any of the people downstairs still cleaning out my mid-tier spirits, they'd do it in a heartbeat, even if she was in the wrong.

"When I left, I called Mom from the road, but she tried to convince me to come back. Swore she was looking out for me. Helping." Lily scoffs.

"I'm sure in her own way—"

"She was oh so helpful with the invasive questions," Lily snaps, staring into the distance. "'Did you make sure he was fulfilled sexually? Were you working on your cooking enough? Was the house spotless? Were you too needy? Moody?'"

I hop up and grab the box of tissues from the counter, then quickly return to her side.

With a grateful smile, she plucks one out. She blows her nose, and when she's finished, the disdain has drained completely. "No, my so-called mom was happy to take it out on me. Poor Grant, poor heartbroken Landan, poor everyone but me. Fuck, Mom demanded I beg for his forgiveness," she says, her voice growing low and her cheeks heating.

The more of the story Lily shares, the more the fortress around her comes into view. Grant's betrayal was the tip of the iceberg. Her parents were the pain under the surface.

Damn, I missed so much. We all did.

As I listen, Nessa's voice from her Feminist Romance Book Club speaks in the back of my mind, explaining the trap of being the 'good girl' for the adults growing up.

Lily goes on, and when she's finished, the roller coaster of emotions turns back to shaking and quiet tears.

I tug her in closer again. I like being the shoulder she cries on. "That's about her. You know that, right? The strong, friendly, courageous traveler I know, the one who's circled the globe, is nowhere near weak or unworthy."

Eyes rimmed red, she give me the tiniest smile. Then she leans back against my chest.

My heart races. I'm angry, but not with her. I'm afraid, because this isn't my moment, but I want it to be.

"You aren't broken. Can I tell you a bunch of things you probably know, but I think you should hear?"

She nods, her head brushing my chest.

I hold her tighter and we sink into the pillows. "You're amazing. I've thought that since elementary school. Traveling and maintaining these friendships is so much work. I've been a bad friend for not keeping up. You haven't, though."

A soft snore from Pete cuts the silence as I consider my next words.

"The girls bring in the gifts, postcards, and trinkets you mail them. You've never missed a video call brunch. You've made the effort for them. I should have made that effort too. I'm sorry, Lil."

Our gazes meet. The intensity of this moment isn't lost on me. I am in awe, and she looks completely confused.

I wish I could explain how I've been destroyed by guilt for the last decade over not stopping the wedding. Over how I should have begged her to not walk down the aisle. I could have spoken up when the priest asked.

But I can't. Because that all means I also played a part in destroying her relationship with her parents.

Gravity has evaporated and I'm dizzy. My pulse jumps and the weight of it all is heavier than ever. I'm still stumbling through what to say when she presses the softest kiss on my cheek.

I pull her so she's nestled against my side, curled in on herself like a little ball. Just like Pete, who's curled up in his dog bed across the room.

With a soft and low laugh, I ask, "Anyone ever tell you that you and your dog are pretty much the same?"

She giggles. "In my previous life, I think I was a Shiba. I'm high energy, emotional, and I want to be touched, but on my terms only. Oh, and I love naps. Thank you." She kisses my cheek again.

This time I contemplate turning my head slightly and capturing her mouth with mine. Before I can, though, she yawns and closes her eyes.

According to my phone, it's 3:33 a.m. So I reluctantly tuck her into my bed. I have every intention of sleeping on the couch, but she clutches my arm and sleepily begs me to hold her. So I drift to sleep with her in my arms one more time.

fall

fourteen

Lily

I **SPEND** Monday recovering from the party and the emotions that overtook me. On Tuesday, I have a meeting in New York and then I'm free. Until the next wedding-related event, that is. I'll pretend I won't have to return for another decade between now and then.

My phone lights up, and a notification appears on the screen.

RIVER:

Kick ass and take names

The ugliness of the Philadelphia to New York line is why folks have the wrong impression of the state. Each stop is more densely populated than the last. Once the train hits the airport, it's all a blur of industrial parks and old graffiti. It's impossible to know what to expect at Penn Station. The last few years have brought about near-constant construction, which make it a chore to leave the building. I find the familiar exits boarded off, so I go with the flow of people toward the next set of doors. Thankfully, my friends warned me of the construction yesterday, so I built in ample time to make my way and get in the zone before this interview.

Smiling at his text, I type out a response. Then my nerves take over and I delete it. I want to reply to River, but nothing is right. A like is too casual, but a heart feels weird. Just *Thanks!* is flippant, but a *TYSM!* is lame too. "Ugh, fuck it." I drop my phone into my bag and focus on the sidewalk in front of me. Coffee. Coffee might help me think.

I snag a venti iced coffee, then sit at a table in the corner and skim through potential gigs for the fall and winter. I quickly accept a few of the opportunities, like the nepo-baby bachelorette party. It may even include cute and expensive *bride* items to swipe for Stef.

Tulum, Mexico, here I come.

I add "check passport expiration date" to my to-do list, then "find passport" on the next line.

I can't help but whoop quietly when I find an email from the client who has to cancel or reschedule 99.9 percent of the time. He's aware that I don't think his wife and daughters want my services, but he keeps shelling out the 75 percent deposit anyway. Honestly, it doesn't get much better than that, so I quickly send a reply with a heads-up that my prices were raised due to completing a new training.

When my phone vibrates in my bag, I dig it out and find another text.

RIVER:

BTW this is River

Shit. I forgot to reply, so I type out all of my thoughts and hit Send.

LILY:

We exchanged numbers three days ago. I haven't deleted it yet <wink emoji>. But thank you. For the place to crash and everything else. See you and Petey later.

Hope he's good for you today!

I lose track of time at the coffee shop, then find myself jogging through the studio doors in Hudson Yards and up to the sleek white and gray marble counter. Out of breath, I hand my ID over to the surly attendant. The steel turnstiles that require swipe badges for access may be intended to make people feel safer, but they only make me tense. They make the place so sterile.

Already, I'm picking up vibes I don't like. My gut instinct is to skip the meeting, but I've come this far, so I pull my spine straight and roll my shoulders back, then tell myself I'm ready.

I check my reflection in the stainless-steel door of the elevator and take inventory of myself. This is my nicest workout outfit; buttery soft leggings and matching longline bra in a coppery color topped with an unbuttoned autumn-colored flannel. It's reminiscent of that Evermore coat, giving low hanging fruit to chitchat about all things Taylor Swift.

I've learned to strategically place hints to steer the conversation to topics I'm comfortable with. It's why my large water bottle is covered in stickers of all the places I've been.

My ponytail is the perfect mix of cute and undone and my understated makeup is camera ready, so I'm prepared for test shoots if things are going well.

When the doors open, I'm greeted by a modern pair of iron-and-glass doors and a large neon logo. Once the perky receptionist checks me in, I'm guided to an open kitchen and waiting area. It's full of everything a fitness minded person could want, from cold brew and kombucha on tap to a glass-front fridge filled with pressed juices, waters, and electrolyte drinks. In separate wicker baskets are a variety of snack options. Damn, I could live in this kitchen.

I contemplate a green juice but am snapped out of my thoughts by an irritated man.

He spends the next forty-five minutes on photos, measurements, and documents, his intensity making it feel like onboarding, not an interview.

When I get back to reception, I'm craving some form of comfort, so I snag one of those juices from the fridge. I've just cracked it open when the founder and CEO, Kara, strides in. She's a beautiful, leggy blond woman whose signature outfit is head-to-toe white workout gear. I've idolized her entrepreneurship for years, and I've often felt like I'm chasing her tailwinds.

I stand to shake her hand, only to trip on my bag at my feet. As I lurch forward, green liquid sails through the air and lands down the front of the all-white outfit, leaving her looking like an outfielder at the end of a championship baseball game.

Mortified, all I can do is stand, frozen to the spot. My face is hot and I can hardly meet her eyes. The tension in the room builds, deadly silent. *This is bad.*

An assistant rushes over to clean things up and another brings her a fresh set of clothes. The twenty minutes that follow are filled with terse formality. When I'm finally released, I slip out the glass doors, ride the elevator to the main floor, and stride out to the busy sidewalk knowing I won't be back.

Person after person bumps into me, everyone in a hurry to get somewhere. The air smells vaguely of trash, and there's too much noise. This is why I'm not a Manhattan person. I have never experienced the magic so many movies claim this city possesses.

I hustle to the train station, eager to get back to Pete and open air. Far from all of this. My luck seems to turn a corner, because by the skin of my teeth, I make it through the station and find a seat on the departing train.

With a breath out, I think the day may just get better. Instead, I notice my seatmate, and it gets so much worse.

"Grant?"

fifteen
Lily

MY INNER MONOLOGUE is a slew of curses.

Beside me, Grant blinks slowly. An awkward silence lingers a beat too long. Then a chilling grin stretches across his face, causing a new layer of sweat to form on my skin and mix with the bits lingering from jogging here. This is the cold kind of sweat. My stomach bottoms out. I know that smile. Nothing good follows it. I thought town was bad, but the desire to flee ratchets up exponentially. It's like all those years ago, when I was desperate to get out.

I guide myself through the talking points meant to calm my nerves. He won't hurt me physically. Even if his words are meant to cut me down, they are meaningless.

A gust of patchouli breezes over us as another passenger drops into the three-seat row. Paisley sheer fabric brushes my side and tickles my face and arm.

Prudence Cleary, the Peacock Springs tea shop owner and tarot reader, breaks into a husky laugh. Between the Puritanical name and infrequent but very noticeable use of odd and outdated phrases, the likelihood that she is truly a three-hundred-year-old witch is a topic that's been discussed among the children of

Peacock Springs for decades. Her beautiful dark skin is an umber as warm as her personality, and the few wrinkles she does have add to the allure.

A thread of relief works its way through me. Her arrival helps to momentarily cut the tension.

"Hold these, will you dear?" She digs through an oversized tote, then, without waiting for a reply, tosses item after item onto my lap or shoves them into my hands. In a matter of seconds, I'm juggling a large pink crystal, a vial of essential oils, at least three mini bags of salt-and-vinegar chips, and a T-shirt with a well-worn spell book screen-printed on it.

Finally, she produces a journal and a pen with a flourish. "I knew I needed to be on this train today. Did I know why? Of course not. This is why I follow where the spirit takes me."

I gape, jaw slack, my head spinning after the events of the last few hours.

Breaking the silence, Pru nudges the conversation along. "Go on, go on. Don't allow me to interrupt this reunion."

I fold the shirt around her items and slide them into her tote.

Pru cackles, the sound causing an anxious giggle to spontaneously escape from my lips.

Wrapping my arm sidelong around Pru, I ask her, "What sort of witch are you?"

Pointedly looking past me, Pru says, "Grant, is this the first you've seen Lily? Spoken to her in a decade? Apologized to her?"

A small zip of excitement hits me. Okay, I'm good with putting him in the hot seat.

Grant coughs and shifts, uncrossing his legs, making the small space tighter. With a sneer, he says, "Oh no. Lily, I didn't. I was a total child then."

Pru tuts, shaking her head.

He searches my face like he's waiting for something from me.

My jaw clenches and my ears ring. I've tried every method I've come across to release trapped anger, but it's here. Lingering.

And he still can't pretend to apologize.

Pru homes in on him. "You'll do better than that. This girl was run out of her home because you can't keep your willy in your pants. You can't fool this old woman."

"Old?" he interjects, turning on the charm to take the heat off himself. "What are you, forty? Forty-five?"

She cackles, and as she quiets, I take advantage of the subject change and blurt out, "Whatever it is you're doing, keep it up. I need that skin tincture. I'll swing by."

She drops a tiny bottle into my hand label side up. It reads Boy Tears. With a grin she returns to glaring at Grant and nudges me softly in the ribs, as if signaling me to take over.

Looks like I'm going for it.

"Thanks, Grant, for whatever that was. Though I didn't hear you apologize."

Warmth radiates through my body. Is this pride in the face of a challenge? It feels like when I finally mastered the crow pose, so probably. The flood of emotions flows from my lips in a chaotic scramble.

"Seriously." I sigh. "Did we get married too young? Of course. But you cheated. That's on you. Only you. You had zero consequences and then let everyone villainize me. They literally wanted to throw me in the stocks." Anger rises in my chest, the warmth of pride turning into fiery fury. "At no point did you even try to come to my defense. You hurt me. Badly. For many years."

His smarmy smile fades, his brows knitting and his eyes narrowing. I can feel his cruel response brewing, like a change in air pressure.

Cocking his head, he lowers his voice, allowing the condescension to seep through his false confusion. "How is your inability to get into college or maintain a relationship with your parents on me?"

He tentatively reaches out, like he might brush away the hair falling in my face. I flinch and retreat, my blood running cold at the idea of his hand on me.

"Lily, sweetheart. You only get one set of parents. Don't you think it's time you take accountability for your anger issues? You can act high and mighty, like some centered hippie, online. But we know the truth. Your drama queen antics caused you to embarrass yourself."

Blood boiling, I clench my fists, my nails digging into my palms. I want to punch him in his smug little face. I should have expected this. Emotional baiting is his signature move.

The train lurches to a hard stop at the first station and the doors open, allowing people to enter and exit the car. The muffled conductor announcement comes over the speakers. All the while, we're locked in a standoff, and it's my turn to make a move.

When the train rocks, then picks up speed, I stand, shifting toward the aisle. "Yeah? I also only had one appendix, but when it was infected, the doctors removed it. Toxicity becomes septic and kills. I'm not swallowing your poison again."

As I slip past Pru, I say, "Do you need a ride? I'm parked at the next station."

She shakes her head, her eyes locking on mine, conveying a message. I'm hypnotized enough to zero in on my ex and say, "You've never defined me, and you never will. Apologies are only as good as the changes a person makes. Do I have regrets? Sure. Don't worry, I don't need your lip service apology. I forgive you. But don't confuse forgiveness with permission to continue the behavior. Pretend you don't know me, since you don't. You will see me again. Soon. I'll be damned if you make me miss this for my friend." With those words, I turn away.

I wait by the exit, and when the door opens at the next stop, I dash down the stairs. In the car, I turn the music up loud and drive. I keep driving until I reach the banks of the Delaware River and find a low pedestrian bridge.

I park nearby and walk to the middle, where I sit with music blasting through my headphones. The meditative rhythm of the river gliding over rocks, the wind in the plants, the clouds thick and white in the sky above make me feel like myself again. I lose all sense of time and enjoy existing until my phone's virtual voice cuts the song.

"You've received a text message from River. It says, 'Hey. Expected to hear from you by now. You survive the city?'"

Whoops. Giggling, I close my eyes and consider how to explain my day to him.

Before I can dig my phone out of my bag, it says, "River sent a photo message."

It's a picture of Pete sitting at the bar with a smug look on his face. He's balanced on a barstool with his paws on the surface, and it looks like he even let River drape one of the bar rags over him.

RIVER:

Petey is making a solid bartender, but he was wondering when you'll be back

LILY:

Baby pup!! Of course I will be back for you my love

My interview was a disaster. I ran into Grant on the train <puke face emoji>

< sends a photo of her feet dangling above the water >

Was getting some air. I can be back in 10

RIVER:

Take your time <heart emoji>

sixteen

River

SEPTEMBER

Email Chain

FROM: Stef
Subject: Wedding Party Details

BEAUTIFUL WEDDING PARTY MEMBERS,

We just met with Mrs. Sherman at the Honeybee Inn, and it's official: the wedding will be Memorial Day weekend! So what comes next?

1. Colors, dresses, suits, etc. A second note coming soon :)
2. Susan would like to host a formal engagement party. Word is sometime around Valentine's Day/Presidents' Day Weekend.
   a. River: she'll probably talk to you or Delia about this.

3. We're going to have a joint celebration in Atlantic City
   the weekend of May 5th, so save up if you are a gambler
   and get ready to party!

———

FROM: Seth
   Subject: RE: Wedding Party Details

UNSUBSCRIBE

———

FROM: Lee
   Subject: RE: RE: Wedding Party Details

NO

———

FROM: Lily
   To: Stef, Nessa, Delia, River
   Subject: RE: Wedding Party Details (No Boys)

THANKS, babe! So excited for you. Just wanted to confirm dates
for my calendar. I'll head back for:

- One week in February for the engagement party and
  catching up
- Month of May for everything from the bachelorette
  through the big day!

What about a shower? Is that separate from February?

———

FROM: Stef
    To: Lily, Nessa, Delia, River
    Subject: RE: RE: Wedding Party Details (No Boys)

STILL TBD. IDK, you are the maid of honor. Don't you plan that?

———

FROM: Nessa
    To: Stef, Lily, Delia, River
    Subject: RE: RE: RE: Wedding Party Details (No Boys)

JUST MOVE HOME, K. THANKS. BYEEEEE

DR. NESSA RABIN, PsyD

———

FROM: River
    To: Stef, Nessa, Delia, Lily
    Subject: RE: RE: RE: RE: Wedding Party Details (No Boys)

LAST I CHECKED, I'm still a boy.

———

MY PHONE VIBRATES on the nightstand and when I roll over and scoop it up, the photo I took of Pete sitting at the bar appears on the screen. Scrubbing the sleep out of my eyes, I sit up. My heart flutters when I confirm this isn't a dream. Lily is calling me. I accept the call and realize a moment too late it's a video call.

"Oh my god, I'm so, so sorry," she rushes out. "I didn't mean to wake you. Oh shit, it's early, isn't it?"

Still groggy, I croak out, "What time is it?"

"Eight. I just finished doing a live workout up here in Vermont. I took this for the fall foliage. Check it out," she says, flipping the camera to show the view. "Or whatever." Her tone goes from excited to a terrible facsimile of nonchalant.

"It's cool. Scout is supposed to be here today to take a look at the cottage with me." I rub a hand through my hair and scratch the back of my neck.

"Your brother still goes by Scout?" she asks, smiling wide.

"Oh yeah. You know we do as Mom says," I say, breaking into a grin that matches her. Falling back on a pillow, I relax into our conversation.

"River, Scout, and Leaf," she muses, listing off the three of us Hendrix boys by our middle names.

"It's still River and Scout, but the middle-child is a shot banker who goes by Robert these days." I roll my eyes. Ever the compromising pair, our mom chose fun middle names while Dad bestowed on us strong traditional first names.

"What have they been up to lately?" she asks, sliding into a deck chair and propping her phone up.

We spend the next fifteen minutes discussing what each of my brothers has been doing in recent years.

"How is your dad?" she asks, her mouth turned down in concern.

"He's the same cantankerous bastard he's always been," I say, giving a little shrug.

"River," she says, dragging out my name.

"Lily," I reply, matching her tone.

I sigh and scrub a hand down my face before diving into the details of his stroke recovery.

"The stroke affected the left side of Dad's brain, damaging his language, reason, and logic centers. It also left him with weakness in his right-side limbs. He finds light and sound more difficult to process, so my parents' house is always bathed in low lamp lighting. He's generally in a pair of noise-canceling headphones, drowning out the world around him." Scratching the back of my neck, I roll through the rest of the topline details. "Robert." I roll my eyes and scoff. "He hired some giant guy, Gary, to help with some of the physical care and PT stuff. Mom's working with Gary on some veteran support group things too. We'll see. I don't know."

"That's good, though, right?" Her question is so sweet and genuine.

"Maybe. If that means he won't be such an ass."

She laughs and my chest feels lighter from the sound. In my half-awake, relaxed state, my mind drifts to daydreams of her bright smile and the twinkle of her eyes. After several seconds, Lily says, "River? You still here?"

Yawning, I shake my head. "Sorry. Tired. I spent too much time researching ideas for fall beers for Sunflower Fest."

In a flash, her magnetic smile is replaced by the slowly shifting foliage behind her. "Nothing says fall like New England. Can you sneak away for a day or two?"

I want to say yes so badly, but I'm nervous to step away right now. Wavering, I offer, "Maybe?"

With a sugary singsong voice, she adds, "I had a local maple beer last night that would be perfect for the festival. You could say it's a business trip."

With that dangling suggestion, I'm a goner.

seventeen

Lily

WHEN I FIRST SAW THE black saltbox house on a hill with its mossy green door, I knew I was home. At least for now. The shared space for travelers like me houses a mix of people, including writers and artists and people wandering through life, finding themselves. It's the perfect space to find inspiration and reset after the disaster that was New Jersey. And now one of the very few parts of Jersey I miss is coming here, to me.

My stomach flutters. I hope he enjoys how magical this place is.

At sunrise, I record a class, taking advantage of the twinkling amber threads of light between the birch and beech trees in the background. Then I shower, edit content, separate into "social pages" and "paywall." Yesterday I took a midday hike with Pete, allowing myself to get lost in the trees as the natural world prepares to hibernate.

Today, however. I'm skipping the hike. While I wait for River to arrive, my phone buzzes, and a notification appears on the screen.

PIPER IS PLANNING an intuition humming ritual, which requires choosing a personal focus. She suggested gratitude, mourning, or healing to keep it simple for River, since this is probably new for him. I can do that. Just as long as I don't forget to touch on the topic between now and then.

I'm standing on the front stone patio as River's old pickup truck crests the hill. The well-maintained but ancient beast shines cherry red against the mix of deep greens and yellowing leaves. His arrival looks like the final embers of a bonfire glowing against the deepening darkness. He's like a beacon of hope.

He parks and ducks out of the cab, a duffel in hand.

At the sight of him, my heart stops.

"Hey." He gives me a sheepish smile.

Air whooshes from my lungs, and my pulse ticks up a beat. "Hi," I reply. "It's my turn to show you around."

I lead him to the bedroom I've been sharing with Piper so he can drop his bag on my bed and I can crate Pete.

My little buddy's whine pulls at my heartstrings, but for now, this is the best place for him. "I know, pup. I'm sorry," I say as I close the door.

———

ON THE SHORT drive to the brewery, I fill him in on everything I've learned about the area. I love watching his reactions, the way his smile reaches his eyes and how the fine lines around them crinkle. He looks relaxed and so handsome. But I refuse to screw up our friendship. So I clench my thighs, trying to ignore the tingling sensation that hits me when he's near.

The brewery is a converted garage with lifted glass doors and a gray stone patio with string lights strung above the picnic tables. From the look of things, the sustainability practices that River's spoken about with such passion are in effect here. His dreams for his place are completely within reach.

"What do you think of the menus being digital only?" I nudge, curious if he's seeing what I do.

"Seems like the place is stuck in 2020," River mutters. He scans the code and with his eyes locked on his phone, he reviews the list. A few moments later he taps my hand, and electricity seems to zing between us.

I chew my lower lip and find it impossible to take my eyes off him. The intensity of his focus is mesmerizing, but I'm second- and third-guessing if this was the best place to show him.

"You were hoping I'd see something else, weren't you?" He cups my chin and presses his thumb on my lip, forcing me to release it.

"I hoped that if your dad is putting down your sustainability plans, this could be, um, a compromise. Like, if you keep a standard menu physically and then specials online?"

Our server appears, greeting us with a smile. "What can I get you two?"

"I'll have a flight, please. Can you include some of the new fall seasonals?" I ask. "My only requirement is the maple porter."

He suggests rounding the flight out with the sunflower hefeweizen, hard apple cider, and a Sip of Sunshine IPA.

"I'll try others so we get the full experience," River says. "I'll go with the red ale, the Oktoberfest, and…" River tilts his head before committing to his order. "And the pumpkin ale."

"You don't have to get pumpkin if it's not your thing," the server says. "We have plenty of year-rounds too."

"No, it's okay. We came here for a seasonal tasting. I've got to give it a shot."

As the server heads back to the bar, River fidgets with the beer list on his phone, worrying his lip, his knee bouncing.

After a moment, he stands, frowning, and excuses himself. He walks up to the server and bartender and extends his hand. They shake, and as they chat, his shoulders relax a bit. I want to make my way over to listen, but I don't want to intrude, so I force myself to remain seated.

When he returns, River's demeanor is far more casual. "Sorry," he says. "I felt like a jerk, and I needed to make it right. I hate being rude." He runs his hands through his hair.

Rude? That's the last word I'd use to describe him.

"I don't think you're rude at all," I say, reaching for him mindlessly. My hand lands on his knee. The heat of his skin through the denim sparks something confusing, and I quickly retract my hand. I make a mental note to try to figure out what it is in therapy.

Before long, the server returns with our flights, two pint glasses of water, and a basket of apple cider donuts.

Warmth blooms in my chest. Being here with River is so damn

easy. This feels like being home but not the home that gives me anxiety. It's a sensation I've been searching for. Maybe it's Vermont?

Or maybe it's River, a small voice whispers.

———

RIVER and I gather around the fire pit with my housemates. Evening light casts a lavender and sapphire hue over the world, ushering in the peaceful end of day.

Piper, in a dark violet cape, her fiery copper curls wild, looks bewitching.

"Tonight," she says, "we're going to step outside our comfort zones and welcome the coming season. You all should have prepared a meditation on an autumnal theme."

My heart lurches. Crap. The meditation I meant to explain to River. I forgot all about it.

"This is a time to invite wisdom," she continues. "To ground yourself and prepare for the hibernation of winter. This is the season for gratitude and healing. Remember that healing comes from inviting balance into your life. It comes from planning and preparation, providing self-care, and mourning what ends. Like summer's inevitable exit, all things that enter our lives will eventually take their leave. Thankfully, that allows space for something newer."

The whole group is nodding, entranced by Piper and the musicality of her lithe voice.

Everyone except River, who's watching me from the corner of his eye.

"Take a few moments to reconnect with the information you prepared," she suggests. "Then you will spread out, finding spaces where you can still hear my instructions but have some solitude." She pauses, giving the group time to disperse.

"Lily," River says, dragging out my name, eyes narrowed.

"It's fine. I didn't get a chance to tell you about this part, but you know what your goal is for the new season: to create a new era of the Featherweight." Smiling reassuringly, I pat his hand. Again that heat zaps me, and I pull back.

What is going on?

"And your goal?" he asks, his focus on me like a heavy weight.

Sighing, I admit, "I want to feel at home. Somewhere. Anywhere. Moving is exhausting."

He only gives me a sympathetic smile. Now that I've made the moment awkward, I stand and drag my chair to the edge of the patio. River does the same, positioning himself so we face one another.

Piper relays instructions, speaking about change, comfort zones, and the familiar and unfamiliar bridges we take. She suggests that those who are typically the loudest in the room should focus on remaining quiet more often. Those of us who are still should add movement, and so forth. Then she guides us to inhale a deep breath. Then, collectively, we let out long noisy hums, like the *ohm* in a yoga class.

Most people have their eyes closed, but River is looking at me, and I can't look away from him. Locked in his gaze, my insides shift, and suddenly, I feel like the little girl I used to be. The one playing on the muddy banks of the water. I'm overcome with giggles, and despite the poor timing, I can't stop. The harder I laugh, the wider his eyes get and the firmer he presses his lips together, trying to suppress his own outburst.

"What's so amusing over there?" Piper snaps.

A wave of emotions hits me. A storm of shame, embarrassment, resentment, and helplessness, along with a deep desire to be the kind of person others approve of.

Nothing is funny. No, the laughter is because the humming brought up being young. Spending time with my friend, for once letting go of all my cares. Being unashamed of who I am and how I don't quite fit into any of the boxes I'm presented with.

But this is not the time to explain that. Not to mention my heart is racing. I don't think I could speak if I tried. I hate being the center of attention like this. My lungs can't take in enough air, and my mouth is too dry to talk. So I do what I do best. I stand and dart for the forest path. Once I'm out of sight of the group, I bend at the waist and dry heave.

When I'm finished, I stand and turn around. Only now do I realize how dark it is. There's no way I could find my way back like this. I can't move, since I can't figure out where the house is. So I sit on the leaves and dry dirt, head hanging.

I'm collecting dried curls of birchwood, thinking about how perfect they'd be for bonfire kindling, when a phone flashlight appears above me. Then I find myself face-to-toe with River's boots.

He crouches, and for a moment I think he's going to kiss me. I want him to kiss me. I want to ask him to be my home and travel with me.

Except that wouldn't be fair to him. He's earned the right to his steady life, to build his legacy. Instead, I ask, "Want to watch the world burn with me?"

eighteen

River

THE FEATHERWEIGHT'S exterior is decorated with dried corn stalks, pumpkins, and gourds in a variety of oranges, yellows, and greens. The baskets of mums that line the walkway amplify the sunny look of the building. It's picture perfect, so I take the opportunity to snap a few photos for social media. The place feels like the last moments of sunshine before the darkness takes over. Despite the beauty of the moment, I can't shake this ominous feeling. Maybe it's the October chill setting in. Or seasonal depression. Can someone who's never had it before experience it randomly like this?

I've turned a few of the front lawn seating boxes into a festival station, and today, Delia is out there training our newest servers.

Phone still out, I wander over to take a few shots.

"Hey." Delia says, holding out a hand. "I haven't touched up my makeup. Don't put that on social media."

"This one's just for Lily. We can redo it for marketing later. Maybe wearing our new fleece jackets. You'll have ample time to primp before that, promise," I say, my hands up like she's got a weapon pointed at me.

See, Officer Shane? I have nothing to hide.

Smirking to myself about the joke, I type out a quick text to Lily with the photo attached.

RIVER:

Check it out. The Sunflower Fest is about to have a whole new tasting menu thanks to you and Vermont

Wish you were here

THE THREE DOTS that signal she's responding pop up, then disappear once, then again. I stare at my phone, hoping she's just crafting a reply.

"Hey, boss," one of the new guys shouts, fumbling as he maneuvers a keg to its ice bin. I pocket my phone and rush over to help before he puts a dent in the hardwoods. Lifting in tandem, we heave it into place. Then I show him how to hook up the taps. These aren't traditional fall beers; there's nothing pumpkin spiced here, and that, actually, has my dad making faces at me. He's not fond of the craft brew concept, but he's resigned to it, though it irks him more when our selections don't line up with whatever he hears is on trend. He worries that working to stand out the way I do puts me too far outside of what the market wants. I'm hoping to show him otherwise today. The maple porter and the sunflower seed hefeweizen I came up with, inspired by the trip last month, turned out really well.

Dad immediately balked at these new ideas and tried to tell me they would flop.

Thankfully, he's quickly proven wrong.

We've officially had one of our strongest Saturdays in ages. The tables indoors and out were full from the early side of lunch until the vendors were packing up their booths. Even then, the vendors clamored for the dinner buffet the business council and I set up as a thank-you for their participation, and many said they'd be back for future events.

The only thing that could have made today better would have been a response from Lily. I can't help but think of her that night in Vermont, on the forest floor, gasping for air. Her body bent and breaking from the inside. Then the instant change when she realized I was there. A playfulness returned to the corners of her eyes. She made a joke and wouldn't speak of the incident after. We still haven't discussed what happened, instead sticking to exchanging memes and missed calls.

I was tempted to pull her in and kiss her that night, but she was vulnerable, and it didn't feel right. Now I'm stuck waiting for the chill between us to lift. For our interactions to get comfortable again, if that is even possible. The potential that she could conveniently miss the upcoming events for Stefanie and Lee feels more real than ever. I just want to shake her, to wake her up to the truth. The truth as far as I'm concerned, at least.

Maybe if I tell her what happened at Grant's bachelor party, she'll understand that she was never at fault. She might hate me afterward, but she'd have every right to. All I'm certain of is a deep exhaustion has set into my bones and my thoughts are jumbled, making it difficult to drag myself up the stairs. I don't even strip out of my clothes before I crash.

In the morning, I have a reply.

LILY:

> Looks gorgeous! I can't believe Delia let you take a picture of her without mascara

nineteen
Lily

THE PANIC ATTACK in Vermont was not the kind of blast from the past anyone would enjoy. I was so embarrassed that I packed up shortly after River left. I've been bopping around from one temp gig and town to another so much that I wake up some mornings unsure of where I am.

I went down a rabbit hole scrolling anxiety content one afternoon and landed in a slew of memes and informational posts on gifted kid burnout. It seems like I'm not the only one who was full of potential as a child that is drifting. Burnout posts morphed into content on ADHD and autism. My content is all neurodivergence all the time: understanding it, laughing at its idiosyncrasies, videos, infographics, personal stories, and ads for virtual therapy. It finally pushed me to schedule an appointment.

I meet with Dorothea virtually every week, and I'm working hard to unpack the events that landed me here. We've discussed my childhood, parental relationships, Grant, and the last ten years, as well as what I think I want for the next ten. But we've only scratched the surface of those subjects. Now I'm going to dip my toe in the deep end.

"Can social media lead to accurate self-diagnosis?"

Dorothea gives me her "elaborate on this" look.

So I do, twisting my fingers into the fringes on my scarf and pulling my legs up in the chair. "So, like—" My heart stutters. So I take a deep, calming breath in, and on the exhale, I try again. "River came to visit and we talked about how being in our hometown turns me into a totally different person. The person I used to be. After that, these videos keep coming my way. There's gifted kid burnout, good girl syndrome, and then more extreme terms like emotional abuse, neurodiversity, ADHD, autism spectrum, and complex post-traumatic stress disorder. I was curious if there's any validity to the algorithm sending this all my way?"

As is her style, she asks me to think about where some of these questions may be coming from. Then we break down as much of the complicated mess as we can in the remaining half hour.

The following week, we pick up where we left off, and I dissect the young Lily who triggered my giggle fit: a carefree girl playing with River, as well as the anxious child who always reached for teachers' and parents' approval. Then the young woman who got married immediately after high school.

"From what I've gathered, good girls are people pleasers who struggle to speak up for themselves for fear of upsetting others or being socially rejected. Instead, they focus on their loyalty and warm obedience. That's exactly the kind of person I was when I left home. So of all the titles, being a pathological people pleaser is definitely on my list of traits. But is that a bad thing? I've always thought of it as putting kindness out into the world, not instigating when there's no need to cause trouble. I'm not really concerned about it..." Head down, I wring my hands in my lap.

Wow, even I don't believe me there.

A look of skepticism flashes across Dorothea's face, though she quickly resumes a neutral look. "If you aren't concerned about it, then is it important to discuss?"

Sighing, I admit, "No, it's not always a positive. Sometimes my need to be liked has led me to do things like date people who I know are not looking for something serious. Except, every fucking time—" I clap my hand over my mouth. "Sorry, I didn't mean to curse."

"Keep going. Don't apologize," she encourages.

I nod once. "It seems like I always end up playing house with casual partners. We get together and agree it's just for fun, but then we get attached quickly. We're always together, and I start to feel like maybe I don't have to always be alone. Except I end up alone."

"What do you mean that you are always alone?" she gently prods.

I stare at the wall in front of me and consider. This is really hard. "Um, well." My insides twist as I search for words to explain. "I just wish that I knew there was a person out there who finds me worth sticking around for." The moment the words are out, I wish I could take them back. It's pathetic, I know, but it's the truth. I fidget with the hem of my pants as I sit cross-legged. Then I adjust my posture a few times, but nothing brings me comfort.

"Who told you that you were not worth sticking around for?" The question sounds harsh, but Dorothea's eyes are soft.

"Um, nobody said it, exactly, but when Grant cheated, my folks took his side. The entire town did, really. I was berated and swamped with comments about how I didn't perform as a wife. Every person I talked to poked holes into every corner of my actions."

My anger flares hot, my spine stiffening.

"But I don't think I could have done anything to stop him from cheating." I lick my lips. "Sure, I could have said no more often. Like when our moms pushed me to delay college and when they pushed me to have the wedding so quickly. But I was young and naive enough to think playing house would be an adventure."

Tears prick at the backs of my eyes.

"I figured we were adults on paper, so we were in charge. I didn't realize how little power or control over my own life I would have. Since I left, I've floated from place to place and thing to thing. Sometimes it is amazing. Everything I own fits inside my Wrangler, and Peter Pan is always at my side so I'm never lonely. Except that's not true. Sometimes, I am lonely. I can't understand how my parents could write me off the way they did. My mom walked away like I was made of air when I saw her in September. That hurt. A lot…"

The tears well in my eyes now, a dull ache pulsing in my chest.

"It was really brave of you to be so open and vulnerable with me," she encourages.

Great. I'm glad, I guess, but could she now tell me what to do next? That would be amazing.

"Unfortunately, I can't tell you what to do from here," she says, as if reading my mind. "If I did, I'd be yet another person you felt you had to please. Another person whose opinion you either weigh more important than your own, or someone to run from. Instead, I want to know what an adventurous and entrepreneurial woman like you sees that has made you wonder about each of these diagnoses. What feels true to you, and what feels like a stretch. Take the next week and write it all down. When we meet again, we can compare your feelings with what I've observed and come up with a plan together."

twenty
River

WHEN I LEFT VERMONT, I did my best to return to a somewhat normal rhythm of life. Our evening chats have become stilted, and the two of us have made a lot of excuses to shorten them, but they haven't fully disappeared. During closing most nights, my fingers take on a mind of their own and I hover over her contact. As I'm considering it once again, a notification pops up.

LILY:

Hello from the Moab desert!

RIVER:

Hello from the basement

LILY:

<photo of Pete with large red stone arches in the background>

RIVER:

<photo of whiskey barrels>

. . .

I TRY to discuss the nothingness of each day now that I've discovered that her online life is a complete ruse. She has so few genuine connections in the world, but I'm dedicated to being one of them. I will not admit my crush, turning myself into another horny man whose focus is *dat ass*.

It's a fantastic ass, don't get me wrong. Her last photo is of her with a mirror behind her, the angle making both her face and back visible. Her hair has grown longer in the last couple months and cascades over her shoulders and skims the swell of her breasts in that sports bra. It's a rich emerald green, reminding me of the pine trees everyone has been dragging home for holiday events.

I wonder what it's like for her to spend holidays without family.

Standing like this, the tiniest bit of cleavage is visible, showing off her perfectly round and perky tits. Damn, do I want to know how they would feel—

I slap myself, willing the thought away. *What the hell is wrong with me?*

IT'S a Monday afternoon and the bar is closed, as is the industry standard, but I'm here unloading deliveries and organizing them in storage and stock locations.

The first George to own and operate the Featherweight did so with his wife, Molly. Every time I consider that, along with the husband-and-wife duos who've done the same over the generations, it reminds me of how badly I want to have a partner, a real one. Delia is an amazing employee, but this isn't her dream. She's still finding her way, and eventually she will, and she'll leave the bar.

The cool stones of the basement hold in the necessary chill for the aging home-distilled spirits and brewed beers. While I'm down here, I take all of the practical steps, checking inventory and ensuring things are stored and working properly, just like Grandpa taught me starting when I was nine years old.

The stones and tiny dark alcoves are nostalgic. When I was a teenager, Grandpa would hide a secret stash of alcohol down here and I would swipe for my friends. He had watered down the bottles and they were hardly alcoholic by the time we got a hold of them. Grant, Seth, and I would play truth or dare and I'd wait for them to request these terrible drinks.

I'd sit in that circle, palms sweating, wanting to ask them to be my wingmen but too afraid of rejection. I always hoped that she'd be the brave one, or that Nessa would instigate a game of spin the bottle since she teased the idea so often. My prayer that someone else could intervene and make this happen for us remains unanswered.

"Shit." I huff, roughing a hand over my head. The song echoes into the darkness as the complicated layers of time, friends, parents, and the opinions of others swirl inside my head.

I climb up the steps to meet Carmine Salvatore for our biweekly delivery from the butcher shop, and as I hit the top, Ava Marie's and Bella Salvatore's voices drift through the open doorway.

Irritated, Bella pushes the empty hand truck my way. "Nonna needs to talk to you. I'll drive, but I'm not doing the heavy lifting." She unwraps a piece of gum and pops it into her mouth, then proceeds to chew with loud pops and snaps.

Ava Marie purrs with a mix of faux sweetness. She reminds me of Meryl Streep in *The Devil Wears Prada*, down to the oversized sunglasses she keeps on indoors. Despite the polite words, she's bitter and indifferent.

"Sugar, we're going to need to reserve the Featherweight for an upcoming town meeting."

"Of course. Your standing weekly reservations and the setup

are on the books. Delia can add any supplemental meetings you need for the committee," I tell her. "She'll be here tomorrow. I'm sorry you came all this way when Carmine and the boys could have handled the lifting for Bella." With my most charming smile, I do my best to warm her a bit.

Bella's bloodred nails look so sharp I fear she could stab someone.

Ava Marie breaks into Cheshire cat grin, happy on the surface but sinister behind the eyes, then chuckles, Bella joining in. "Due to the nature of the town business, this can't be handled by anyone other than the owner," Ava Marie argues. "The proposal party indicates that Lily Long is back, and she'll need to be held accountable for her previous actions. Pending a vote, of course. It's not up to the council alone. We'll need to gather the town elders and a few others, so we need the whole space and we need to ensure she isn't tipped off. She's not invited, and we're concerned Delia is compromised there."

Bella cracks her gum and snarls, "We can trust you to keep this to yourself, can't we? You wouldn't want to do something as silly as tip her off when you need Nonna and the mayor to sign off on your upcoming renovations."

Fuck. She's correct, so I pull out the book from under the counter and flip pages. Rumor has it that Carmine has connections to the mob, although if we're being honest, Ava Marie is far scarier than he is.

"I'm booked solid for the next several weeks. If you want that much privacy, we'll probably need to look at next year." I point to the calendar as evidence. "Plus," I say, "the party was in September. Why are you tackling the issue three months later? You've waited this long. Can it wait a little longer? She won't be home for Christmas, if that's the concern."

Ava Marie hums, the room then falling silent except for the occasional smacking of Bella's chewing gum.

Filling the discomfort with oversharing is a rookie move, yet I find myself doing it anyway. "Listen, I am the best man and she's the maid of honor."

Bella scoffs "dishonor" under her breath.

My lips twitch into a grin, until I remember my use of it was playful and hers is venomous.

"Anyhow, I have it on good authority she won't be back until at least February." I point to February's penciled-in events. "Susan has put a hold on the weekends before and after Valentine's Day for a formal engagement party, but the exact date hasn't been confirmed. Should we touch base when she locks it in? Since there's no need to rush, why don't you focus on the holidays for now?" I pray this stalling tactic will work so I can formulate a way to intervene.

Bella has looked completely indifferent if not bored throughout this fifteen-minute ordeal, but she gives a small wink as they turn to leave. Halfway across the room, she pauses and peers at me over her shoulder, popping a large bubble. "Don't go tipping off your girlfriend. You'll just hurt her more."

Leaning my forearms onto the counter, I allow my head to flop into my hands and lean my weight onto the bar. I don't want to keep another secret from Lily. I want to break down barriers between us, not add new layers.

I'm not sure how long I stay slouched and numb, but before I can decide what to do next, Seth slides onto a barstool. As usual, he's arrived with a book in hand.

"Beer me," he says as the book drops with a thump onto the wood.

I pop the top off my attempt at a Thanksgiving red ale and slide the bottle to him.

"Fall beer season is almost up, so help clear this inventory while you're here."

He takes a long look at the amber glass, sniffs, and winces. "Pumpkin Spice?"

"Jersey cranberry Thanksgiving red ale," I correct him.

With a nod, he takes a drink. When he sets the bottle down, he asks, "Dude, what is happening with you lately? Is this still about Lily?"

"Ava Marie made Carmine's delivery with Bella. So I unloaded the truck myself, and Nonna Ava wanted to discuss Lily." I open a second bottle and sip, grimacing after I swallow. "This was better in concept than execution. I went with too much nutmeg. And it's too tart."

"But drinkable," Seth says. We clink the glass necks and sip again.

"The Salvatore stuff is an after-Christmas problem. I pushed them off until February for now. Today, my biggest issues are clearing out these beers, so thanks."

Seth raises his again in a show of solidarity and takes another long pull from the bottle.

"On today's agenda is also housing plans since Scout's talking about moving in upstairs after college," I say and lift my head, as though he doesn't know where my apartment is.

Our cottage behind the Featherweight sits close to the banks of the Delaware. My parents lived there for a few years, back before they had three rowdy boys. When they were ready to grow our family, they found a bigger place, and it fell into disrepair. Over the last few years I've made the bigger updates to the structure, electricity, and plumbing.

Following my next sip, I say, "I guess I should call your sister?"

"Hell yes. Gemma will be so excited. This is her slow season. She's itching for a project. Please hire her. She keeps trying to redecorate my place and I need her out of my hair," Seth says.

Gemma and her wife Alice renovated the Featherweight and their family bookstore, Pages. Since then, it's been hard to grow her portfolio. One of many the downsides to living in a small town is the lack of job opportunities.

"She did a great job with both our businesses," I say, giving him a smile.

"Yeah, she did, but even *Alice* is saying she's tired of the constant changes to their home."

"That bad?" I confirm, knowing his sister-in-law is the most easygoing woman.

With a nod, he lets out a sigh.

———

RIVER:

Wish me luck. It's family dinner night and Dad wants an update on the bar.

LILY:

You don't need luck, you've got places to run away to <wink emoji>

<photo of Lily and Pete at the US/Canada border>

Made it to Vancouver today. Going to edit some photos and unpack. Should this be where I finally invest in an actual laundry basket?

<photo>

National Geographic called this one of the world's most iconic places to stay :)

VANCOUVER? *I thought she was staying in Utah.* Rather than ask, worried I'll spook her, I keep the conversation lighthearted.

RIVER:

Isn't citizenship hard to come by?

LILY:

I guess. Maybe not the time for a laundry basket after all...

SINCE OUR FAMILY business is busiest on the weekends, Mondays and Tuesdays are our weekend. Mom staunchly believes that a homecooked meal made to a Sinatra song has the power to improve even the worst day, and family dinner is mandatory.

"Smells amazing in here, Mama," I gush with a peck to her cheek.

She turns to the beat, snagging the bottle of red, then pours a glass for me. "Try this. It's new from Harry."

I arch my brows. Why did the distributor go to her instead of me?

"He still brings the samples to me," she says, as if reading my mind. "And I will not correct it when it means free wine. I had to push your large head out of my body, so you can pry sample bottles from my cold, dead hands." She finishes the statement with a wink.

I give a playful salute. "Yes, ma'am." Bringing the glass to my lips, I take a sip and close my eyes, focusing on the flavor, then hum a pleased note. "This is good." After I polish off the glass with one more gulp, I reach for the bottle.

"See? Since they come to me first, I can weed out the bad samples. It might be worth looking at the inventory list and swapping this in as the house red for the holidays."

From there, she goes on to update me on the lives of Dad, his nurse, and my brothers.

I am about to tell her about the lingering effects of Lily's visit and my subsequent trip north when we're interrupted.

"Betty." Dad hollers from the other room, using his nickname for her.

She sets her glass down and shuffles out of the kitchen, waving for me to follow. "Hold that thought and help me."

Given Dad's much less chipper disposition, I won't mention the Salvatore delivery change earlier. I worry Dad would personally deliver Lily to the town leadership. Instead I stick to the usuals like the books after our Halloween party and holidays decorating plans at the bar.

"We're completely booked through the new year too," I say, my chest filled with pride.

He nods once, unimpressed. "Good, as you should be. If you find you are slowing down, let me know and we'll review things together."

————

AT THE END of the night, after I've slipped into my coat and shoes, Mom follows me out onto the cold porch. With her maternal instincts apparently on high alert, she sweeps the hair off my forehead, her eyes locked with mine.

"Sweetheart, what is going on? The anxiety around you is palpable. I kept hoping you'd tell me during dinner, but I realize now it must be something you don't want Dad to know."

I swat her hand away gently. "Enough, enough." Sighing, I say, "Dad wearing his noise-canceling headphones?"

"He's listening to his book with those DJ-sized headphones you got him on. Now, please, tell me what is going on. If you don't, I'll call you hourly until I break you. Don't think I won't. You can ask Leaf."

"*Robert*," I interject, the name laced with sarcasm.

Laughing while lightly tapping my arm, she says, "I grew you three. I call you what I want. Stop deflecting. Out with it, George River Hendrix."

The deep exhale comes out in a puff of white given the chill in the air as I gesture at the two wicker chairs on the porch.

Once we're seated, I turn to face her and let the story tumble out of me. "I assume you could tell Lily was my first crush. But what you might not realize is that I still had a thing for her when I was the best man at her wedding."

Laughing gently, Mama says, "Oh honey, I had a feeling."

My chest tightens. "At the bachelor party, Grant was drunk, and he admitted he still had feelings for Landan. I should have stopped the wedding after that, but I didn't. I've hated myself for it for so long."

She nods, making a soothing humming noise, encouraging me to go on.

"Seeing her reignited our friendship, and since I visited her in Vermont, I can't stop thinking about how she'll be alone for the holidays."

My mom's gentle face, now deeply lined with age, is still bright and youthful. With her maroon glasses and short gray bob with matching maroon stripes peeking through from the bottom, she's chic and relaxed.

"Mama, are you aware that Belinda doesn't talk to her?" I ask, my chest aching for my friend. "She ignored her during the party, and Lily spent the night crying in my apartment."

She clicks her tongue and shakes her head. "Damn shame. I always wanted a daughter like her. She's smart and hardworking and always so helpful. I don't know what your grades would have looked like without her." Blowing out a breath of her own, she sighs. "I'm sorry to hear that."

"I hate that she will keep confronting this over and over because she's committed to being Stef's maid of honor."

I'm leaving out so much, but this is enough to placate her for the moment.

"This isn't over." She points a finger at me. "But I will accept that for tonight. When those men from Woodbury come in to antagonize Jim this week, you take care to listen. Latest gossip out of Curl Up & Dye is that it's about which town will get the county craft fair this spring. So if you hear more, you will…" She stares at me, waiting for a response.

Expression flat, I repeat the message I have heard since I

started working at the bar. "Take copious notes and tell my mother immediately after my shift."

"That's right, my bestest boy. Go home, get warm." She rises and heads in.

winter

twenty-one
Lily

"[T]HE WAY THE symptoms are expressed in their behaviors can appear different from their expression in men and boys. This difference in expression has historically been one of the reasons girls and women are underdiagnosed.[i]"

I continue to scroll through resources from qualified medical professionals and blog posts. I wound up so focused I forgot to stop for meals and drink water.

One statement more than the others has really struck me. Hyperactivity is not only restricted to little boys bouncing off the walls. It is possible to have a hyperactive mind. Between that and the explanation of rejection sensitivity dysphoria, I'm hearing so many clicks that my mind sounds like a ticking clock.

During my weekly call with Dorothea, I blurt out a question without even greeting her.

"Can we discuss RSD? Um, I mean rejection sensitivity dysphoria?" I ask, then grimace and add, "Also. Hi. Nice to see you."

"Hi. Of course. We can discuss anything you'd like, you know that," she hedges, and my face starts to feel impossibly hot.

"You don't seem like you want me to. We can start with your agenda," I say, glancing at my hands while they fidget with a pen.

"No, it's interesting that you skipped right to this specific topic from the many you mentioned last time," she says. "I'm guessing it hit home for you, and I'm happy to hear what you think."

A slight sense of ease threads through me, making my muscles loosen a little. "From what I've read, all of these reactions are connected. If I followed correctly, the perception of being rejected or failing is physically painful. Pain is unpleasant. We cope with fight or flight, and with my frequent moves, it's like I try to escape pain by getting as far away as possible."

My background has changed again. I'm sure she's noticed that since leaving Vermont, I've visited a few places. My cancellation-guaranteed clients did, in fact, cancel, so the pay day from that has kept me afloat during this challenging time. I'm on my third resort job in a single season. I haven't worked this circuit in almost five years.

"I guess I wonder if I think I need to keep moving. Or am I moving to avoid something?" I can't meet her gaze. Instead my eyes bounce around what is behind the screen.

I walk her through the experiences in Utah and Vancouver that landed me here. Utah was far more religious than I expected, so, inspired by all the books I've devoured, I headed to Vancouver. I hoped to have my own meet-cute turned found family story, but all I got was completely triggered. While I was there, I found myself face-to-face with a man easily confused for Grant and ended up unleashing years of resentment on this stranger.

"A grainy video of the incident went viral, and in addition to being escorted out by security, I was terminated," I admit, my voice breaking. "I miss my girls. I miss River. I could use their support after that embarrassment."

The virality only lasted a few days before another scandal

overshadowed mine, but it didn't erase the chest ache and insomnia. My nights are haunted by reminders that someone blogged about it, saying "mid-tier fitness influencer Lily Long falls from grace and sponsorships are dropping fast." Between that and the spill at Karma Fitness, my professional contacts have become eerily quiet.

Late to the season, and on my third resort town, I had to start from the bottom again. I'm doing more desk work than usual and trying to substitute teach as many classes as they need. At least Denver offers ample opportunity to hike with Pete. But nothing is silencing these obsessive thoughts, not even my favorite THC gummies.

"After being in Peacock Springs, it feels like I'm moving backward. I can't find that feeling of empowerment. I don't feel capable. I'm haunted by loss and longing mixed with rage and resentment," I say.

She shifts, bumping her desk and making her computer's camera jostle a little.

"Sorry, dear. All right. I've taken all of our interactions over the last few months into account, and I agree with your suspicions about ADHD. I think that you've developed a number of coping skills, like many young women do, that have allowed you to mask or hide the impact of your symptoms. Even if setting fire to Grant's prized Wayne Gretzky autographed photo," she says, grinning teasingly, "was beyond a fair exchange for infidelity, it was an extreme reaction."

Dorothea walks me through information on grieving the living and what it truly means to be triggered. She explains that after feeling numb for so long, shock and grief have likely been reignited inside me. "You've been so dedicated to your mental health these last several years, and you are capable of rebuilding coping skills, but I recommend considering a medication consult. With the high-stress events coming up, it would likely benefit you to consider medicine. Even as a temporary tool to enhance successful symptom management."

The conversation continues as she discusses what I should expect as I move forward on this journey. It is both exhausting and validating to find out. So many moments of my life make more sense in this framework. Along with my preference for large, open, quiet places and big feelings, so much has come together. The more I examine it all, even my preference for THC over alcohol is there. It helps to slow the anxiety, it allows me to eat when I forget, it brings my nervous system to neutral. Everything I've been drawn to is either a product of this wiring in my brain or something those with ADHD do constructively or destructively to themselves.

"I know that your birthday is coming up," she says, bringing me out of my thoughts. "As is Christmas. What do you have planned?"

"I'm not sure. Honestly, I feel so lost right now. I barely know where I am mentally."

"Remember that days like these can be a trigger for big feelings, and anger deserves to be felt. When we try to keep it in, we become like a shaken-up Coke bottle. The pressure will reach a tipping point and explode, and sometimes we blow up on the wrong person."

"Like a greasy-haired, tattooed Canadian man?" I grumble.

"Exactly." She keeps her expression neutral. "You've elaborated on the conversation you had with Grant on the train, but is there anything else you want to say to him?"

I suck in a big breath and shake my head. "Sober me has nothing left to say."

"Well, then. What about to your parents?"

She holds space for me to think. The exercise is one I struggle with. I'm used to trying to fill silences, but she's helped me work on allowing myself to take my time. To not feel like I must rush the conversation to say it all.

Blinking, I ask, "What about them?"

"Let's use the magic wand question. Imagine that tomorrow you wake up back in your hometown, and you have a magic wand that allows you to say anything you want to your parents. What do you say? And what happens after you say it?"

"I… I don't know." My stomach twists at the thought. "While I was there in September, I found out that there's a chance the town council will still want me to sit in those ankle stocks." I blow out a puff of air. How is it that a decade later, this subject still hasn't died?

She leans forward, moving closer to the camera, her expression genuine. "There's something I need to ask you, and please don't take this the wrong way."

Heart in my throat, I wait.

Finally she says, "Does your hometown really use stocks for punishment? So much of this sounds like a fever dream, making me worry that you may need to see a therapist in person."

Laughing, I pull up my web browser. Then, sharing my screen, I show her our town's website. There on the home page is a photo of town hall, a tiny red brick building that used to be a church. In front of it is a golden peacock statue on a pillar and the stocks.

"They really do. In the summer they let tourists use them for photos, but there is a giant lock on it overnight and the brass key comes out to make it usable each morning."

"All right, that's… unique." Blinking, she sits back and adjusts her glasses. "This week, I'd like you to write a letter to your parents. Rather than send it, I'd like you to share it with me during our next session so we can discuss it. This writing exercise is often very helpful on its own. Often sending these words hurts more than helps. My theory is that while there are many things we need to say, the other person doesn't always need to hear them."

With those words of wisdom, we part for the week.

After I've signed off, my mind races. Should I tell anyone that my therapist has basically confirmed that I have ADHD? I don't want to disturb Stef while she's planning her wedding, Delia doesn't usually do well with this sort of thing, and Nessa is a professional. I don't need a second therapist. I need a friend.

Looking down at my phone, I sigh and consider telling River.

LILY:

I got some news… I don't know how I feel about it

RIVER:

What's up? I'm in the office doing schedules. I can talk

LILY:

No. I don't even know what I'd say, I… I have ADHD? But like, the girl kind?

DK, that's not exactly what I mean… from what I've read, I guess it's looks different for girls and women

My phone rings in my hand, and I answer immediately, stumbling through the new information while River listens.

---

i. Children and Adults with Attention Deficit/Hyperactivity Disorder (CHADD) Page: Women & Girls https://chadd.org/for-adults/symptoms-of-adhd-in-women-and-girls/

twenty-two
Lily

GROUP CHAT: BAD BITCHES [STEF SANTOS MANOLO, LILY LONG, DELIA SHANE, NESSA RABIN]

STEF:

Happy Birthday [Taylor Swift, unknown late-night show, scrunching nose & smiling GIF]

NESSA:

[Taylor Swift, 2023 Football Season Chiefs Super Bowl Win, Taylor kissing Travis Kelce GIF]

Me, your face, next time we're in the same place.

DELIA:

SHUT UP. SOME OF US WORK SUPER LATE NIGHTS WITH AN EXTRA ANXIOUS BOSS BECAUSE HE'S DEFINITELY CRUSHING ON THE BIRTHDAY GIRL…

NESSA:

[Taylor Swift, innocent face, GIF]

I SMILE AT MY PHONE. My friends mean well by making a big deal out of my birthday, despite my discomfort. I'm loud and engaging and my career involves social media, yet deep down I dislike being the center of attention. Yes, I, Lily Jayne Long, share a birthday with the pop superstar of the era. Yes, I, like nearly every other red-blooded female, could not escape falling in love with her, despite trying. It's not that I don't want to be like other girls, though. In fact, I think that the collective love for the pop star shows how universally and fundamentally similar we are as human beings.

STRETCHING, I stand and pull the curtains open wide to allow more slices of golden morning light into my space, taking in the view of the Rocky Mountains.

Pete stirs as I pass by him to turn on the coffee pot, but instead of popping up and begging to go out to potty, he yawns and snuggles deeper into the pile of blankets on the couch.

While I wait for the coffee to brew, I dig out my journal for my birthday ritual.

Happy Birthday to me! Let's do this.

Roses:

I have seen more of the world than most people my age

The Jeep Wrangler lives (thanks to my strict maintenance schedule for her)

Pete turning 4 means the puppy zoomies are less frequent and he's a little calmer

Stef & Lee got engaged. I was brave. I went back to NJ and celebrated. I saw Nessa, Delia, Seth & River

Seeing River rekindled our friendship. We had another visit in VT, and we text and video chat regularly now

Thorns:

Belinda Long walked past me like I was air

Grant Morgan is still a total asshole. He tried to blame me for his cheating and suggested that it's my fault that my parents don't speak to me

I'm still struggling to remove these toxic things from my brain. The insecurities creep in on their own, but hearing and seeing their sources made it worse. I'm practically ready to scrape my memories with bleach

Manifesting:

Being in Peacock Springs can be as good or bad as I allow it to be. For the coming year, I will remember the woman I am beyond the town. The confidence and self-love I've cultivated lives within me, and I can drown out the naysayers. My open heart offers kindness and empathy to those who need it, and I will accept only that energy in return

I will welcome love in all its forms in my 29th year, and I will continue to watch it bloom like flowers in a well-tended garden. Love for myself, for my friends who are my family, and love for those who cannot show the same love back

WHEN I'M FINISHED, I move on to the assignment from Dorothea and scribble all my thoughts and emotions—logical or not—onto the page. All that matters is writing.

> *Mom (and Dad),*
>
> *Grant chose Landan and broke up our marriage. Which was embarrassing and painful. I looked around at my friends and couldn't help but compare myself. What was I doing? I was cleaning up after a grown man. Sitting around, alone, wondering how I'd gotten there. It was like everyone else had moved forward and I was stuck.*
>
> *Landan is superficial, selfish, and cruel. But wait. Why am I faulting her? Is this on her? Has anyone else noticed that our comments are directed at the wife and the mistress? Where is the outrage for him?*
>
> *Have you ever noticed that Grant's horrible actions mostly go ignored?*
>
> *Yes, burning a few of Grant's possessions on our lawn wasn't my best idea. I'm in no way trying to excuse that choice. It was an embarrassing moment of rage due to the betrayal I experienced. But his betrayal pales in comparison to yours. You could have loved me unconditionally and supported my hopes for higher education. Instead, you were more concerned with how the situation reflected on you. So much so that you were willing to turn me in for public shaming. How in the world would your daughter sitting in the stocks to be humiliated help? What kind of parent wants to see their child punished for being hurt?*
>
> *I used to think returning was impossible. The panic*

that hit me while driving back for Stef's party was almost too strong to fight huge. But I powered through. Then I saw you at the proposal and you acted like I was invisible. Seeing you reopened so many old wounds. Worse, it reminded me of all the times I've felt like a child over the years, thinking "I want my mommy."

Whether it was missing an opportunity to share something good or needing comfort, I still wanted some version of you. I see now, though, that there is no comfort left between us. I hate that, but it's the truth.

So my cards are on the table: I won't let you keep me from the people who love me unconditionally. Stef & Lee, Delia, Nessa, Seth, and River are too important to me. I can't let ghosts stop me from loving them in return.

Love is a two-way street, yet you have always held me to conditional love, and so this is me saying goodbye. My friends are all I need. I see that now. They've loved me unconditionally through those hard times and have cheered for me as I've succeeded.

Goodbye, Mom. Goodbye, Dad. I appreciate that I exist. Thank you for creating me. It's such a shame you can't see the person I truly am. I'll follow your lead and ignore you next time I'm in town.

The following week I read the letter to Dorothea.

"Very powerful," she praises me, wearing an impressed look. "Do you believe you'll feel that way when you go back? You mentioned before that you wonder if it's the physical distance that gives you strength."

My body stills, uncertainty flooding and my heart thumping. The unease makes it hard to contemplate the chances. I can see scales with poker chips in my mind. One side is labeled *you can do it* and on the other, a person laughs hysterically at me.

Each thought I weigh adds another chip. With River, my friends, what I'm learning about how my brain works, I can do this. But if I see Grant or Belinda, I'll crack. It doesn't matter who is holding my hand. I failed. I didn't fail; they failed me.

"Probably not," I admit. "But I want to." It comes out a whisper.

Dorothea nods and makes a note on her pad. When the appointment is over, I'm left to wrestle with all kinds of mixed feelings.

My phone rings, and a video call request from River appears, so I quickly swipe at my tears and try to put on a happy face.

He is beaming when I pick up, though his expression falls quickly. No doubt because my eyes are rimmed red and I can't stop sniffling.

"Oh, Lily," he says, his tone soft. "Why are you upset?"

I sniffle, and he waits patiently, always so willing to let me sort through my words and figure them out while I think out loud.

"You caught me at the end of therapy, and I've been thinking about what you told me." I wipe my eyes again. "It's total bullshit that I had to disappear when Grant was the one who fucked up, not me."

I'm exhausted after the first heavily emotional conversation I had today, so I'm not even sure what I say to River specifically. Time becomes fuzzy and unreal.

"Gemma and Alice are planning to renovate the back cottage," he says after a few minutes, blessedly changing the subject. "Don't be alone. Come here. You don't have to miss things. You can have us."

Shaking my head and wiping my nose on my hoodie sleeve, I say, "No, I committed to the ski resort here. I love it here. I want to stick out the season. Maybe in March?"

"That'll give all those bones time to heal, I guess. I'll make sure there's a comfortable place for you to sleep. The view of the river is incredible, and we'll even get a pole and runner set up so Petey can have freedom without fencing in the yard. You'll consider it, right?"

My chest pangs. I can't say no to him, so I tentatively agree that I'll give it some thought. He sounds so confident that we can fix this together. But that means I'd have to be there. After the letter I wrote and the last few sessions with Dorothea, I know it is time to reclaim my place. I'm so thankful for River. Without his support, I don't know that I could make it through the coming months.

twenty-three
River

"SHIT," I curse after I disconnect the call, slamming a fist on the bar.

Delia runs into my office, a look of concern on her face. I wave my hands in surrender. I can't form a verbal explanation, so I pull out my phone and wave it in her direction, then start a new group text.

GROUP CHAT: PS HS+ [RIVER HENDRIX, NESSA RABIN, DELIA SHANE, SETH WHITTER, LEE CARTER, STEF SANTOS MANOLO]

RIVER:

I'm an idiot

I told Lily to move into the cottage out back after her job in Denver ends and stay here till the wedding

I also said we can fix things with the town

SETH:

Total idiot. You calling Gemma and Alice now?

Or am I gonna watch you build an Ikea dresser and blow up an air mattress?

LEE:

[Baby walking, entering room and quickly turning around to leave GIF]

STEF:

Enough, boys. Don't ruin this. Bride's orders. Understand me?

< hand covering mouth giggling emoji>

I love playing the bride card! Yay!! Let's bring our girl home!! <pink heart emoji>

SETH:

More like bridezilla <dragon emoji>

RIVER:

If the town elders hear, it will be bad so <zipper face emoji>

Delia, participate. You might have gone back downstairs to roll silverware for tonight, but I know you're reading these

DELIA:

<middle finger emoji x5>

I stalk downstairs, and as anticipated, Delia has her phone out on the bar and she's watching the conversation as she places a knife, spoon, and fork onto the napkin and then rolls them up with precision. These mundane chores are far more enjoyable for me than they should be, so I join her. Delia has been an asset here over the years, so even though this isn't what she wants to do forever, I will keep her here for as long as I can. We've built a series of silent cues to keep things quiet before and after shifts or to communicate when the crowds make it hard to hear.

She signals me to talk, and when I ignore it, she tries again. Repeatedly. She clears her throat every second or third set of silverware she wraps until I can't take it anymore.

"Spit it out, Cordelia, before this becomes a new form of torture the feds borrow for investigations."

A look of anger flashes across her face, but it's gone quickly. Then, subdued, she lowers her eyes, focusing on her work. "It's interesting that you've got Lily moving in with you, that's all. Don't get me wrong. I love Lily. But come on. She's a mess. I think she's gotten worse since she moved away. So is this what we want for her or is it for someone else?"

I swallow thickly. Does she mean me? Or Stef?

"Belinda is never going to forgive her," she goes on. "And I don't know how Lily is going to feel about that. Plus," she says, dropping another rolled set of silverware in the tub, "it's obvious that you've never gotten over her."

My throat closes up, and I choke. Dropping the silverware in my hand to the bar top with a clang, I scrub a hand over my face. I scoop a pint glass up and use the bar gun to fill it with water, then take a large gulp.

Fuck me.

I did ask her to speak up, so what now? *Do I argue?* She isn't wrong, but I didn't realize she knew. *Do I admit it? Ask for her help?* Rather than cause more trouble, I point toward the steps awkwardly.

"Seems like you have things sorted here for the day," I force out, still choking. "Headed back upstairs." With a wave, I dart away and I don't stop until I'm in my office with the door closed. *Shit*, that was not what I expected.

I sit and open up the calendar where we keep track of reservations. Then I stare at invoices. Order reports. But every one swims with letters, just as jumbled as my thoughts.

When my heart rate has slowed to a normal pace, I pull open the calendar again. Susan wanted to have the engagement party in February, but Lily is considering March, so how can I convince Susan to push the date back a month? I'm desperate to ask my mom to help, but this is something I should do on my own.

With a groan, I lean back and plot out a few routes that could successfully delay the party. I jot down the ideas, and along with each one, I make a list of who would have to buy in and who could help me convince them.

Figuring I'll get back to it another time, I shove the notebook into a locked drawer and put it aside for Future River to deal with. Then I head downstairs to help Delia with the lunch rush. Descending the winding wooden staircase, I focus on all the work we did to the place. How Seth, Gemma, and I collaborated on a mix of Victorian opulence and contemporary simplicity.

Black and white photos in ornate gold frames line the wall, illustrating the history of both the Hendrix family and Peacock Springs. I know these faces almost as well as my own after spending so much of my life here.

There's George and Molly when they opened up the home to entertain folks, then men and women in military uniforms during both WWI and WWII. The grouping of color photos starts with my dad as a kid, a teen, and then as a husband and father himself. So many of the photos in this section include the Long family, the sight of Lily's parents making anger flare inside me. Our group of young business owners consists of descendants of founding families. As the current leadership, we are more powerful than we allow ourselves to be. *So why do those gossip queens get to dictate to us?*

I'm lost in my thoughts as I hit the last step and nearly collide with Pru as she approaches the hostess stand. She deftly grabs my elbow and guides me to the kitchen, where she fixes two cups of tea. Despite the cold December weather, she picks up the mugs and shoos me out the back door. Outside, I shiver, quickly deciding to settle in the igloo we set up for outdoor seating in the winter.

Inside, she shrugs her oversized tote off her shoulder and drops it onto a chair. The slightly frayed beige woven straps look like they could snap any minute under its weight. I feel like one of those straps, strained and unraveling. Without speaking, she roots around in the bag. Finally, she presses a small stone and a business card into my palm.

I'm examining the smooth, cold edges of the brown-striped rock, a tiger's eye, she tells me, as she returns to digging through her bag.

After a moment, she overturns the bag and sends its contents skittering across the table. A book, a feather, a sage smudge stick, a journal, a deck of tarot cards, odds and ends like buttons and receipts, some loose change, and a candle tumble over the once neat place settings.

"Ah. Perfect." She picks up her card deck and shuffles.

Frowning, I study her. This is so very Prudence to ambush me with something supernatural. But I learned long ago that the fastest way out is to listen. Shuffling this way and that, bridging the cards and mixing chunks, she tells me of her train encounter with Lily before she left in September.

Pru shoves the deck into my hands and says, "Kid, you've loved that girl since you were too young to know what love was. So let me tell you what is going to happen from here." I divide it into three neat piles for her and tap the one to my right.

She pulls three cards, a classic Rider-Waite style. The first, the one on the far left, says Temperance, with an image of an angel mixing liquid from cup to cup, like a bartender for the spirits.

The next one says The Tower. This one looks far more ominous. A dark background, gray clouds, and lightning striking a building. One either side, a figure falls from the sky. The third card is much brighter, with a cheery yellow background. The Four of Wands. Four poles that create a structure with garlands of greens and flowers on top. A couple in the background tossing flowers into the air. It looks like the end of a wedding ceremony.

As she lays them out, another card falls on top of the pile, causing her to cackle loudly.

"The Chariot has a message for you, dear," she croons.

The carrier is sideways, neither upright nor reversed. Two sphinxes sit at the foot of the sled manned by a man in armor. I'm trying to recall if cards can even be considered sideways when she interrupts my train of thought.

"A choice you will make soon could set in motion a large part of your life to come. This can be the start of great destruction or a great love story. But the Chariot means you have to make a decision and follow it through. No matter what or who gets in your way."

Nerves skitter through me. "Does this mean that Grant and the salon will get in the way of Lily staying around again? What about this place? Am I going to lose my business, the family legacy, because of a girl? That's the last thing I would do, Pru. You know that I am steady and responsible..." I babble, my brain spinning.

With a calming hand on my shoulder she says, "Honey, I do not make the future. I read its signs. And the signs point to major changes that will only occur if you stick up for yourself and cling to your truth. If your truth is that you want to leave and follow the girl around the globe, then that is your truth. If your truth is you want her to return home and stay here with you, then you will have to unmake and remake many things. However the Four of Wands and the Chariot tell me that you're in the driver's seat. It'll just take a little tenacity and follow-through. Whatever your destination, it's yours. Nobody else's. So make a choice, Georgie Boy. The other Georges would expect nothing less."

She says it as if she knows them all. Like she was around when the original George opened this place in the 1860s. No one knows just how old she is, but there's no way she was around then, right? If I ask, she will make a joke and brush me aside.

Ignoring the thought, I turn the worry stone's smooth texture over and over in my hand, considering the implication of the cards in front of me.

"Make a choice and stick with it," I whisper.

As I continue to mindlessly turn the stone over in my hand, she sweeps all her belongings from the table, rewraps her cards in ornate silk, and vanishes as quickly as she arrived. Leaving me with the stone, a business card, and a table to turn over.

135

twenty-four
River

THE DINNER RUSH will hit at any time, yet rather than prepping, Delia and I are having another staring contest from opposite ends of the bar. Her eyes have narrowed in a look that usually means she's going to drop a truth bomb. No getting around it. Anxious for the shoe to drop, I noisily exhale, hoping she'll get on with it. She quietly slides an envelope my way. On the front, in elaborate green and gold lettering, it reads Merry Christmas, Love your Framily. The flourish of the script rivals that of her eyeliner.

When I open the envelope, a thick piece of paper falls to the floor. Bending at the waist, I pick it up quickly, along with the other object that fluttered out. My heart stops when I realize the first item is a plane ticket to Denver.

The note is written in Nessa's messy scrawl.

Didn't wrap my extra gift, but please wrap yours. We love you guys, but neither of you are ready for tiny humans. K, thankssss.

Attached to the note is Nessa's thoughtful gift. A variety of condoms, with staples in the center of each one, as if she isn't well aware that poking holes in condoms could easily lead to those tiny humans she mentioned.

"Does she," I ask, my throat closing up. "Does she know about this?"

Delia, who's applying makeup using a hand mirror, looks up and rolls her eyes skyward.

My muscles tense as irritation rolls through me. I'm about to call her out when she uncaps her mascara and applies it, her mouth popping open.

"Why do women hold their mouths open like dead fish for mascara?" I wonder out loud.

She snags a damp, smelly bar towel and hits me with it. Then, trying to school her expression, she resumes her routine. "Nope. That's on you. We decided you needed this push. I'm sick of your face, *George.*"

"Wait, really?" I stammer, my pulse tipping up.

"Yeah. Spend time with her. Stay at a Motel 6. They leave a light on for you. Whatever. Merry Christmas, boss. Go pack and get the fuck out of here. You're cut from this shift. I have a crew coming to help tonight."

Stef and Lee enter, followed by a gust of cold air, then hang up their coats.

Heart thumping, I study the ticket. The flight is set for the day after Christmas. If I go, I will be in the same city as Lily. Again. Soon.

"What about the rest of the week?" I push back.

"Don't you trust me? Scout's home from school. With his help, I'll keep the place running. Get out of here. Go," she says, glaring at me.

I head upstairs and dig through my closet for my duffel bag. I pull out the necessities—boxers and socks, T-shirts, a couple of sweaters, sweatpants, and jeans. I'm crawling on the floor of my closet, searching for my weather-proof boots, when my heart starts to beat loudly in my ears. There are dark spots in my vision and my lungs can't get enough air.

I fall back onto my haunches and slide against the wall. I place my head between my knees and focus on not suffocating. Breathe in. Breathe out.

Slumped over, I wonder if I'm having a heart attack. I gasp and sweat drips down my neck. I scratch the damp hair and start to question if I need a haircut. A slew of incoherent questions flood my thoughts. Is it because I'm leaving Peacock Springs? The bar? Or is it the idea of seeing Lily?

When the noise subsides, I can finally take a proper breath. In a daze, I stare at the off-white wall and hanging clothing, waiting for feeling to return to my hands. Shaking my head, I force myself up and shuffle to the bathroom.

I splash cold water on my face, and when I'm thinking more clearly, I peer into the mirror above the vanity.

The modern touch is one of my favorite parts of this place. The black iron frame of the mirror is shaped like an archway with a round top and rectangular bottom. Above the curve of the arch is a series of small windows, allowing natural light in, and a deep iron pendant hangs above, its Mercury glass both vintage and warped to cast beautiful shadows on the room.

I picked each item. This place is mine. It's a reminder. The Featherweight is mine. The thought awakens a primal part of me.

Pru's advice, despite being like all fortunes—about the listener and not the reading itself—is exceptionally relevant. I have to steer the chariot to my next destination. If I don't want to lose the family business *or* the girl, I have to make the effort. I have to make this place appealing to her, for her sake and mine.

Examining my face in the mirror, I note both the boy she knew in school and the man I am today. My beard is fuller than its usual stubble. Mostly brown, with tiny bits of copper mixed in. My heavy dark brows are now accompanied by light forehead lines and crow's feet. My eyes are the same deep teal-green color they've always been, with flecks of blue noticeable in some light.

My mom has always said they're the color of the pines and sky. The tiny scar on my earlobe is a reminder of the earring I got and stopped wearing several years ago.

Morning workouts and evening runs help keep me busy between shifts at the bar. Compared to seventeen-year-old me, I'd consider myself broad, my chest and shoulders filled out. Before his stroke, Dad's default setting was stressed. Always because of the bar. So I decided early on that I'd take preventative measures to ensure I wouldn't do the same.

Though I can't say I have much more of a life than he did. I'm not a saint. I've had my fair share of short-lived relationships and casual hookups over the years. Just, not since September. Actually, not since I took over renovations here. Since Dad signed it all over, I've completely drowned myself in this place, proving myself to him to ease something knotted inside me.

Once Lily slept here alongside me and I held her throughout that night, not one flirty patron or app-based match has appealed to me. I'd rather chase the release from my own fist if needed. I'd rather be chatting with Lily about nothing at all. I often stop swiping to scroll Lily's feed for the umpteenth time.

Just tell her! There is no good reason not to. I *want* to see her.

It doesn't have to be about chasing her, although maybe that's what she needs. None of us have shown up and offered to hold her hand as she walks back in that door. We've left her alone too long.

The longer I assess myself, the surer I become. I am getting on that plane. I am going to get my girl.

I move around with purpose, packing, while images of us over the years run through my mind, from the little girl with pigtail braids all those years ago to the flexible woman in workout gear. I don't know if she'll want me, too, but I won't know if I don't try.

CHRISTMAS MORNING

. . .

I'VE DELAYED LONG ENOUGH. I need to call her. Sitting on the couch, I let out a long groan. *Fuck, stop procrastinating.*

As I open the video chat app, I run a hand through my hair, trying to make it the right amount of messy and neat. *Who even am I, preening and primping?*

Before I can overthink it, I hit her contact and send up a silent prayer she answers quickly.

twenty-five
Lily

SOMEONE BETTER BE in a serious pinch. It's way too early for phone calls. Groaning, I roll over and reach for my phone. Instead I accidentally knock the damn thing onto the floor. Across the room, my tablet and laptop are making noises too, the sounds making me wince. It's like I was dropped into the middle of the alarm clock torture circle of hell. With a growl, I throw off the covers so I can snag the closest device and make this noise stop.

This is the worst week of the season. Christmas week. When the guests are all parts of big, happy families and every staffer is talking about what they miss about their family, or their family visits.

Family.

Those of us who don't spend the holiday with loved ones end up having our own sad party, usually with too many drinks. One benefit of being in Denver is meeting new friends who are happy to smoke a bowl, turn on a comedy, and eat snacks before going to sleep. I shouldn't be so cranky after doing exactly that last night, but I have never been a morning person, especially when there isn't something exciting on the other side of the alarm.

Grumbling, I snatch my phone off the floor and stab at the screen to stop the ringing. The instant before I dismiss the call, I note the caller, and a thrill shoots through me.

I stretch my arms overhead, then answer, grinning like a fool. My mood plummets, though, when I notice his slumped posture. Is someone hurt? His dad? His hair is mussed, like he's been finger combing it—a sign that he's stressed—and his expression is almost sheepish.

Ducking, he scratches at the back of his neck. When the move causes his arms to flex and show off the corded muscles that he's honed by hauling boxes, I try not to drool.

"Hey." His voice is soft, almost breathy. "Um, so, our troublemaker friends gave me my gift at closing the other night. It's a ticket to Denver." His cheeks go pink, his eyes darting to the side. "There are a handful of breweries I've wanted to check out that way, and I've heard really good things about Voodoo Donuts, and well… are you up for a visitor?"

"Of course. When is the trip? I bet I can get you set up with a room. But why do you look so overwhelmed? And why are you calling so early?" I snap my mouth shut, trying to reel myself in.

I've gone from half asleep to as excited as a kid on, well, on Christmas morning. That thought brings with it a bout of nerves. Am I being too enthusiastic?

River gives another hesitant breath. "That's the thing. The flight… it's first thing in the morning. I'll be there tomorrow. Would that totally ruin your week?"

A tiny part of my lizard brain urges me to flirt. Thankfully, the part of me that notices his anxiety wins out and I give him a megawatt smile.

"Ruin my plans? There's nothing to ruin. I don't have many shifts this week because I worked last night and I'll work again later today. I could probably trade a couple of shifts later this week so I can hang out with you during most of your trip." I pull up my calendar to confirm and nod aggressive affirmation.

His teeth are sunken into his bottom lip, the pulse in his throat fluttering wildly. "I'll be there until the thirtieth, and, um, I think we did okay when you were here. Can you handle a roommate for a few days?"

Anxiety washes over me as I survey my room. The lumpy full-size mattress is nothing remotely like his comfortable king. It's going to be a tight fit.

Would he be okay with that? I'm too scared to ask. But we can make it work. It will just be extra snuggly.

I eye the kitchenette, realizing I only have snack foods. There are dishes in the sink. The pile of laundry on the floor is practically a mountain, because I never bothered to buy myself a hamper. Is the laundromat even open today?

Oh shit. My battery powered boyfriends are all stashed under my pillow. Need to move those.

Can I have River Hendrix in my space for multiple nights? Will this add up to a complete disaster?

Before my brain can tell my mouth what to do, it opens and says, "Absolutely. I can't wait."

After the call, I switch on music and rush to clean up, dancing as I go. This is officially the best Christmas I've had in a very long time.

GROUP CHAT: BAD BITCHES [STEF SANTOS MANOLO, LILY LONG, DELIA SHANE, NESSA RABIN]

LILY:

I don't know why you did this, and it may be a terrible idea. But thanks?

DELIA:

He actually called?

STEF:

Clearly!!

WHEN I RIP the sheets off the mattress, my toys roll to the floor. I toss open my suitcase and shove the laundry and sheets inside it. Then I block the door with the suitcase so I won't forget to head to the laundry room. Next, I collect my toys and set them on the in-shower shelf so I remember to clean them while I'm showering and put them away.

I'm always behind on these kinds of tasks. I'm easily distracted, and once I walk away, I forget. In the kitchenette, I toss anything that cannot be salvaged into the trash. As much as I value my nomadic lifestyle and using only what I need, I'm terrible without good motivators. It feels like I'm always rushing. From what I've read, this is a classic symptom of ADHD. It's an executive dysfunction, meaning task initiation and time blindness. It's a fancy way of saying *it was never about being lazy.*

My first step is to throw out anything with mold growing on it. Then I turn the faucet on, and once the water is scalding, I rinse out the containers that can be saved and toss them into the mini-countertop dishwasher, silently thanking the previous tenant for leaving it behind.

Suitcase in hand, I walk to the laundry room and cheer when I discover the door isn't locked.

While the machines swirl, I sit in a plastic chair and listen to the audiobook from Nessa's latest pick for her book club. It's fun and a little spicy, so time passes easily. I have no trouble powering through multiple loads because nobody else does laundry alone on Christmas Day, making finishing up and hauling it back upstairs not too challenging.

As I unpack the now-clean clothes, the husky male narrator says something I can't help but laugh at. The character's friends tell him to rub one out to avoid being tense before his big date with the female protagonist.

The micro-trope his hilariously gendered. It's always the men who suggest or make cracks about being a "two-pump chump" or complain about being unable to focus. As if women don't also get worked up when time with a love interest is on the horizon. Like a childhood best friend who'll be sharing a full-size bed with this protagonist soon.

Eyes shut, I release an audible groan of frustration. These are the last thoughts I should be having.

As I drop the fresh hand towels over the bathroom rack, I catch sight of my toys. Shit, I need to clean and store them. Since it's front and center, I'm thinking about it, but that's another executive dysfunction I struggle with: out of sight, out of mind.

This task is an important one. Too much potential for embarrassment if I don't complete it. I remove my earbuds and connect my phone to my Bluetooth speaker and start the shower. Might as well wash them and myself at the same time. This will not be *the* shower, though: no shaving, nothing that encourages me to give into impulse. *That will work, right?*

My pulse goes a million miles per hour as I clean each device and rinse them. With the narration taking a turn further into the spicy parts of the story, that pulse drifts, settling low in my belly.

Maybe the character's friends' advice isn't so bad after all, since River will be in my bed tomorrow night.

I sit on the shower floor, choose the water safe wand toy, and power it on. Water droplets sluice down my body, warming me and adding prickles of sensation I can't anticipate. One thing I've learned since the mechanical sex life Grant and I had is that my brain and body crave variety. For too long, sex was like cheat code orgasm video games for me. Click A-B-X-B-X and finish. After my first anonymous hookup with a guy at a fraternity party, I knew it could be different. Fun. Unexpected each time. With the audiobook narration behind me, I force myself to focus on what I hear and feel. To settle into my body and ignore my brain's nonstop commentary. To simply allow the tension to swell within me.

Except my brain refuses to cooperate. One fleeting thought of Grant and… ugh. *No. No thinking about Grant, I scold myself. Focus on the gravelly nature of the narrator's deep voice. He's in the shower too, he's got his palm against cold tiles. Feel the cold on your back.*

Before long, I find myself almost present again. Is it normal to have to redirect my brain to stay focused on something as good as this? Maybe I should ask Dorothea next… no… shower, cold tiles.

Okay. *His broad chest with a small patch of curly dark hair. Soft and smooth.*

Like when I accidentally touched River in bed. River's emotion-laden eyes looking right into mine. The way he ran his hands over my hair and consoled me.

"Fuck," I moan. Sticking to the thought is my best bet right now. It's only a flight of fantasy. It's not real. My nipples get even tighter, and the warm spray continues to tease them softly like wet kisses. My body tingles and my breath hitches, my mind drifting back to the morning I found myself lying in River's strong arms. The soft bit of hair below his belly button leading down toward his boxer briefs… and lower. I'm imagining what peeling him out of his boxer briefs would be like when that big cresting wave hits me.

Relief and relaxation course throughout my body and I slam my head back against the wall with a chuckle. Either I just got it out of my system, or this is going to be an interesting few days.

twenty-six
Lily

I'M CIRCLING the arrivals lots at Denver International Airport, again, checking for River in the distance, when my phone vibrates and a robot voice blares from my speakers.

RIVER:

Arrivals is a zoo, can you meet me at departures?

WHEN IT ASKS me if I want to reply, I say yes, then slowly say "you've got it," so the message comes through clearly.

Flicking on my turn signal, I merge back into the flow of traffic headed toward departures. Toward River. I brush my hair back from my face, then adjust it forward again. I spot him from a distance. His gray knit hat is pulled low on his forehead, and he's dressed in a deep blue wool peacoat, jeans, and a pair of weather-proof work boots. He's so effortlessly handsome. A brown leather duffel sits at his feet and he's got a matching backpack slung over one shoulder. I'm white knuckling the steering wheel as butterflies erupt in my stomach.

I signal right and pull over to the curb. Once the Jeep is in park, I hop out to open the trunk and greet him. I move like a magnet toward him, and I swear he does the same.

I'm immediately engulfed in a firm hug—the kind that knocks me off balance. Before I know it, my feet leave the ground. Despite the cold air surrounding us, I'm convinced that I'm wearing a ski suit on the equator at noon. My face must be turning all kinds of pink hues, but with any luck, he'll think it's the cold chapping my skin.

He sets me down, his focus fixed on my face. Then he leans in to kiss my cheek, but at the same time, I turn to talk, inadvertently making him press his lips to the side of my mouth. The near-kiss shocks us apart, and we use the cold as an excuse to get in the car quickly.

As we buckle our seat belts, we mutter apologies and I begin to worry that this is what the whole week will be like. If so, I will absolutely die from a combination of sexual frustration and embarrassment. As we pull onto I-70, I pass him the auxiliary cord, "Hey, DJ, surprise me."

We cruise along, singing along to every song, from boy band hits to classics to Disney anthems. The awkwardness dissipates quickly, leaving two old friends relaxed and playful. When a familiar drumbeat begins, I gasp.

"Is this—"

"I've carried you home a few times now," he teases. "Figured it was fitting to revisit the old group anthem."

"We Are Young" by fun. featuring Janelle Monáe plays. When we were teenagers, we'd utter the phrase "we are young" for every silly, extreme, or unexpected idea. With twin smiles, we shout about setting the world on fire. The irony of it isn't lost on me.

Months after this song played on the radio once an hour every hour, I really would set a fire. And it became a catalyst for every change I've been through in the last decade.

I pull up to my assigned parking spot, and we sit outside my apartment silently. I should get out and lead the way, but I'm suddenly frozen in place. Teeth gritted, I will myself to move. With jerky actions, I scramble out of my seat belt, nearly hitting myself in the face with the metal latch plate, then scurry out of the Jeep.

Outside the passenger door, he stretches and declares, "I need a shower. I hate the way I feel after sitting on a plane."

"One hundred percent, me too," I splutter out. "It's the recycled air. And how inefficiently they clean. And being breathed on by strangers while I'm trying to watch a cheesy movie so I can forget that we're hurtling through the air in a tin can. It doesn't make sense, how something so large and heavy can remain in the air like that."

Rather than look annoyed with my rambling, he smiles and nods as he plucks his stuff out of the cargo area of my Jeep. As we head inside, a wave of nervousness hits me. It'll be strange to have someone in my personal space like this. I haven't even unlocked the door before I'm apologizing.

"I did my best, but I'm sure I forgot plenty of things. I'm not the neatest, but I really, really try."

On the other side of the door, Pete scratches at the beige painted wood eagerly.

"Calm down, pup. It's Mommy." I nudge him back as we enter, and he stretches into a downward dog pose with paws forward and his head bowed.

Crouching, I give him a few scratches on his head and thank him for being a good boy while I was out.

His body goes rigid and he pulls his lips back, exposing his longest, sharpest canine tooth. There is no snarl, implying he's looking to attack, meaning that he's uncertain. He's assessing the likelihood that I need his protection. Thankfully, after giving a slight warning growl, Pete sniffs at River and switches to wiggling his hips and tail.

"Better give the man what he wants," I tell River. "He's asking for you to scratch his booty, and if you ignore him, he'll hate you. It only takes minutes for him to decide whether you'll be allowed back. What he says goes around here." I wink at Pete.

River joins me on the floor, shrugging the backpack off his shoulder and placing it on his duffel.

Side by side like this with Pete squirming in front of us, my small place feels downright claustrophobic.

Pointing to the only other door in the apartment, I say, "Feel free to use anything you need to wash off the plane feeling. Clean towels are in a basket. You'll see them."

Once the bathroom door clicks shut, I climb onto my daybed-slash-couch to listen to a guided meditation in hopes of calming down before River returns. Relaxing would be a lot easier if I weren't drenched in his pine scent. And if that aroma didn't grow stronger every minute he's in the shower. *Note to self: read his soap bottle and purchase your own so you can drown in it.*

I've banished that thought and have convinced my body to relax when another thought pops into my mind, sending my heart thundering. I snap up straight, eyes wide. I put everything away yesterday. Right?

I didn't wash the toys and leave them on the shelf, like a giant invitation to… what? Think about me masturbating? Tease me for it, in the most non-sexual way? Think it's an invitation to something more?

I should check that everything is in the lock box.

Tilting to the side, I feel under the bed frame, and my stomach bottoms out. It's not there. *Shit.* That means it's under the sink.

Lying back down, I force myself to rest my hands light on my belly and follow the meditation's coaching. Breathe in, breathe out. This particular track is listed as heart opener: a journey to your true desires. Instead of listening to the instructions, though, my mind drifts to the man in my shower.

All morning while he was on the plane, the girls shared tidbits about River that he probably wouldn't think to point out about.

. . .

DELIA WENT on to talk about River's focus and determination when it comes to the Featherweight's legacy. According to her, it's impressive and it's been pushing her to think about what she actually wants. She mentioned the idea of starting her own makeup and styling company but quickly diverted back to the topic of River. She suggested we visit breweries and sustainable farm-to-table eateries while he's here, saying the research was the primary reason she sent him. It seems the Vermont trip was helpful with his menu planning, so it wouldn't hurt to try that again. That's pretty cool to know, honestly.

Stef jumped in, talking about how River dedicates far too much of his limited free time to caring for his dad, mentioning that Lee and Seth have been pushing him to step back a little, especially since Robert pays Gary to provide nursing support. According to her, he puts the needs of everyone else above his own.

GROUP CHAT: BAD BITCHES [STEF SANTOS MANOLO, LILY LONG, DELIA SHANE, NESSA RABIN]

NESSA:

I've got a client coming in soon, then I have to sort through listener questions. Unless one of you wants advice about sex and relationships…

Maybe someone who hasn't been in a serious relationship in at least five years?

THEY TALKED MORE about River this morning than they have in nearly a decade, and honestly, it made me wonder whether they were trying to convince me to date him or encourage him to relax. Or both.

NESSA (VOICE TEXT): "Ouch. Delia. She knows we are being heavy handed, doesn't she? You didn't think this was subtle?" [Nessa unsent voice message]

TOO BAD I saw the transcript. That settles it. Their conversation had its intended impact, making it impossible not to question what I want.

WHAT IS *my heart trying to tell me?*
    I don't know.
    What is my heart asking me to see?
    I do not know.

A DROP of sweat rolls down my face as I silently curse the meditation app again. Great. I'm so nervous that I'm sweating. Wait. The drop was cool, not hot, and it hit my cheek. Like it came from somewhere else. Pete? Maybe?

Cracking one eye ever so slightly, I find River standing over me, searching through his duffel, wearing only a towel. It sits low on his waist, in danger of falling, causing my heartbeat to pick up and my breath to hitch.

I close my eyes again quickly, hoping he was too distracted to notice that I was watching him. An internal war rages inside me, half of me hoping the towel will fall and reveal River to me in his full, naked glory, the other half staunchly against the idea.

Maybe I can fake sleep if I keep my eyes closed. The narration ends, and I'm thrown into silence. Though it's cut a second later when his laugh takes over my every sense, causing goose bumps to prickle on my skin.

Another drip of water. Then another and another. Like he's shaking out his shaggy hair. He removes one of my earbuds and says, "Wakey, wakey, maid of dishonor," the taunt reverberating through me.

With sweaty hands, I return my earbuds to their case. When I sit up, I discover that the towel has been swapped for a pair of black boxer briefs tight enough that if he turned a little farther to the side, I would get a quick glimpse of what he is packing. A white T-shirt comes over his head and floats down his back, and he steps into his gray sweatpants.

"Much better." He sighs. He eyes me, his expression going a little concerned as he sits next to me.

twenty-seven
River

AFTER MY SHOWER, I find Lily sitting with her back against the wall and her legs hanging over the side of her daybed, using it as a couch. She holds her stomach, her breaths slow and controlled rise. Like this I could almost believe she's sleeping, yet her fingers twitch every so often, telling me otherwise. Testing this theory, I first grab my duffel and place it next to her. She doesn't seem to notice. Then I dig for my clothes and turn my head, sending droplets of water flying at her.

After that, she stopped pretending. I sat beside her, the two of us facing her kitchen island. The bar stools tucked beneath it don't match. This place is nothing like the share house in Vermont. It's nothing like any of the glamorous places she posts about on social media either. *Has she been hiding more struggles than we realized this whole time?*

She pats my knee, the simple touch sending ripples throughout my body, then unlocks her phone and peers down at it, then starts rambling.

"All right, I have specific instructions from everyone for this week," she says. Her words are confusing at first, though I quickly realize she's talking about the wedding. "My texts were going haywire while you were in the air."

Trapped and staring like a deer in headlights, I'm unable to blink. Did our friends tell her about the condoms? About the comments they've made about my feelings for her? Swallowing thickly, the best I can offer is a nod of encouragement.

She worries her lip, her expression hesitant, but she goes on. "Stef asked us to run some interference. Something about the February party being unreasonable?"

"Oh yeah, there's some construction on the property, so I'll handle it." I brighten. If this conversation is strictly about the wedding, I might survive being so close to her lavender chamomile scent and the warmth radiating from her skin.

"Check. Next, the couple has decided to do a joint trip to Atlantic City for pre-wedding festivities. They'd rather have us all together and break into smaller groups for the more gendered stuff. I already reached out to a few hotels with inquiries about connecting suites. We'll want three: one for the guys, one for the girls from home, and one for the bevy of Santos and Manolo cousins who'll be in attendance. I'll keep you posted. Can you figure out some dinner options and a guys' night out?"

She's so focused, her tone serious, her body tense. Shifting her weight, she rocks on her hips, causing her to teeter toward me and then move away in a dance that may or may not be intentional.

"That sounds like a good split. When you come out east, we can go over some of the final details. It'll be easier when we're in the same place for longer." I lightly elbow her, hoping she doesn't regret agreeing to stay with me once the work out back is done.

"What did Delia say during your conversation? Knowing her, she had strong opinions. She better not have been complaining about the new kid. Kyle will eventually learn how to tap a keg."

"No, she demanded that I take you to bars and restaurants while you're here. For inspiration."

I try to stifle it, but a sigh of relief slips from me. Unfortunately, that sensation vanishes when she mentions our most unpredictable friend.

"Nessa," she says, and my hands ball themselves into fists.

"Oh god, what did Nessa say?" I hang my head, any hint of cool I've maintained evaporating. I might as well have a jaw full of acne and a retainer again with the way Lily looks at me. Nessa, a relationship and sex therapist who is a big fan of troublemaking? This could go in many different directions.

Her face softens in the low light from the lamp behind her, and she looks practically angelic, eyes rounded and full of innocence.

"Whatever could you mean? Concerns?" she teases. "About Nessa? Why, George River Hendrix. She only has the loveliest things to say in regard to your trip." She sticks her bottom lip out in an over-emphasized pout.

I'm hit with the urge to capture it in my teeth. To yank her toward me and tell her how much of a brat she's being.

Whoa, I want to what?

I blink a few times for good measure. Has it suddenly gotten warmer in here? Heart thumping, I rake a hand through my hair. I swear her pupils dilate and she sticks the tip of her tongue out and slowly licks across her bottom lip.

Then she snaps out of it and with a giggle, bumps her shoulder against mine. "She wants you to bring edibles back with you in gummy vitamin containers. The dispensaries back home don't carry a specific brand she likes. She was making jokes about mules. Did she do that to you, too?"

Oh, thank you, sweet lord. This is my out. "Yeah," I scratch at the back of my neck, face lowered. "Yep. Uh-huh. That's all. You know, Elizabeth wouldn't care, but if George Jonathan Hendrix discovered that I was less than perfect, he'd give Robert another gold star and lecture me about being more like my brother. Again."

Lily, in all her infinite gentle kindness, smiles. "Not really worth testing the FAA anyway. It's still a federal felony to cross state lines with products, even from one legalized state to another. It's not a risk you need to take on."

———

LIKE WHEN SHE was my desk mate, Lily meticulously checks off items on the list and adjusts the next steps needed with light movements of her wrist. Next, she looks at the week ahead.

"I traded a couple of shifts, so I'm all yours this week." She points to the scratched-out lines in her calendar and notes about who she traded with.

She's all mine. A thrill shoots through me. It's not at all what she meant, but it's late, and I spent the day traveling, so now my mind is running wild.

"The weather looks nice tomorrow," I point out, glancing at my phone to keep from staring at her.

"You never know out here. It changes on a dime. Since you're beat and we have a few small plans to work through, let's lay low tonight. We can focus on the Atlantic City trip and order take out. Then I thought we'd check out this spot tomorrow." She passes me her laptop with a bar website pulled up.

"That is perfect." My chest aches. I want so badly to believe that Lily suggested this because she wanted to care for my needs.

The local distillery she found is part of the River North Art District. According to their site, the RiNO graffiti walking tour group ends their route there every night.

I pull out my phone and call their business line. When the owner's daughter answers, we fall into conversation about the industry and family legacy. We discuss what my visit tomorrow will look like, and I agree to come in at nine p.m. since she expects it to be a slow night.

As I pocket my phone, I smile at Lily. "For a bunch of shit-stirrers, our friends really were on to something."

She breaks into a full, toothy smile. The light behind her eyes has me fully captivated, and the swell of her lower lip taunts me, challenging me to press my mouth to hers the way it did when we were fifteen.

It's easy to get lost in the unknown—the future of my family legacy and whether Lily could love me enough to come home—and I have plenty of time to overthink it all when I'm at home wiping down bar tops. This is the first true vacation I've taken in ages. It's time to focus on relaxing.

My goal this week is to be someone new. To banish the always-worried-about-optics, sweep-it-under-the-rug River. Maybe Robert has the right idea after all. That River has been nothing but serious and over-worked for six years.

I clear my throat and force out a question before I change my mind. "Would it be weird to use my first name?"

Head tilted, she presses her mouth into the cutest little pout and examines me, fidgeting as she considers the question.

Like I knew I would, I regret the question immediately. It was out of left field for me. That's for sure.

She whispers a confused "Huh?"

"Never mind," I say. "Just a silly idea. Since I'm in a new place, I thought maybe I could be someone new. Give hardworking, responsible, overthinking River a break. See how George Hendrix enjoys a vacation."

A devious little smile curls around her lips. "You absolutely cannot go by George. That name is just not you, darling." She taps her chin with one long finger, her dark purple polish shimmering, and hums quietly. "No, no, you are certainly more of a River than a George." She leans back, humming again, and uses her hands to frame me in view like a movie director, her smile growing. "Let's do it. Let's use fake names this week. We can be completely different people." She turns, facing me head on, our knees touching, burning the brightest I've seen in a long, long time, and I'm like a moth to her flame. I'm lost in the mirth in her eyes, fully mesmerized by the beauty, until she yanks me back to reality by saying, "But I will find a name for you."

Sweat pools under my arms, not enough to show but more than I'd like, especially when I'm this close to the woman of my dreams. I twist the throw pillow next to me, my worst-case-scenario-prone brain trying to convince me that her selection will be a subtle jab. Perhaps she'll take a page from tween River's attendance sheets on substitute teacher days. She'd always roll her eyes when I'd use Harry Dick, Eaton Beaver, or Willie B. Hardigan.

Based on the mischievous look brewing behind her eyes, there's a good chance my middle school jokes will be thrown back in my face.

To keep this from going sideways, I use a maneuver I hope will prevent her from using the worst suggestion that comes to her mind.

"Darling," I say, matching her sugary and somewhat condescending tone, and stroke my stubbly beard. "You can name me, but only if I name you back. Do we have a deal?"

She smirks, and damn do I want to kiss it right off her face. "Deal. This week, you'll be Pacey, like that show I made you watch with me. The series one my cousins left at the beach."

I remember the show. She made me watch the DVDs on repeat in middle school. Stef and Lily would argue about the love triangle all the time. Which team was she on again? I want to make sure I react properly. Thankfully I don't have to think too hard because she continues.

"It's because he chases what sounds fun in the moment. Plus, he was *wicked smart*. Smarter than anyone gave him credit for. Let those snarky jokes you've texted me out."

Shit, now I regret the quid pro quo I insisted on. *Do I want her to know how I feel yet?*

"Hey, Pace." She cocks a brow, hands fisted at her hips. "You aren't allowed to overthink. Name me. Now."

Maybe it's the way she looks at me. Or the idea of being someone else. Or maybe it's a force stronger than I can control. Whatever the reason, I move closer, as if we're magnets with opposite poles, turning my body so I'm fully facing her. My voice is quiet, deeper than usual, my lips skimming her ear.

The pulse in her throat quickens and a line of pinpricks rises on her flesh as it turns pink.

Emboldened by her reaction, I let the words I've been holding back since my shower leave my lips. "Is that whose name you moan when you are using the rainbow of surprises you left for me in the shower?"

She jolts, her eyes going wide, her pupils so large her dark brown eyes are nearly black. I swallow hard, trying to read her but second-guessing myself instantly.

Has she ever thought about me like that before? Did I cross a line? Was the move not intentional? Am I embarrassing her?

She leans forward.

Is it possible she's tempting me to cross the line?

I need her words. I can't do this without them. Time stretches on. An eternity has gone by before she licks her bottom lip, her eyes sparkling. This is a version of her I've never met.

This woman has a fire in her eyes and I'd willingly let her consume me. I yearn to close the gap and capture her lips with mine, but I hold back. I've wanted this for longer than any man should be able to bear, but I'm statue-still.

She surprises me by swinging one leg over mine and slipping onto my lap. Legs wide and pushing her hips lightly against the thin material of my gray sweatpants, she drapes her arms over my shoulders in a hug that sends electricity crackling between us.

I wrap my own arms around her back, accidentally causing her hips to grind against me and sending all the blood in my body rushing for my groin.

Who is this goddess? This beautiful woman who exists outside of

Peacock Springs and is right here with me? There's nothing shy or timid about her.

"Fucking exquisite," I whisper to the crown of her head. As if they have a mind of their own, my hands roam up and down her back, then grasp a handful of hair at her nape and angle her face toward mine.

It's clear: we're playing chicken.

Lightly, I yank her hair again, eliciting a light gasp from her, the move forcing her hips into mine.

I'm thirty years old and dry-humping my lifelong friend that I've been secretly in love with, and I can't just kiss her? This is ridiculous.

I graze the tip of my nose against the soft skin of her neck, relishing the scents of lavender, sandalwood, and chamomile. The way her breath hitches and her thighs clench suggests we are on the same page.

"*Darling,*" I say, sticking with the term of endearment, "I need you to tell me what you want. Do you want to play pretend with me this week?"

Panting, she nods. "Who am I?"

There's no blood left in my brain. It's all relocated to my erect cock. It strains against my boxer briefs and sweatpants, nestling itself between her parted legs, twitching in complaint because there are too many layers between us.

There's no doubt she's enjoying our standoff when she swivels her hips again. This time it's blatantly intentional. Call it: time of death.

Too caught up in the moment, I let my words tumble out fully raw and honest.

"You, *my darling,* are the first girl who ever gave me tingly feelings. The ones that caused me to wake up to sticky sheets too often in middle school."

Her eyes search mine, swimming with vulnerable curiosity. Even after I told her she was the star of my wet dreams during puberty.

Keep talking. Keep it moving.

"You are the most beautiful flower, and I had the honor of watching you blossom from a shy new student to my personal shusher. Then you were my secret keeper. I looked for you in the stands at every hockey game," I admit. "Even when you were with *him.*"

That last word is full of the ire and derision the man deserves.

She shivers ever so slightly.

Pressing on with an increased fervor, I nip at her jaw. "Who are you? You are the most beautiful woman I've ever met. It killed me to watch a man so fucking unworthy of your drive, your love for your friends, and your ability to float on so lightly through this world claim you as his. But I kept quiet. Remained patient. Because I always knew. You are destined for so much more than he offered you. You deserve a life filled with the type of color you bring with you. Playfulness. Joy. You deserve a partner who remembers your coffee order."

Her eyes widen.

"Yes, I caught that look on your face in September." Feral. Enraged. I am nearing lecturing territory or a firm reprimand. "You are the woman who turned every mistreatment you received inward, who fled from home blaming yourself when the house made of paper you and that asshole lived in didn't stand up to the rain."

Now that I've cracked the lid on these emotions, the all-consuming torment plaguing me bubbles over. My pulse quickens to the speed of a hummingbird's wings.

My tone is commanding and harsh, but she doesn't look afraid.

I hold her tighter, watching for any sign of discomfort. *Am I scaring her? Hurting her?*

Her knees fall farther apart and she locks her ankles behind my back and grips my shoulders more firmly, like if we get close enough, the two of us can be squeezed into a singular being.

Hands on her ass, I haul myself up and turn. Then I drop her onto the mattress and crawl over her. I graze my palm against her cheek, pushing my weight into her as she did to me, and grind against her, savoring each ripple of expectation between us.

"Do you not realize, *darling*, that you've always been it for me? When you went quiet for two years, the girls kept me updated on your every move. Not to be kind, but because I was annoying the life out of them. Pretty sure Nessa blocked my number for a while." I huff. "Where the fuck were you?"

Our eyes are locked and we're intimately wrapped around each other, yet she hasn't interrupted this overdone speech.

"When you popped back up online like you never left and started posting pictures?" I growl and shake my head. "You looked fucking delicious. Good enough to eat. Still do. And I'd happily make a meal out of you over and over until it's time to fly back to New Jersey, but first you have to tell me you want this too."

A strand of hair falls in her face, and without slowing my frantic movements, I brush it aside, skimming her forehead and cheek with the pads of my fingers and tracking the freckles across her nose.

Eyelids heavy, she parts her lips on a soft breath, like maybe she is waiting for me to finish my monologue, or maybe she's trying to find her words.

She raises her hips, chasing the friction, but I pull back, despite how badly I want to bury myself inside her. Cupping my cheeks, she brings her face to mine, our noses touching. We are close enough to kiss, but I remind her, "I need to hear that you want this. I can't guess."

Finally, she nods, lightly grazing my lips with a nearly there kiss. "Please."

That is all the permission I need to steal the sound from her mouth.

With her tongue, she parts my lips, and our bodies move together, setting a rhythm that is both brand new and familiar, like the remix of a favorite song. Slipping her hands beneath the hem of my T-shirt, she drags her nails over the lower part of my ribs lightly and swirls patterns up the sides of my body. When she moves to my shoulders, she presses her nails harder into the skin, the sharp sting urging me to pull her lower lip between my teeth with a soft nip.

"Like to be a little prickly, do you, darling?" I laugh against her mouth.

She cocks an eyebrow. "Mm-hmm, you'll figure it out. We have time. Five days, huh? Do we tell…" Her breath hitches. "Um, everyone? Back at h…in Peacock Springs? Or…" She trails off, searching my eyes, uncertainty written all over her face. She wants to ask me if this is a secret, a vacation hookup only or something more. I'm just not certain what answer she wants from me.

All I can do is tell her how I feel, so I let the words pour out. "This ass has teased me on Instagram for far too long. Bent over, twisted, legs in the sky. I've wanted to be over, under, or alongside you in each of those shapes. The only one who sees your face in the throes of pleasure and hears your moans. I thought you'd never come home. I'm this generation's George. I'll never be anywhere but there. So I gave up on the idea."

Equal parts vulnerable and turned on, I force myself to make sure she understands where I'm coming from.

"When you slammed into my chest in September, all my fears disappeared. It didn't matter that having you once wouldn't be enough. You snuggled into me that night and I knew for certain that I am a masochist. Whether I have you for one night, one week, or one lifetime, the idea of going another fifteen years without ever kissing you, never having you in my arms, is too much. I will take what you'll offer me, for as long as you're offering it."

twenty-eight
Lily

"I DON'T KNOW if I can come back for good." With my lip caught between my teeth, I consider what this could mean. *Holy shit, I need this to happen. Shut up and don't prevent this.* "I *am* confident that I can make you come. Tonight, tomorrow, for as long as you're here." Before I can say too much or blurt out the wrong thing, I pull him in and place kisses, little licks, and nips up and down the column of his throat.

Together we work his shirt over his head. Then I resume my trail of kisses from beneath him, pausing over his heart.

"I don't know what else we will have, but I know that I want this so badly," I gasp out. "I want you so badly. If you're someone else, you're here for a good time, not a long time. So follow the dopamine, darling. Keep touching me. Kissing me. Do you want to keep touching me?"

"You always did keep me on task." Chuckling, he dips down and claims my mouth. It's the permission he needed to drop the sweet, sincere persona and revel in his basic desires. He hops off the bed and tries to take off my leggings from the ankles, but they barely move.

I lift my hips and peel away the waistband so that his next

yank causes them to spring free in one swipe. The soft clingy black fabric is gone, leaving me in a tiny dusty blue mesh thong and a gray T-shirt that's ridden up, showing my stomach.

In a flash of insecurity, I survey my legs, mumbling, "I really didn't expect. I mean… I didn't know, and…"

He runs his hands from my waist along the inside of my thighs to my calves, chuckling again. The second the sound is out, he blushes.

"Darling." He steps in and prods my knees farther apart. "Not the first time I've seen a woman naked. I do not care that you didn't plan to let me taste you. I only care that the wet spot growing on your panties is for me."

My mind is screaming "holy shit," but my lungs are unable to get enough air.

He runs his hands lightly up and down my calves as he studies me. I've never had a poker face, and while I can't think, speak, or breathe, he's still the one who knows me inside out, and he manages to make me laugh and relax a bit further.

Rubbing his beard against the stubble down my legs, he leaves a trail of kisses, adding in moments of deep skin sucking and light bites along the way. When he's hovering over my core, he meets my eyes.

"I didn't shave my legs for you either," he murmurs, "so we're even. Now relax. I need to know how you sound when you are getting everything you deserve."

Fuck, I can't keep track of what he can hear at this moment. I yank off my shirt, exposing the bralette that matches the panties. The set is comfortable, but it's also smooth, soft, and a little sheer.

Eyes flaring, he catalogs me, studying every curve and divot, every marking of the passage of time since the last time we swam together in our teens.

His perusal is interrupted by a streak of auburn fuzz, and as Pete zooms past, hops over next to me, and hops off the bed, I fight the instinct to cover myself.

I slip out from under River and snag a cheese stick from the shelf, then toss a bit toward Pete. As he inhales it, I drop the rest into his crate, and as I hoped, he chases it in. River slams the door shut, then drapes a blanket over the entire thing.

"That's one jealous man I'll have to contend with eventually," he teases, pulling me into a hug.

"And how many fans do you have?" I ask, splaying my hands over his warm, muscular back. "A bartender as hot as you are? You must have ladies throwing themselves at you all the time."

He presses me against the wall, looking intensely into my eyes. "I haven't been with anyone in months. Not since I saw you that night in the square. Couldn't even consider it. I was tested this fall and am all clear." Hands cupped at the sides of my breasts, he dips his head and gently clamps his teeth around my nipple through the mesh. "Also, I cringed when you mentioned Nessa because she added condoms to the plane ticket. With staples puncturing the middle of each one."

I do my best to reply between gasps and spontaneous intrusive thoughts about babies and what my friends know about this trip.

"Me too," I breathe out. "Tested. Always after each partner. But *fuck*, since September, I haven't been with anyone… other than my friends in the shower, who you met earlier."

Finding pieces of the self-assured woman I usually am with partners, I add the important things like "And I have an IUD. Trust issues, you know. Daddy issues. I don't need to add a person to this mess until it's a bit more figured out. So tell me more about these other fun things and we'll see what happens as we go. There's no rush."

Despite the words, every action we take suggests otherwise.

twenty-nine
River

AS I RELEASE HER NIPPLE, gearing up to give the other the same attention, she surprises me by sliding down my body and kneeling before me. She runs her hands along my thighs, every tiny touch making my muscles flex and shake. When she reaches the waistband of my sweatpants and fitted black boxer briefs, she peers up at me. "These." She tugs. "Off. Now."

We do the awkward pushing and stepping that comes with these moments, then I kick my boxers away, distracting myself from how her hand feels fisted around the base of my cock.

Fuck, I'm afraid I'll explode on her face immediately.

Gingerly, she licks from the base to tip where the earliest drop of pre-cum is leaking from the head. She swirls me in her mouth like her favorite dessert, and when she takes me into her mouth in earnest, letting her jaw fully extend, I know I need to reverse things here. I want to get the focus back on her.

"This feels. Fucking. Amazing," I groan, throwing my arms out to steady myself on the wall. I want to stabilize myself. I want to take back control. I like that she is trusting me that way.

Suddenly, a sharp noise cuts through the room, causing Pete to bark from his crate. We jump apart like two teenagers caught by their parents. It takes another two blares of the obnoxious horn noise before Lily jumps up, eyes wide. "That's the delivery. Oh shit."

I reach down and pull on my sweatpants before gently turning her back toward the mattress. "Hold that thought. I'll be right back." I shuffle to the old-school intercom and buzz the delivery person in. When the buzzing stops, I get an idea.

I crack the door, unsure of how much of Lily could be exposed if I open it more. I haven't turned around for fear of abandoning this task and returning to the meal I'd prefer to eat instead. After I've thanked the delivery person and locked the door, I drop the food onto the counter, then open the oven to stick the takeout boxes inside to stay warm. *Seriously, River, are you concerned about the food?*

Lily sits in the center of the mattress watching me with her feet together, knees wide, and her arms behind her, propping her up, looking casual, unaffected, and completely sexy in the most unintentional way.

Winking, I say, "Give me one sec." And I slip into her bathroom.

I study the shelf as if I didn't do this during my shower, then pick up the toy that looks the least intimidating, a shiny little device that looks like those acne face brushes or a toothbrush without bristles. With my thumb, I press the power button and assess the way the little circle attaches to my palm and creates a tickling pressure. Continuing my search, I eye a toy that looks like a Brookstone muscle massager. A star-shaped curved silicone item with lots of bumps and ridges sits next to the tiny bullet-shaped leopard vibrator. I grab the last one because it's the most simplistic and exit the bathroom.

As I step into the main room of her apartment, I find her lying on her back, completely bared to me, one hand between her legs while the other rests palm up across her forehead. She's getting started without me.

The sight sends a rush of adrenaline through me. It's the kind of sensation I usually tamp down, but this feels like the right time to let it out. So I pull my shoulders back and bark, "Who said you could move?" My authoritative tone is unfamiliar, but after years of dreaming about this moment, I need to keep control. The possibility of it being less than perfect for her won't stand.

She removes her hand from her face and cocks a brow. "What are you going to do about it?"

Her teasing lilt takes my straining dick to a level I could have never anticipated. My balls tighten, and my stomach and spine contract.

Thoughts of all the dirty things I can do to her flit through my mind. *What should I do first? I'd like to spank that luscious ass... but I'm not ready to go there just yet. Instead, I'll take a page out of her TV boyfriend's book and open up and show her my vulnerable side.*

thirty
Lily

"COLLIDING into you that night at the square didn't just shake me up physically. You jump-started emotions I buried years ago. And I can't contain them anymore." River's stare is soft but firm. "You want to play? Act bratty? Then I'll happily give you my demands: I demand you show up for yourself. Want to be loud? Great. Quiet? That's perfectly fine too. Just be honest with me. Because my goal is to make this perfect for you. I want to know every inch of this..." He bites his knuckles and mumbles, "This fucking amazing body. I've dreamed about seeing you like this, about feeling you respond to me, for so long. I've dreamed of this perfect pussy." He kneels between my legs. "And all the ways I can make you wet like this." He runs a hand up and down my now exposed center. I undressed myself while he was turned around, growing impatient with the interruptions.

"I'm going to examine every single inch of your skin and find where you are ticklish and what turns you on, and I'm going to give you the time and attention a fucking masterpiece like you deserves."

I nod, though I can't speak at this point.

"Anything off-limits?" he asks. "Tell me now so I can focus on making you come." Brow arched, he smirks devilishly. Deliciously.

"About that," I croak, covering my face. "What if I don't?" A pit forms in my stomach at the thought, but it's a possibility.

In some of Nessa's books, the alpha-hole male main character grabs the heroine and assures her that he not only can but will make it happen more than once. Then he's just perfect at it all. There's no fumbling. No, the entire encounter is magical and she's coming on his fingers, his lips, and his cock.

The men I've met who've made those same assurances are the least likely to have succeeded at making me orgasm, and I've only ever had sapphic lovers who accept that it's not the end all, be all.

But I should have known better than to compare River to those men. Unfazed, he grasps my wrists and pulls my hands away from my face. With a softness that shows he understands that this isn't the moment to keep the dominant tone, he says, "If you don't come, but you enjoyed yourself, and you tell me you're done, then we are done."

He winks, then his expression hardens again, the deep seriousness in his eyes causing me to become increasingly turned on.

"You are not allowed to fake things for my ego, got that?" he asks. "That's not how we do things. No lies. Nothing fake. In fact, if you don't touch me back, I'll just... I'll need a few minutes alone in your bathroom, but I'll live."

Shit, that's sexy.

My body heats further at that admission.

"I'm going to trail kisses all over your body now, and I won't stop until I make you squirm and smile." He presses his lips to mine. "Got it?"

All I can do is nod woodenly, too entranced to find words.

"Good, darling. Very good," he growls out. "Now..." He traces his lips up my calf to my knee, running his fingers up the outside of my thigh and sliding his hand under me to grab my ass. But he stops short of where I'm aching for him and starts over with the other ankle.

Hovering over me, he kisses my sternum, and when he pulls back, he studies the delicate peacock feather adorning the cage around my heart.

Gently tracing the lines with a single finger, he whispers, "The night you came back, you were stuck in your sports bra, and I saw a faint hint of this. I've been wondering what it was but was afraid to ask. It's beautiful. Though I'm surprised you'd go with a peacock feather."

"Just because I didn't plan to come back home didn't mean home wasn't in my heart. You know?" My chest tightens. "Sorry, I can share the rest another time. This is what I do. My brain goes in a million directions even when all I really want to do is be here with you." I drop one hand to his cheek and softly stroke his beard.

Sincerity emanates from his eyes, his voice, and his posture. "We are here together. I was tracing your body art. I'm the one who brought it up. Now you're giving me the story. Please tell me all your stories. I want nothing more than to be the keeper of them and your secrets again. I want to do that and this," he says, bringing his lips to mine in a soft and sweet kiss.

The anxiety beginning to build eases again. River always knows exactly what to say.

I drag my hand to his nape, raking my nails up into his hair. I pull back for a beat to marvel at this moment, to try and capture his handsome and kind ways.

His tongue traces a zigzag line to the lower areas of my stomach before detouring and making slow sucking and nipping stops along the curves of each hip bone. He repeats the action down my bikini line to my inner thigh and pulls my skin into his mouth. He sucks hard enough to leave a mark, causing me to squirm.

Finally he touches me where I am aching for him most, the

pads of his fingers moving my own lubrication to my clit, then making firm circles. Eyes rolling back, I lose the ability to think clearly. The more he uses the steady pressure, the stronger the pulsing between my legs grows. I can't believe I am this close already. Usually the only men who can get me to relax enough so that I can orgasm are run by batteries and USB chargers.

Changing things up, he pushes two fingers deep inside me, and while the fullness feels amazing, I lose that near-orgasm feeling. I focus on the new sensations, relaxing into them, eager to find that place of near release again.

He licks a long line against the most sensitive spots of my pussy, and a moan escapes my lips, loud and feral, a sound I've never made.

"Good," he praises. "Keep moaning for me, darling. Tell me what you like. Just like that." He repeats the motion. Between long, languid laps over every sensitive inch of skin there are rougher digs of teeth and nails, making it impossible to anticipate his next move.

At a cool, smooth sensation between my legs, I crack open my eyes. "I didn't know you invited someone else to the party. River, meet the ocelot. In Texas, I loved getting glimpses of the wildcats, and with the spots, this toy looked like them. Figured it was better than calling her Kitty or Pussy."

"Her?" He holds the device up, surveying its multicolored neon spots and tiny turn dial, and laughs. "Never seen a woman who looked like this."

"My ex-girlfriend did." The words escape me without thought. "I mean, she had a leopard-spot heart tattoo..." I drift off, waiting for his reaction. When he seems to be stuck, I snatch the toy from him and turn it on. "While you are glitching, I'm going to just..." I place the vibrator exactly where I need it: directly over the bundle of nerves that will allow the wave of an orgasm to crest. This does the job, and within seconds, my pulse speeds up and my muscles tense, my lower belly clenching. It's not *not* with him, just—

"What the? Whoa..."

A sharp sensation hits my chest. River's teeth clamped around my nipple. I lurch forward, dropping the vibrator to the mattress. Stifling a scream, I bury my face in his neck. His forest scent overtakes me, his pheromones taunting me, telling me that a few days won't be enough but it's probably all I have.

He follows the bite with soft kisses and continues to massage my breast and tweak at my nipples.

"No need to work," he says. "Just relax."

"Trust me, I couldn't be more relaxed if I tried," I gasp.

Pulling him closer, I push at the waistband of his sweats. He helps, and then I line the throbbing head of his cock against my entrance. He's thick and heavy in my hand.

Finally, he pushes in and fills me, pressing his chest to mine roughly, like the day we reunited in the square. It feels like we were always supposed to be like this, heart to heart.

I'm lost in every move, and when he finds his own release, I'm entranced by him, watching the flutter of his lashes. As he rolls to the bed beside me, his face is soft, almost boyish again. I turn on my side so I'm facing him, relishing the peacefulness that demands to not be disturbed. Eventually, I slink over to grab the towel he abandoned and wipe myself down, then gently drape it over him to let him do the same.

I kick my discarded clothes into the corner—*I really need a hamper*—and pull on his T-shirt, then pluck a pair of boy short underwear out of the drawer and wander into the bathroom.

Once I close the door behind me, I relieve myself and wash up. After, I'm unable to calm myself, so I start reheating the takeout, my mind racing.

River comes up behind me, wearing only his boxers, and wraps me in his arms.

"Sorry," I huff. "I have too much energy to sit still. I figured you could relax while I reheat our dinner. I didn't think to ask if you wanted me to stay and snuggle."

With a kiss to my temple, he squeezes me closer. Instead of wading into the anxiety with me, he holds me firmly and moves the conversation along. "Ocelots, huh? Have you ever seen *Archer*?"

Twenty minutes later, with our plates in our laps, we sit side by side, watching the cartoon he says mentions ocelots. Snuggled close and in the easy rhythm of friendship, I drift back to those old love triangles we watched and wonder: *Did I choose the wrong friend last time?*

thirty-one

Lily

I **SNEAK OUT OF BED**, hoping I can brush my teeth and slip back in before River wakes up. But as I rinse my toothbrush, I catch his large form in the mirror. He steps behind me at the tiny pedestal sink and holds my hip lightly while reaching for his toothbrush. I mindlessly list back into his chest, my boy shorts pushing against his boxers.

It doesn't take long for things to heat up between us again, and we find ourselves touching and kissing throughout our shower together. We spend the morning like this, teasing, touching, whispering, and bringing one another to the edge of climax and over the cliff again. This continues until our stomachs are rumbling with hunger and we've broken into epic fits of giggles, making me feel like we are grade schoolers again.

"Guess I better feed you," I say once I've caught my breath.

He gives me a wicked grin and points to his face. "I've eaten a few times already, but hop on up."

Shaking my head, I walk away to get dressed. "It's been almost a full day since you got here," I call over my shoulder. "We're going to a place that serves the best breakfast. We've got that brewery tour later, and we can't drink on an empty stomach, bartender."

———

I ORDER the most decadent dessert-like strawberry shortcake biscuit stack and coffee, and once our food arrives, he's asking serious questions. This conversation started in the shower. He's clearly not going to let it go, and my way of pushing the subject off won't work here.

River takes a large forkful of whipped cream, strawberries, and biscuit together while waiting for me to answer.

"What do I do for fun?" I repeat to buy time to come up with a good response. It's not that I don't enjoy my life, but I have a feeling that he will realize that just because it seems fun doesn't mean it is. I am always on the move, heading toward the next adventure. I meet amazing people, see places beyond my wildest dreams, and spend time with nature's most astounding treasures. I build temporary connections to people and places, but before anything gets too familiar, I move on.

The longer I wait to reply, the more likely he is to dig, and it takes just one question to shake me.

My fork clatters to the plate as I process his words. *Do you ever want to stay put?*

He looks at me like he can tell that my lifestyle isn't as fun as it used to be.

I play off the fork drop as intentional by picking up the coffee. With a deep sip, I continue to stall. Before I can figure out what to say, he goes on.

"As awed as I am by your career," he says, wearing a hesitant look, "sometimes, I feel like your life would be different if we'd protected you. That you've had to be a hustler, on your own, and it's our fault." Head lowered, he examines his breakfast. "Or maybe this is exactly where you were meant to be and I'm completely off base. Sorry, maybe I shouldn't have asked. It's just, the last few years with my family haven't been easy, but I've been fortunate to have a support system. I just feel guilty that we were so distant when you may have needed us."

Lips pressed together, I focus on the responsibilities he has at home, choosing to steer the conversation away from me.

"Are you asking because you want to stay on vacation forever? Or is this because you want your brothers to do more?" I reach for his hand and trace circles on the back of it.

He peers over his mug, the emerald color of his T-shirt making his eyes more green than blue today, and smirks. "Yes to both. The last twenty-four hours have been some of the best of my life. But also, it's because I let Robert"—he rolls his eyes at the formal name—"pay Gary to work a few extra days so Mom isn't taking care of Dad on her own. He really thinks his money makes up for his absence. I don't know how to explain that it's nice but it's not all there is. Sometimes it would be nice to feel like I had a partner in things. Yeah, Scout does a lot when he's on break, but I hate pressuring him. Peacock Springs is not for everyone." He smirks, knowing that I'm cornered.

Giving a dramatic sigh, I wave my napkin like a white flag. "I surrender, fine. Yes, being there again was weird. It shook my belief that I had healed, that I'd moved on. You know this. You know how I reacted when I saw my mom, but I also saw Grant. On the train after that terrible interview," I admit. "It was a clusterfuck. Pru Cleary was there too. Probably snooping so she could tell the whole town that I was—"

He cuts me off. "What? Incredible? That you told him that his lack of remorse isn't your issue anymore? I heard. I was impressed. I wish I had seen it. I wish I had done something about it sooner."

"Yet I'm also the arsonist they still want to put in the stocks." I huff. "My therapist has encouraged me to try it, though. To come for the spring and stay, like you suggested. I just have to be sure, for myself, that I can survive being so close by for so long. To butcher a quote from *Gilmore Girls,* 'look, we live in a teeny tiny little hamlet here, it makes avoiding people tough and uncomfortable.' Being there means I have to figure out how not to panic if those ghosts are near me again."

He flips my hand over on his, then traces the underside of my ring finger toward my palm, following the lines there.

"All right, that's a lot of vulnerability." He interlaces our fingers and gives me a soft kiss on the knuckles. "And it makes sense. When we were kids, you were quiet, a rule follower, but that was not for you, was it?" Head tilted, he studies me like he's solving a puzzle. "Delia likes to clean the bar while listening to podcasts, and Nessa runs a teen girls group upstairs. I hear things. You promise to keep what I learned between us?"

His expression turns conspiratorial, like we're about to cause trouble.

"They have been discussing *nice girl syndrome* and *good girl complex* lately," he says. "It's all about people-pleasing and boundary setting. I'm pretty sure Delia was trying to passive-aggressively kick me off the property, and when I didn't get it, she handed me a literal plane ticket. I think she was hinting that I need to work on setting boundaries and worry less about being perfect. But I think it applies to you too. It's time for us to stop being who we think other people want us to be." He swallows thickly. "It's unfair that your family expected you to be perfect, neat, quiet, or pretty to be loved. Not then. Not now. Not ever."

He squeezes my hand tighter, his eyes turning stormy, darkening in color. With his jaw set like this, he looks more like a man than ever before. He's strong and solid, and yet he has control of his emotions.

"You deserve only good things. Fuck. Them." He scoffs. "Grant. Belinda. Neal's cowardice. All of them. They don't deserve your time and energy. They don't deserve your pain or tears. They sure as shit don't deserve to force you away from…" He inhales deeply. "From your girls who are like sisters."

He left himself off the list. Why? Maybe because we agreed to scratch an itch this week, to get the mutual attraction out of our systems? I just have to tell myself it's no big deal. And push back any hope that he was making a grand declaration.

I learned long ago that if someone wants to keep another person, they will try. And based on my track record with love interests, after me, River will find a real partner and settle down. She'll have less baggage and won't be an issue for his future success.

"Thank you for saying that." My voice is barely a whisper.

thirty-two
Rriver

GROUP CHAT: THE FEATHERWEIGHT MGMT

[12/26 12:00 P.M.]

How are things going so far?

DELIA:

Go away.

[12/26 8:04 P.M.]

Can I get an update?

No.

[12/27 1:37 P.M.]

River: Do you want to keep getting paychecks?

You'd never.

Stop tempting me

Everything is fine. I've worked here for as long as
you have, dude. Best manager you have. You
can't lose me. Well-oiled machine. Still in the
black. Go away

Tell Lily I said hi.

[12/27 9:30 P.M.]

Update me after close

[12/27 11:59 P.M.]

Cordelia...

[12/28 12:22 A.M.]

Hello?

[12/28 7:47 P.M.]

I'm cutting my trip short if I don't hear from you

DELIA:

[sends photo of Seth reading with a beer, the town elders at their usual table eating lunch over his shoulder]

The building is still standing, things are fine, it's two more days

thirty-three
Lily

EVERY DAY, we make stops, checking out new beers, whiskey, and food to see how establishments tie details relevant to the city into their offerings. Our afternoons are spent exploring and noting ideas for the Featherweight. The public hugs and hand holding continue, but in the back of my mind, a small voice is whispering that I should be cautious. My heart has a way of forgetting what it signed up for and daydreaming in places that are very far from reality. Despite the warning, we spend the evenings fooling around and fall asleep snuggled together. It's all so easy, I wish I could bottle these moments up and keep them with me.

———

DECEMBER 29TH

AS DAWN BREAKS on our final full day together in this little bubble, I'm determined to take full advantage of it. Like every morning this week, we brush our teeth, and our mouths and bodies are pressed together before we even make it to the shower.

Once in the warmth of the water, I wash his shoulders, relishing the swell of his muscles, then the bumps and veins of his biceps and the planes of his pecs. The soft tufts of dark chest hair clump and swirl under my sudsy touch. I run my hands along his sides, his back, and down his bubble butt, giggling.

With a soft kiss to my mouth, River asks, "What's so amusing?"

"The last book club pick was a sports romance, and I am starting to understand the obsession with hockey butts, that's all. Wait, do you still skate?" I ask. "What do you do when you aren't at the bar? What do you want Vacation River to keep doing at home?"

He cups my chin and uses his thumb to pull my lip from between my teeth.

More often than not, when someone I've made a connection with wants more, they find it after me, so I'm holding my breath. As much as I can't stand giving him up to another woman, he deserves the good luck.

He slips his hands down to my ass, and with a little squeeze, he presses me closer.

"What do I want?" he repeats, pressing his hard length against my thigh with a little grin.

Head bowed, I survey his impressive manhood. Then I smirk up at him. "Well, yes. I know that part. You haven't exactly hidden this desire. I meant beyond this. But I guess we can talk about it another time."

We continue to wash each other's bodies, fingers lingering, memorizing one another in the event that this is our last encounter before his flight tomorrow.

As he slips a soapy hand between my legs, I clutch his wrist and pull it away. "Dude, no. You are basically promising to give me a UTI if you use soap as lube."

Eyes wide, he raises his hands like he is surrendering to the police. I reach over him to remove the shower head, first spraying him down, then myself. I linger a moment longer than needed over my pussy, humming as pressure builds against my clit.

Hands clear of soap, River touches me until I'm panting and moaning in his arms. When my knees wobble, he presses his weight against me, pushing me against the tiles. The cold sensation is a reminder of the morning before he arrived.

"My toys were supposed to be put away that first day. I wasn't expecting this, and I had tried to get it out of my system before. I just messed up cleaning up, as usual."

He throws his head back, laughing. "I've never been so happy that you forgot to put something away, now put those legs around me."

Breath catching, I ask, "Won't we fall?"

With just a hint of force, he drags one of my legs around his hip, then hauls me up into his arms. He holds me up with one hand while he turns off the water, then he carries me over to the sink and pushes himself in to the hilt. "No, darling, but we might fly." With a snap of his hips, he fucks me like he's also afraid he'll never be given the chance again.

———

AFTER WE CLEAN up for the second time that morning, he asks a vague "You... did? Didn't you?"

Focus fixed on the bathmat, I repeat his words from the start of the week. "Honesty over ego, right?" I curl my toes, watching the fibers of the mat move rather than meeting his eyes.

"Yes, honesty. Always be honest with me." He tilts my chin so our eyes meet.

"Then honestly, no, I didn't, but I'm happy this way. So though you might want to move this to the bed, we don't have time. I've had a little surprise up my sleeve." I can't help but grin. "A resort client, the Hayden Group, was supposed to be here for the new year, but their travel plans were disrupted by a snowstorm. So instead of sending them on a tour of a local aero-garden and community farm project, I'm taking you."

I don't mention the Michelin Star restaurant on-site. I called and convinced the team to keep the reservation and reduce it to two. Dinner at the highly coveted Japanese restaurant, where they use vegetables grown directly on-site in vertical hydroponic planters, will be the most wonderful way to cap off the week for River.

When we arrive, we're met by a slender man with a bushy mustache and day-old stubble. He's dressed in skinny jeans, boots, and woolly socks. His hat is pulled low over his glasses, and he's popped his coat collar up to protect his neck from the wind. Despite the usual warm weather, a cold front moved in this morning. He introduces himself as Silas, and once the pleasantries are out of the way, he leads us toward a small garden shed with heat lamps attached outside.

"Thank you for keeping this on the books," I say as we follow. "Since it's so chilly, we're happy to keep the outdoor portion quick."

With a relieved smile, he guides us down the dirt path past the now-empty garden beds, promising that it's no trouble on his part.

"River's family has owned and operated the Featherweight out in Peacock Springs, New Jersey, since the end of the Civil War. He's in town doing research regarding expanding their operation and bringing back sustainability. Nobody does it like the folks out here, so we're grateful for your time."

Silas's shoulders relax. Clearly the flattery and move indoors, out of the wind, are working in our favor. The raised aero-beds are like nothing else and could easily be replicated for the Featherweight.

We take a lot of shit for being a joke of a state, but New Jersey is known as the Garden State because of the vast farmlands in many places. River's property could easily handle the outdoor beds, allowing the restaurant to move to an on-site farm-to-table style service.

Over dinner, we discuss all we've discovered with the eager enthusiasm of watching our favorite team win the championships combined with kids at Disney *on* Christmas morning.

"This would allow you to raise the prices," I toss out there.

Smiling, River says, "My dad would be so proud of this profit-minded conversation. I'm surprised you aren't espousing the values of keeping things affordable for those who need it."

"That's the best part." I say a little too loudly. Shit. I can't contain myself. When I get excited about an idea, I can go from zero to sixty faster than a Maserati.

"By pricing your food and drinks fairly, you'll be able to pay the staff in the restaurant and those who maintain the garden a fair and living wage. The overall staff meals can improve, and any produce just past the quality you'd use in food service but still edible can become part of an on-site community pantry. There are so many ways to turn the Featherweight into the sort of socially conscious place you want without sacrificing quality. In fact, when we ignore the value of our own work, we often end up losing out. It also means you aren't price gouging others. There's always a balance."

Eyes full of happy tears, he stifles a slight laugh.

A flash of nerves hit me. Worried I said something wrong, I bite out, "What?"

River leans forward, cupping my cheek, and brushes his nose with mine in an affectionate gesture. "You're a passionate adventurer. It has always inspired and awed me. You bring me so much happiness, and I can't contain it within myself." He softly places a kiss on the tip of my nose before pulling back again.

thirty-four
Lily

WHILE DRIVING River to the airport in Denver, nerves skitter through me. The upcoming town meeting and the unknown surrounding it hang heavy in the air.

His phone rings, and he flashes the screen my way so I can see Delia's name. The second he answers, I say, "Hello, Deedee. I'm about to drop your boss off at the airport."

"Hi, there. I have good news," she says. "River, Ava Marie has decided that you've been compromised, so she discussed the town meeting dates with me." Her words are staccato, emphasized. "She still doesn't want Lily to know about the decisions that will be made. She doesn't want to spook her, but they've agreed anything they try to enact will match the original timelines and line up with some sort of festival. It'll be like when we used to dress as soldiers on the Fourth of July or whatever."

She scoffs on the last bit.

"Not even the most biased of the crowd could argue." She sighs. "And there's one other thing. It's being pushed out to late spring, which is good. You mentioned Lily might be willing to help you, and since you've been gone, it's become clear that the guys I've been training are on top of things. And…" she says, dragging out the word. "Well, I got into a huge bridal makeup program. It's twelve weeks long, but it's the best in the world. I didn't think they'd accept me." she lets out a long breath, then her usual brash confidence returns. "So Lily, gotta lean on you, girl. Please don't flake."

A squeak escapes my lips. Maybe from fear, or maybe hesitation. Because I forgot about all of this.

Delia sighs. "River, you told her about the stuff with Ava, right?"

"I did, don't worry. I got this from here. We'll talk tonight, Deals." River disconnects the call as I pull the into a parking lot, hands shaking, my thoughts spinning out of control, my lungs shrinking, making it a chore just to breathe. My mouth goes dry, and I can't decide if I want to scream, run away, leave River on the side of the road in this parking lot, or disappear into thin air.

Gingerly, he puts a hand over mine and ducks, urging me to look at him.

I continue to stare straight ahead at the windshield. I can't truly see anything, my vision clouding. Slumping over the steering wheel, I close my eyes.

The thought that this time was all I'll have with him has been weighing on me.

The frustration from those early days after Grant, the loneliness, the sense of betrayal by the people I thought I loved most returns. Every bit of it comes flooding back into my veins.

Cold dread surges through me, the emotions jumbling with a longing to feel loved and protected, a desperation to believe in my own worthiness.

I've long resigned myself to a lifetime of temporary attachments, but I had genuinely considered moving home. I had hoped that if I could move on, the town could to. But maybe they can't.

River reaches across the center console, cautious not to

dislodge the half-empty water bottles, ChapSticks, and random receipts, and rubs soft circles across my back.

I float between leaning into the soothing touch and wanting to be as far from him as possible. Eventually, my nerves win out, feeling like they've been lit on fire. I shriek to stop and he jerks away, his hand floating in midair.

As my vision clears, I look at his stupidly pretty face. Cataloging the soft stubble that's edging toward a full beard now. His jade- and aqua-colored irises fill with their own tears as they bore into me, and his skin loses color quickly.

"You knew this?" The question is violently ripped from my vocal cords.

His eyes are rimmed red now, and slow, steady, quiet tears fall.

"I told you," he whispers. When I called ..." He withdraws into himself, his shoulders rounding.

I blink, at a loss for where to go from here. And suddenly I process what he said. *I knew. He told me before he came here.*

It felt fake. One awkward conversation I shoved into the back of my mind, set aside, pushed so far down I'd forgotten about it.

All the magic is gone now. Reality has crashed in and is catching up to us. The bubble we created to protect us has popped.

thirty-five
Lily

I'M BORED, but thankfully, I've always been a bit of a daydreamer.

Clients trickle in and out in the usual rhythm, leaving me with little to do between them except overthink about therapy sessions and the upcoming expectations in New Jersey.

When I left, I was running from the ridicule, from the perception of who I am. I'm smart, but my motivation is inconsistent. I like people, but they can be exhausting. Traveling means that the people I love have continued to love me. Because I don't spend extended periods with them, I never overwhelm them with my messy feelings or cluttered space.

I've impressed each boss for weeks or months, but I've never been asked to stay or return. I've done just enough before moving on. Though I suppose they haven't asked me to come back either. *Is that on them or me?* I'm not sure.

I'd like someone to love my messy parts, even if my ability to believe I'm lovable is broken. After experiencing my mother's conditional love, my father's unwavering allegiance to his wife, and my first boyfriend-turned-husband's betrayal, it's impossible to not feel responsible. The fire was fueled by my parents' questions and their lack of empathy or concern for me. The way Mom never looked back put the final nail in the coffin of my self-esteem. At least that's the story I've told myself.

I'm so deeply lost in thoughts that I'm only snapped out of them when a woman standing across from me aggressively clears her throat. Shit. Based on the extreme irritation vibrating off her, that wasn't the first time she tried to get my attention. The prim older woman shoots daggers at me while clutching a bag worth more than all of my possessions combined. But the person behind her snags my attention before I can check her in, and I nearly fall off my seat when I take in the familiar long blond waves and sharp dark eyebrows.

"What the hell, Nessa?" I practically shout.

My manager scurries out of her office, shushing me, her look almost as stern as Birkin Bag Lady's. "I am so sorry, miss," she says to the older woman. "I will have a serious talk with her."

"I'm so sorry, ma'am," I add. "The guest behind you is a childhood friend who should be in New Jersey right now. I'll let Joanne get you situated." With the most innocent smile I can muster, I focus on my manager. "May I take my lunch now to see what brings her west?"

Nessa gives me her signature smirk and quips, "Nope, you've got to check me in next. I booked a couple's massage for Barbie and…" She clears her throat and peers over her shoulder.

A sheepish Stef slinks forward from the hallway, giving me a finger wave.

"Barbie and Kendall Roberts."

With a laugh, I shake my head. This is so something Nessa would do—use the dolls names to ambush me.

———

AFTER MY FRIENDS have been pampered thoroughly and my shift is over, they drag me to the hotel bar.

"Happy long weekend. How was the massage?" I hedge, hoping to keep this conversation light.

"Amazing. Ugh, I needed a break from wedding planning," Stef says, pulling her iPad out of her bag. "It's the worst and the best all at the same time. We've been living together forever, so sometimes I wonder why I'm bothering with—"

"Nope," Nessa snaps, silencing Stef. "Nice try, Ms. Long, leaning into wedding talk to distract us. The only wedding-related topic we're open to discussing is your role."

"I told River I'd come back sometime in March. I haven't figured out specific dates, so let's focus on April and May and the events we have to plan, okay?" I ask, going for calm and cool, scanning the calendar on Stef's tablet. "Susan isn't that mad about having a little more time to prepare, is she? Maybe we can consolidate the events in April."

"An argument could be made that she'll have better floral options by doing it in the true spring," Nessa suggests.

"We could also mention that River has construction going on too. What do you think?" Stef peers up at me.

At the sound of his name, the hairs on the back of my neck stand on end.

Play it cool, play it cool, I instruct myself.

River and I have been okay since my embarrassing meltdown in the car, particularly since Dorothea and I started discussing how ADHD impacts memory and mood. He was pretty quick to forgive, having realized how beyond mortified I was.

And mortified is putting it lightly. It took me weeks to stop replaying my embarrassment when I should have been sleeping. Thanks to this conversation, I fear that habit will return tonight, *yay*.

"Given that his plans are based on your Denver tour," Nessa says, wearing a shrewd expression," "he wouldn't have come up with the fancy-pants outdoor setups that'll allow his produce to be grown right there and supporting the community without you."

Straightening, I smile. "We visited Rami Farms while he was here. In the River North District."

She and Stef exchange a smug look.

Stef gently adds, "He is obsessed. The trip, the girl." Her lips twitch with amusement.

My cheeks flame. I sip my ice water, hoping to cool off while shifting the subject back to wedding plans. "He's going to utilize a community garden for farm-to-table options, and the party would be early in the season, so there would be a lot of dirt boxes. How could that work?"

Nessa lifts a shoulder, unbothered. "Don't deflect, Lily Jayne. It's beyond transparent what you are doing right now."

Motherfucker.

"All we know is that he came back with a crush bigger than ever, which, having watched that boy pine for you for years, is saying something," Nessa goes on. "He has Gemma and Alice fixing up the cottage he's ignored for the last two years so you have a place to stay when you're home for wedding festivities. The two of you have clearly fucked by now." She pauses, glaring, hoping to use her therapist tricks to make me admit it or something.

"You spent the week together, but he's been tight-lipped to us," Stef adds. "Which, frankly, after we filled him in on what you were up to during those early years, is an insult. So we'll just have to get the dirt from you. Drink up." She pushes a martini my way.

I pick it up, and they do the same with their drinks.

"Cheers, bitches," I say. "It will take more than caffeine and alcohol to break open this vault."

———

CHALLENGING NESSA WAS AN ABSOLUTELY terrible idea. After another three rounds, we're having a giggle fit as I describe my "housekeeping error."

Light, airy, sighing, I'm a woman obsessed as I say, "He's beautiful, he's dedicated. You can tell from how he treats his parents and the bar, but also his freaking body."

Nessa tosses a napkin at my face. "For the drool."

I sigh at the memory, my eyelids fluttering heavily. "He was so fun, like he was when we were kids. Before puberty and the apparently huge and awkward crush he was hiding."

They laugh. "Hiding? It was Peacock Springs' worst-kept secret for years," Nessa says.

"But he's planted roots, and I'm…" I trail off, my heart aching.

While Stef grasps my hand, always the first to comfort, Nessa says, "Fuck Belinda," using her usual fiery tone.

I cackle, even as my eyes well with tears, and raise my fourth martini. "Fuck Belinda indeed."

Stef clinks our glasses, and then the most shocking words come out of her mouth. "In the ass, with a pineapple!"

I nearly spit my drink out with the hearty laugh that follows.

This right here, this is that home feeling I have been missing so much. Is it possible that I can have it there too?

thirty-six
River

FEBRUARY

RIVER:

It's been a while since I've caught you on video chat. Working a lot lately?

I was sad I missed you yesterday. It's been a long week. I miss hearing from you. We don't have to talk about next month. Let's just watch the next episode of that show we started while I was visiting.

LILY:

Later this week? People keep leaving for new gigs and my schedule changes nonstop...

———

I'M worried Lily is going to bail on her trip to town in March. So I decide to approach the Salvatore women about their meeting plans. Inside Curl Up & Dye, Bella stands at the reception desk with her little sister Sofia and their cousin Chiara.

Looking like Carmela Soprano, Anna Lucia is drinking espresso in the little seating area. She waves me over before I can even greet the group by the door.

I breathe out. If she's involved, then this will be going to the moms to be dealt with rather than to my peers. *My peers seem to agree the punishment is weird, unnecessary, and ridiculous. Why is Ava Marie so hell bent on this?*

Anna Lucia gestures for me to sit beside her, then snaps her fingers at Bella.

Bella rolls her eyes but leaves the reception desk, striding for the kitchenette. A few awkward moments of silence stretch between us before Bella places two espresso cups on the wood and gold cafe table.

The navy ceramic cups are a traditional shape, but the paint matches the town aesthetic, as do the small golden spoons topped with engraved peacock feathers. I'm anxiously tracing the engraving when Anna Lucia breaks the silence finally.

"Are you familiar with the background of the peacock?"

On a deep sigh, I recite the facts every child in town learns growing up. "They are a symbol of eternity and royalty. Peacock Springs was established near the Delaware Crossing, so it was initially because of the Red Coats adoration for King George. Eventually, it became an ironic take on the way that royalty upheld values that were the opposite of ours."

With a giant smile, one that suggests she's about to drop a truth bomb in my lap, Anna Lucia says, "Sure, in regard to this town. But the world is far larger than one shitty little town in New Jersey, am I right?"

I nearly choke on a laugh but manage to nod.

"No, my dear," she goes on. "The peacock goes back much farther. To Roman art, to Jewish folktales, and to India and Iran. The species possesses far more magic than you could ever imagine. In this instance, it's not about royal figures, but about the magic that comes with mediating between the heavens and the ground. The gift of flight. The desire to flee the mundane and reach for more, for the unbelievable and unexpected. To break the chains of what holds us back." She gives me a thoughtful look.

Her philosophical answer causes anger to flare to life inside me. "If the town's original goal was to break chains, then why are we meeting about *literally* chaining Lily to a historical piece of wood for setting her cheating husband's things on fire? She was nineteen, and he cheated on her. Her parents turned away from her. So she's, to keep with this theme, flown the coop. She has not stopped running, and she won't," I say, hating how desperate I sound.

"Exactly," Anna Lucia affirms.

Exactly? What the hell does that mean?

"It's not about the town. It's not about the physical restraints, which she could have tried to talk us out of. It's about the running away. She's still chained to us. She has to face the past. She has to face herself. Until she does that, she's tethered to the pain. From what I hear, you knew a little something about that marriage being destined to fail, and it chains you too, George River Hendrix. I wouldn't be so quick to judge how others handle secrets."

The only person I've ever told about it is my mom. My stomach drops and I clench my jaw to prevent myself from saying something I can't take back.

"The answer to the question you came here to ask, son, is no," she says. "We cannot take it away. We are open to including her in the conversation if she's willing to face us. You can tell her and that witchy little coven of hers too. Make it clear that we'll grab her from her bed or out of the lineup for the wedding if we have to. She cannot run forever. But River, neither can you."

With that, she picks up her espresso cup and her magazine, silently dismissing me.

spring

texting interlude

GROUP CHAT: BAD BITCHES [STEF SANTOS
MANOLO, LILY LONG, DELIA SHANE, NESSA RABIN]

LILY:

In KC. You think I can find a celebrity and do
some networking tonight?

<peace sign emoji> KC

8 hours later

LILY:

Officially in Pitt. You are all weirdly quiet. What is
going on out there?

STEF:

Nothing. I worked yesterday. Admin doesn't like it
when I am on my phone instead of paying
attention to the students in my office.

DELIA:

Your boyfriend has been up my ass since I got
back from London

LILY:

Not my boyfriend

NESSA:

[Jennifer Lawrence yeah, ok with thumbs-up gif]

LILY:

Shut up. See you tomorrow.

MARCH 31ST

GROUP CHAT: BAD BITCHES [STEF SANTOS
MANOLO, LILY LONG, DELIA SHANE, NESSA RABIN]

LILY:

I'll be there around 10 a.m.

Ugh, I can't sleep. I'm too nervous. Nessa, Delia, I'm coming right to you. Will bring coffee, text me your orders.

STEF:

Large, little skim milk, no sugar. I have a gown fitting, and dairy = bloat

NESSA:

I'll have all her dairy, extra-large, extra whipped cream, extra caramel sauce

DELIA:

I hate you all, some of us work late at night.

LILY:

Stuck in traffic but headed to Coffee Crumbs first. What do you want?

DELIA:

Medium iced coffee with cream and sugar.

―――――

MARCH 31ST

204

NESSA:

Seth, dude, grab River and go over to CC first
thing tomorrow.

She's avoiding him.

SETH:

Dude, we already had plans to work on the house

NESSA:

So change the plan. Claim you need coffee or
something. I'll tell you when she gets close.

———

SETH:

Want to get coffee before we work on the
cottage?

RIVER:

K

thirty-seven
River

APRIL FOOL'S DAY

BEYOND EXHAUSTED, I drop into a booth across from Seth. He suggested coffee, and honestly, I'm too tired to ask why he wanted to meet here rather than just bringing takeaway cups with him to the Featherweight.

Between the postponed parties, garden prep, the work on the cottage, and being down a set of hands while Delia was abroad, I've been working nonstop. Add Lily's rumored return to town today, and I need a nap.

Seth's storm-blue eyes are narrowed on the black coffee in his mug as he shuffles the handle back and forth. He's so rarely easygoing, but even this level of wound up is unlike him. Instinct tells me there's irritation simmering beneath the surface. Some anger too. He's pissed, but with Seth, the reason could be anything from a person forgetting to hold the door for a little old lady to having caught his wife cheating. If he had one, I mean.

"Dude, before you break the mug, what is going on?"

On a groan, he sits back and runs a hand through his close-cropped dark blond hair. "I actually wanted to ask you the same thing. You know I don't really do this...this feelings shit. But you've been off for weeks now. You're good at the feelings stuff, so can you just...?" He waves a hand, suggesting we get this over with.

This is the kind of moment that would make Lily refer to us as adorable, while Delia would sharply dissect the ways toxic masculinity is limiting male friendships, and Nessa—

Nessa appears beside the table, making kissing noises at us.

"Where did you come from?" Seth sits up, spine snapping straight.

Without asking to join us, she flips a chair backward and plops down into it.

Seth snorts, looking her up and down. "Okay, A.C. Slater, sure."

Laughing, she winks at Seth. Then she turns to me, mischief sparkling in her eyes. "What your emotionally constipated friend here is trying to ask is: What the hell is going on with you lately? Is it because you got laid—like a lot from what I heard—and now you and Lily are barely speaking?"

Seth's eyebrows hit his hairline as he barks out a laugh and holds out a fist for Nessa to bump.

"That solves the mystery. Thanks, Rabin. The guy's got blue balls." He smirks at me. "Do you have the internet? You can watch something sexy, for free. Rub one out and get your shit together."

Never one to miss an opportunity to lean into her impish nature, Nessa adds, "Or just tell her you need some sexy times over video chat while you're apart. It's not like your *girlfriend* would say no." The way she emphasizes girlfriend, long and musical, makes her sound like an obnoxious middle schooler.

Clearly she's talked to Lily about my trip to Denver, and she's here to stir up shit.

"Oh my god, chill. It's *April first*, River. I'll leave you two to whatever this sobfest is. Gotta run. Later, gents."

She breezes out, and we eye each other, chuckling. If there's one thing Nessa can always be counted on for, it's chaos.

That chaos, surprising, drained some of the tension plaguing me. With an exasperated sigh, I admit, "That's not the issue. I can't get my mind off her,I'd rather not give Nessa credit for being right. So how are things at Pages these days? Distract me from my family, the renovations, and the tenant moving in any day now. I beg you."

Smirking, he brings his coffee to his lips.

"Come on, bruh. Give me something here," I practically whine.

Mocking my tone, he says, "Come on, bruh. Give me something."

He really leans into the *G* sound, sounding even more childish than I am behaving.

Shaking my head, I pick up my own coffee. Right on cue, Seth pulls a worn paperback out of his back pocket and opens it up, fixing his focus on it as if I'm not sitting here.

Quietly, he slides another book across the table. "I can't help you, man. But maybe this will keep you busy."

The book in front of me is *Stargirl* by Jerry Spinelli.

Figuring that checking it out would be better than silence, I open it. Seth and I sit in the companionable quiet, drinking endless mugs of coffee and reading. After about an hour, his phone vibrates.

He sits up, checks the screen, then stands, gives me a nod, and heads out.

That's it. No details, no goodbye. Classic Seth behavior.

Not thirty seconds after he disappears, the door chimes jingle again, snagging my attention.

And I find myself staring into the eyes of my dream girl. Her irises as dark as the coffee in Seth's abandoned mug, and new streaks of caramel and auburn ribbon threaded through her messy waves.

Lily is wearing her signature black leggings and baggy

sweatshirt with a pair of Birkenstock sandals since today is unseasonably warm. She freezes in place when she notices me, then rushes to the counter, asking Goldie for the to-go order for Shane.

As Goldie slides a tray of giant iced coffees, it hits me. Nessa was here, checking that Seth and I were here, and Delia placed the order, god dammit.

The cups on the tray are various shades of beige and brown, with whipped cream on top of one. She balances a set of straws across the middle and picks up a box of pastries and stuffs it under her arm. In her rush to escape Coffee Crumbs, and my gaze, she fumbles with the best way to stack and hold items.

Dropping a twenty-dollar bill on the table to cover my coffee and Seth's, plus an extra generous tip, I stand.

Sidling up to her, I channel the tiniest amount of calm I can dig up. "Need a hand?"

She jumps, shrieking, the tray flying, and between one heartbeat and another, I'm wearing four iced coffees.

Licking my lips, all I can do is laugh. She's gorgeous, even as embarrassment turns her a beautiful face a gentle shade of pink. She's back in Peacock Springs for the next eight weeks, and I need to convince her that what happened in December was not a one-time only thing for me.

With any luck, I can show her that being home again isn't the end of the world. Convince her there is a chance for us. More than a few days of playing a couple, but a genuine connection. Then, maybe, just maybe, she'll be ready to plant her own roots.

"I'm not usually a fan of cinnamon coffee, but mixed with that caramel and whipped cream, it's pretty great," I tease, trying to ease her anxiety.

She blinks wildly, her mouth dropping open once, then again, but no sounds coming out.

"Come on, darling." I drop my voice to a low whisper, a

guttural plea. "Don't act like you don't enjoy the sight of me covered in whipped cream."

Her blush deepens, hopefully because of desire rather than embarrassment this time. Finally, a tiny laugh escapes her lips.

Relief washes over me at the way her lips tip up.

Her eyes darken, and with a lingering sigh and giggle, she exhales "darling." She tears a handful of napkins from the dispenser and pats my neck and shirt. Then, turning toward the countertop, she profusely apologizes and asks Goldie to recreate the order. Of course, Goldie is the most kind and chipper woman in town, so she's already working on round two, and brushes off the concept of being paid again.

I drop another twenty into the tip jar, and Lily glares. "I can cover it."

With a rueful smile, I take a step closer. "You can pay me back. And I know just how you can make us even."

I walk her to Nessa and Delia's place, thankful for the way our friends meddled. They'll steer her back to me again and again. This is better than a kiss during truth or dare.

thirty-eight
Lily

ONCE HE RETREATS down their front path, his jean-clad ass looking even better than I remember, I can't hold back. "Pretty convenient that River was waiting for me."

Delia shuffles away, mumbling lovingly to her coffee.

Nessa smiles and shrugs. "Stef's waiting for us. Let's go."

The four of us gather around the table that's been here since Delia's gran was a little girl. Every piece, from the square shape, the wood, and the wicker chair backs to the metal frames, is nostalgic. A step into the past. The old ivy print border still frames the kitchen, though it's peeling in a few places. The dark wood cabinets and faded white appliances are clean and well cared for but showing their age.

"The king has returned," Nessa says in a deep voice.

Stef taps her phone, and "The Circle of Life" plays.

I raise Pete into the air like he's baby Simba, causing an outpouring of giggles.

"Yeah, yeah, getting out of the mountains was a little harder than expected, but I'm here," I say, going for nonchalance.

"What did you do, hook a covered wagon to Pete and have him

pull you here?" Delia asks, wearing a glare. "It took you nearly a full month to go from Denver to eastern Kansas. That's barely an eight-hour drive."

I fidget, zeroing in on my straw.

"What the hell?" She huffs. "You were supposed to help with coverage. River's drowning because you didn't bother to show up to help in March like you promised."

"I know," I explode. The anger, the fear, the resentment, and the overwhelm of it all bubbles over. "And if you hate me, if he hates me, it's earned. I tried, I swear. I left on time. I made it to Kansas. But then I was too scared. Okay? I have been afraid for years now."

Arms folded over my chest, I hug myself. The rejection I'll get for this behavior is warranted. I created this problem. I keep avoiding the hard parts of my life.

Mirroring my position, they all sit, arms cross over chests around the table.

I shrink further into myself, pulling my knees up to my chest and looping my arms around them. "I've been trying to be a good friend *and* protect myself, but it's hard. I'm really fucking scared. I should have told you all this sooner, but after I left here in September, I had a really hard time. Like as bad as when I left the first time." My voice cracks.

The softest of us, Stef asks the question on everyone's mind, "Why didn't you tell us? You've seen us since then."

"Because I'm supposed to be independent," I mumble, squeezing my eyes shut. "Because I don't need a husband or parents or anyone. I've got this. I can do it on my own..." A lump forms in my throat, making it hard to swallow. "Except I can't. But I did start seeing a new therapist."

"Good," Nessa interjects, her gaze intense.

"We realized... Um, we realized I have ADHD. So sometimes it's hard for me to get started. Sometimes it's hard to manage the size and speed of my emotions. When I yelled a second ago." I blow out a long breath. "I feel foolish, and now I'll worry that all you'll remember when you think about me is my stupid outburst. Then I'll shame spiral. I know these all sounds like excuses—"

"No, it sounds like you've figured out that you have emotional regulation skills to work on," Nessa says, using her therapist tone. "And maybe some rejection sensitivity?"

Delia holds firm. "Yep, sounds like an excuse."

"Not an excuse," Nessa says, her posture softening. "It explains a lot of things we've seen for years. As soon as we graduated, the lack of structure put Lily all over the place," she points out. Eyes soft, she grasps my hand. "Take this with love, okay? I'm on your side. But you were the all-star student, and then you've been sort of tripping your way through this part of your life. We understood that some things looked better from the outside than they were along the way, but we never called you on it. What happened with your folks was hard—dare I say traumatic—and we never gave up on you, but we should have done more. You are our sister."

Leave it to the girl with three siblings to get that loving others can be messy.

Stef holds my other hand in silent support. I nod into my knees, still unable to undo the tight ball I've wound myself into.

"That doesn't excuse the way you ditched River, though," Nessa continues. "He spent the last month extra stressed because he thought he would have help, and I know you care about that. About *him*—"

"I really do," I whisper. "It's what scares me the most."

Three sets of eyes stare at me, waiting. A thick and heavy silence settles over us.

"Because of Grant," I finally force out. "Do you remember Carlie? She didn't want me seriously either. We played pretend. Acted like a couple until she left me for someone serious. After her, I stuck to casual. And time and again, when we parted ways, they'd find the person they wanted to be with forever. And I've never been someone's forever. It's like I help them realize what they wanted. Someone *like me but not actually me*. It's because of..."

I pull my hand from Stef's and put my feet on the floor, waving a hand around my tear-streaked face and crumpled outfit.

"Sweetheart," Stef says. "You have to be honest with yourself."

"It's time to admit you want something that will last is what the nice one means," Delia adds brashly.

Shrugging, I reply, "You don't always get what you want."

Thankfully, instead of arguing, they simply hug me and we move on to other topics.

———

IN THE COTTAGE behind the Featherweight, I stare at a wall covered in sample color swatches, examining each one up close, then stepping back. I close the blinds. Then reopen them.

Turning to Gemma and Alice, I throw my hands up in surrender. "Why am I in charge of this?" I'm trying hard not to whine, but they're the decorators, and seriously, this is only my home for a few weeks. What do my feelings on paint shades matter?

Alice loves peasant dresses and flower crowns, and they give her an eternally airy presence. She practically floats through life, making me feel stiff next to her. Exposing my bohemian façade as a poor man's copy.

As she twirls between the blues and grays, she gives her wife a sweet smile. "Gem, I would pick one of these icy steel colors to match your eyes if I was designing a love nest for us. This one right here." She taps a swatch on the wall. "Or maybe..."

She goes on, complimenting her wife's many wonderful attributes as they relate to each color.

This is not helping me choose, and once she uses the term *love nest*, I can't stop thinking about it. Isn't this going to be a rental property?

Alice quickly kisses her wife, then heads out, graciously taking Pete for a walk by the water. Gemma used to babysit me on occasion, and since I'm exhausted from the conversation, I'm unable to stop myself from letting out a whine.

"I trust you. Whatever you do will be great. Do whatever will draw in a tenant after Memorial Day. Taupe? What's the it-neutral right now? It's not like this is my home and I can have a giant blue wall covered in natural wood shelves and colorful pots of winding vines and plants. Do something for River, not for me."

"Tell me about this blue," she presses. "Maybe this place isn't yours long-term, but I'm bored by neutral rentals, and River said to make this a *home*. He said you owed him, and he wanted your vision."

"A midnight blue, I think. Darker than cerulean but not quite navy. The color of royal sapphires."

"Also," I say, spinning and pointing at the ceiling, "those light fixtures look like boobs, nipples and all. If you don't want to have a boring, everyday rental, you need to change that. With the bright white tile and a midnight blue wall, I would want to bring in some dark gold or copper metals and warmth. Maybe paint the kitchen cabinets a pine or sage color?"

I wander into the kitchen area, dragging my fingers along the small island that separates it from the living space, examining the pattern in the slab.

"Probably something that brings out the browns in the floor planks. River wears lots of black, gray, denim. He's classic. So if he ever considered moving in, using those tones would be nice. He loves those industrial exposed pipes in the bar, so those pipe curtain rods, maybe, with masculine curtains," I say. "Are those a thing?"

I wander the space, stopping near the stone fireplace and examining the wall.

"Bookcases here. Paint them to match the kitchen. Ooh, and what about a reclaimed barnwood beam for the mantel?" My heart stutters at the idea. "Perhaps some wallpaper with a metallic pattern in it to pull the kitchen and living spaces together since it's all open here."

He said it was payback, but dreaming this up is fun.

"Lots of candles. Pillars of every size. I know this is taboo for this town, but maybe even in non-jewel tones. Toss in a bunch of neon and bright colors. Throw everyone off. Add a piece of funky artwork above the fireplace. A really plush rug, a basket full of cozy throw blankets and extra pillows."

As I wander up the steps, I point out the boob light fixture in the entryway.

"Seriously, the tits."

Gemma laughs. "Got it, not a fan of tits. It's a shame. They have only the nicest things to say about you."

I bark out a laugh. "I just don't like them on the ceiling. They're fine, better than fine..." I say, suddenly at a loss for how to finish the sentence. I end up going with "other places. You know, like on a woman."

Could the floor please open and swallow me up now?

Instead of giving me a look of horror, Gemma cackles.

Relief swamps me. This is nice. Why did I think I'd have to hide my bisexuality from Seth's lesbian sister? I have to remember that not everyone in town has been focused on me. Not everyone is judging my every move. Maybe being back can be like this, like my time with River.

I hope for it more than I ever have before, but for now, I push those thoughts away and lean in and play along, acting as though this is my house.

The hall is lined with one door on the left and two to the right. The first is a bedroom overlooking the backyard with a door that opens to a Jack-and-Jill bathroom. This room and the one on the other side of the bathroom must have belonged to River and his brothers when they lived here.

Stepping into the bathroom is like stepping back in time. The tiles are pastel pink, straight out of the 1950s suburban expansion. Fortunately, it looks well preserved.

"Gem," I say, my excitement growing. "You kept these tiles when you redid things in the bar kitchen. Were you leaning into the Danish/Scandinavian pastel retro revival? Or making it more masculine with dark wallpaper? Or are you leaving it as is? Because honestly, it could be cool to preserve the history a little here."

"I could leave this and expand, using the Danish pastel, maximalist, high femme vibes upstairs to contrast the lower level's deep masculinity. Unless that would be too disconnected for you," Gem says.

The *for you* startles me, and a pit opens up in my stomach. Back against the wall, I sink to the floor, dropping my head into my hands. The fun is over. The overthinking has kicked into high gear, and now my brain is spiraling.

So, naturally, I blurt out a stream of emotional word vomit to her.

"I don't know what I'm doing," I whine, "and to be completely honest, I don't want to help decorate what might eventually be the home River shares with someone else. Because that won't be me. I'm the woman people date before they settle down. Grant and Landan—"

She ducks her head, whispering *bitch*, or maybe that's all in my head.

"When River came to Denver, he said what we were doing was for the time we were together. Didn't he? I'm pretty sure. Pretending this could be mine, with him, that's..." My chest cracks, then shatters, breaking into a million little fragments. "I'm thankful for the place to stay for a few weeks, and I'm sure he'll be friendly while I'm here. But then what? I carry with me another ghost keeping me away from home? That doesn't seem like a good idea. I was impulsive as fuck before. Still am. I recently learned I have ADHD, and now those impulse control things are starting to make sense. I can't control them all the time. My new medication has helped a little and I've been learning strategies in therapy. But seriously, I'm not the girl—"

"Woman," Gem interjects.

"Right, I'm not the woman someone picks for the long haul. I'm the one you mess around with, learn how to be in a relationship with, before you go find a real one. It's not me, but that's fine. I'm fine. At least I saved another woman the heartache of being abandoned by a man who didn't know if he could love, right?"

I'm rambling, I know, but I can't seem to stop the words from escaping. My head is dizzy, my body heats, and I start to sweat. I lean forward, trying to still the world and finally force myself to stop talking. Head in my hands, counting my breaths, I return to the present.

Only then do I realize that Gem and I aren't the only people here.

"I think you need to speak to her," she says. She steps away, then adds, "You. Let's go."

Gem places her hand gently on my shoulder and whispers a goodbye, then two sets of feet descend the stairs.

A third set of feet appears in my periphery, and then I'm engulfed in a set of strong arms and a familiar masculine forest scent.

Without thought, I bury my face in River's chest.

He kisses my temple as we listen to Gemma and who I learn is Seth, leave the house. When the front door clicks shut, River exhales my name reverently, like the strength he needs to make this statement is as scary for him as my confession was.

"Darling." He sways from side to side, hugging me closer and repeating my name as I silently cry. He lets out a long breath and pulls back, tipping my chin up so I can meet his eyes.

Too worn out to fight, I meet his gaze, finding that his eyes are watery too.

He places the most gentle kiss on my forehead, the simple act sending waves of relaxation through me, allowing my muscles to relax. I didn't even realize how touch starved I was. Again.

"How do you not see yourself through my eyes yet?" The fire and sincerity behind his statement catch me off guard.

The earnest question raises alarm bells, and out of fear, I bite back, "You probably just want to have fun for a few weeks. Is this another temporary setup? I'm not the one you'll keep. I'm loved best when I'm less present. You'll see."

The fear, disappointment, and anguish swirling inside me create a tornado of pain.

"You already saw that. It's why things got quiet after February, right? It's why we barely spoke at all last month. It's why aren't you more mad that I wasn't here to help. Trust me, when my two months are up, just watch, and you'll see how relieved everyone is—"

I snap my mouth shut. I'm no longer making sense. *Shut up, shut up, shut up.*

Cursing, I burrow deeper into his chest, slightly comforted by the soft fabric of his well-worn bar T-shirt against my arms.

He rubs a hand in circles across my back, making soothing shushing sounds and situates me more comfortably on his lap so my legs are draped over one of his while I sit between his thighs.

The affection in his voice increases. "Gem was having you pick these finishing touches because I want you to be comfortable here. I want this place to feel like a home. *Your home.* To give you a place where you feel protected and at ease. I want you to have a home filled with all the things you love. Because that apartment in Denver? It was… not what you show the world. My goal has only been to *give you* what you deserve."

His right hand winds its way into my hair, softly stroking behind my neck, easing the tension there.

"Also," he says, his tone more firm, "do not disappear on me. You are going to want to be embarrassed about crying, but I won't allow it. You are human. You are allowed to have emotions. Good and bad. You don't have to hide the bad from me."

He looks at me, hard eyes heating, the teal color darkening to jade.

"This is what I want, understand? Move in here and let me be here with you as much as *you* want. You're in control, but please, give me a real chance. Let me show you how easy you are to fall in love with. I'll be sure to thank those other idiots for making it possible for me to try to keep you. Get ready, because I'm going to fight for you until you tell me to stop for good. I was lucky enough to have a small taste, but it wasn't enough."

He presses another kiss to my face, this time on my cheek.

"I want to give this a real shot, and I will do everything I can, even have more awkward espresso meetings with the Salvatore women, to get these stupid conversations about a decade ago dropped."

I gasp, and he holds me tighter, his nose brushing my ear.

"Our conversations didn't slow because I didn't want you anymore. Delia was gone, and you didn't come out to help like I hoped you would. I'm not mad because I know this is hard for you. But between being short-staffed, renovations, and trying to make this place into something more, I was barely hanging on." He leans back, meeting my eye. "I promise you, this is not temporary for me, darling. I'm sorry, I should have been direct. I just… I wanted to show you, not just tell you. So I worked harder, longer hours. Gemma and Alice have been prepping this place for ages. I came home and got them started as soon as I could. I did, however, have to make some decisions on my own. Can I show you?"

Nodding, I wipe at my eyes.

He places another gentle kiss on my cheek, then he scoops me up and sets me on my feet. Hand in mine, he leads me out of the bedroom and across the hall to the owner's suite.

The moment he pushes the door open, I'm in awe. The board and batten walls have been painted a soft cream, with a king-sized antique brass bed laid over a delicate floral rug. The walls are decorated with painted antique frames, each one unique, likely thrifted and revived, in shades of sage, lavender, rose, and sky blue. Some hold art prints, but the gold pair glint in the warm light, catching my eye. On the nightstand, the gold frame holds a photo of us as middle schoolers. Memories of that dance wash over me. Our moms forced us to go together. Not that we complained. The tiny bouquet of spray roses in peach and cream was beautiful. The way he looked at me while I buried my nose in the flowers sparked a tiny fire in my chest all those years ago.

"I don't think I've seen this photo before." I graze the frame's carvings.

"Elizabeth."

His mother. Of course.

"She kept this all these years. Gave it to me after Denver, like she knew all along."

Circling the bed, I pick up the other frame. In this one, we're holding glasses of beer, tapping them together in a toast while snow falls outside the window behind us. Beyond that, a light outline of the Rockies. This image was snapped during our most recent visit, our smiles playful and easy.

"This one," he says, stepping up behind me and reaching around me to tap the frame. "This is one of my favorites from the trip. You look so relaxed. You sparkled when you took me around Denver. I can't promise to make home feel as relaxing as vacation, but I promise to make space for travel. You were so alive that night. You weren't pretending to be someone else. You finally let go and were just yourself. And I was too. Because you gave me space to be myself. I can't lose that, I just can't."

With warm, strong hands, he turns me to face him, the heat of his body seeping into me. His gaze is like fire on my skin, setting me ablaze. My stomach explodes with butterflies in anticipation, yet there's a hint of innocent sweetness, like the girl in that photo on the way to her first dance with that boy.

He leans in close, like he did that day in my studio in Denver, but instead of ruefully heated, this moment is soft and full of heart.

"Lily, I think…" He clears his throat. "I know. I've always loved you," he says, his words full of honesty. "More importantly, you weren't the problem in those relationships. The problem was that none of those people were me."

Holy shit. Did River just say he loves me? What do I feel? Can I get out of my head long enough to feel? Fuck, I mean. I was in tears over the *idea* of him loving someone else. Is that the same as loving him? Am I ready to love someone else? Do I love myself enough yet? My chest tightens, my muscles tense. One part of me screams *I'm not ready.* Another screams *don't you dare leave now.*

Without my permission, my feet move. Instead of letting me self-sabotage, this achingly beautiful, vulnerable, sexy man follows me step for step, like we're dancing, until we wind up with my legs backed against the side of the mattress. My pulse quickens and drops low in my belly. I can't say those words, but I can try to show him.

He buries his face in my neck and inhales. His nose draws its way across my cheek, and then his lips are on mine. The kiss is as sweet as his words, his tongue lightly sweeping into my mouth, dancing against mine. I hope my body will show him since my never-ending stream of words has dried up.

Breaking the kiss, he lays me down, my head near one side of the mattress, my feet at the other. The comforter is white, the sheets the softest shade of rose pink. The pillows are piled high against the rails of the headboard. The foot of the bed is covered with throw blankets in sage and mauves. It reminds me of lying in fields looking at clouds and wildflowers.

"They are damn fools," he murmurs. "I will never treat you as disposable. I'm yours. I've never belonged to anyone like this. You don't need to say anything yet. Right now…" Instead of continuing, he leans down and kisses me again. A kiss that seals his promise. A promise I can accept and melt into.

thirty-nine
River

APRIL 2ND

LILY IS SOFT AND SWEET, her body relaxed in post-orgasmic bliss. Tucked between the sheets, I hold her close as she drifts to sleep.

Not today, I decide. Today isn't the right day to tell her about Grant's bachelor party.

Today is about letting her adjust to being here, about convincing her that this can be her home again. Today is about the comforts we've been missing out on since things became strained by distance and misunderstanding.

Maybe I'll find the right time later this week.

———

APRIL 7TH

. . .

EVERY DAY that we wake up together, I relish the separation of work and home more, even if the space between the two places is mere yards.

After closing, I head to the cottage, using a flashlight so I don't disturb the new garden boxes and beds. Each time I see them, I'm reminded of our time in Denver and the amazing places my beautiful little flower showed me.

Tonight I'm more overwhelmed than usual by a sense of dumb luck and admiration, so as I climb into bed, I pull her close forcefully. Situated as the big spoon behind her, I place a kiss on her neck below her ear. She hums appreciatively, and Pete grumbles as he shifts now that I've disrupted him at the foot of the bed.

"Seeing the construction in the back as I walked home reminds me of Denver." I plan to plant an entire flowerbed dedicated to her. I'll fill it with fragrant tiger lilies and local wildflowers that draw in butterflies. Wild, free, and flying from petal to petal: just like her. There is no list of preapproved emotions. No proper quantity or size to feel them. Just freedom to be.

While she was gone, she didn't lose herself. Nor did she find herself. She just lived. Now I get to live with her, loving her. There's no adventure better.

I know the story from Grant's bachelor party has to be shared, but not now. No, tomorrow may be better.

Tonight, I tell her that every time I walk by these garden beds, I'm reminded of how she has made me better. Nudging her slightly behind the ear again, I whisper, "Lily, do you know what I thought as I walked back here tonight?"

She groans, reminding me that she's teaching a virtual class at six.

I should leave her alone, but I can't fight the urge to kiss her neck again. "We're on the way to improving sustainability, and that's because of you. I am better simply because you exist, darling."

At the word darling, she rolls over like I knew she would. She nuzzles against my chest, breathing in deeply, like she's inhaling her favorite cologne rather than sweat and beer and fried foods.

With a soft kiss to my lips, she sighs. "I can't resist when you call me darling, but I do need sleep, so hold me for now, and we'll pick this up after my class tomorrow. Later today"—her words are cut off by a yawn—"whatever."

Yes, tomorrow will be a better day.

———

APRIL 14TH

TODAY WILL BE THE DAY. I can't let this go on any longer. I can't keep this to myself. I owe her this much.

With all the festivities coming up, the sooner the better. The bridal shower is only a few days away. The Atlantic City trip is in two weeks, and the wedding is in six

Before I dive into that, I have a few other things to do. I quietly slip downstairs, stopping at the bottom to study the living area. The raw beam shelves filled with plants brighten up the midnight blue, making it an ideal spot for Lily's classes.

She records classes in here and also talks to potential clients, and the overstuffed couch she chose is the perfect place for editing, she says. The ability to give her this causes pride to swell in my chest. There's no greater joy than this.

I grab my boots at the bottom step, toss them on, and make my way to the garden beds to check on the progress.

Later today, I think. *Later is good.*

———

APRIL 20TH

"I HAD DELIA CLEAR YOUR SCHEDULE," Lily says, her smile beaming. She doesn't have to work hard to convince me that today is a *holiday* or to sleep in when she pulls the curtains tighter and tells Pete to take over as little spoon. He agrees once I scratch between his ears.

When I wake up again, she is full of barely contained energy, buzzing to share.

"First rule," she says. "You can't do anything today."

Pete yips, as if responding.

"*Well*," she says, dragging out the word, tone playful, "we do have to make sure to take good care of Pete, so I guess we should take a short walk. Beyond that, our plans for today consist of the two joints I snagged, take out, snacks, and movies, starting with *Down to You.*"

I was following for a bit, but the last item on her list confuses me. "*Down to You?*"

She pops up like bread in the toaster, her demeanor bright. My efforts to make her comfortable are working. I see it more every day. Wearing my oversized Featherweight shirt—the one I lent her the first time she shared my bed—and a pair of cotton panties, she's the epitome of at home. Her hair is messy around her shoulders and she's shaking with excitement as she describes her all-time favorite rom-com that not enough people love.

"So," she squeals, "it's a movie about falling in love during college. Imogene and Al are the main characters. They call having sex 'cake,' and they buy these boxed bodega cakes when they plan to hook up."

I soak in her excitement, even if she could tell me a little softer.

"There's also a character who calls himself Jim Morrison, like the lead singer of the Doors. He's so committed to the bit that he's got people thinking he might really be the musician, but I think the real Jim Morrison was dead before then." She whips out her phone to check.

I angle in closer. "And this has to do with today how?"

"Oh right." She actually yells this time. "Imogene and her roommate—Rosario *freaking* Dawson—wear bathing caps, like for swimming, while smoking pot, because they're supposed to hold the smoke in."

She giggles up a storm, and I can't help but mirror her smile.

Tackling her, I kiss a line up her neck. I don't make it far, though, before Pete reminds us that he hasn't been out to pee yet.

It takes all my willpower not to lure him into his kennel so we can have a little quality time. Because Lily is a responsible pet owner, she gets up and dresses. I follow suit, then head to the kitchen where I make a pot of coffee and pull her ADHD medicines out to leave by the mug so she doesn't forget them.

Since she's been here, I find as many of these little moments as I can. She doesn't always remember to take care of herself, and she absolutely puts her needs behind everyone else's. She spends most of her time working and accomplishing maid of honor duties, with random things popping up to distract her.

Her independence was born out of necessity, but I swear it softens a bit more each day, causing a new sense of purpose and fulfillment for me. Our friends have rallied with me to show her our *love* is without condition. My love for her comes without condition.

Love. I won't repeat the phrase again until she says it.

This new focus helps me to back off from my parents a bit too. Frankly, the smiles and gratitude are a hell of a lot nicer than my surly father's complaints.

The pantry door is ajar, with snacks haphazardly scattered on shelves. She chose beautiful earthy greens for the pantry, the color highlighting the natural wood and really enhancing the ambiance. The gold light fixtures pair nicely with the knobs and pulls. Every inch of this space feels like a home. Our home.

God, I hope she sees her vision and chooses to stay. I hope she chooses me, because I'd pick her every damn day if she let me.

Tail wagging, Pete nudges me with his booty in the way his breed is prone to do, demanding scratches. While I give him what he wants, Lily appears, grabbing the coffee mug and downing her medicine for the day. Her smile is so bright, so radiant, that I can't bear to bring up Grant right now.

Tomorrow will be a better day. Today is a day for Lily, a pseudo-holiday to be silly and carefree. This is not the day for old secrets.

So we walk Pete along the river. Afterward, we give him a chewy treat and tuck him into the crate-slash-end table and head back upstairs.

forty
River

INSTEAD OF TURNING into our bedroom like I expect her to, Lily pulls me into my old bedroom across the hall. It looks nothing like it did back then. She chose a lavish purple for the wall color. It's deeper than a pastel purple but still soft and feminine and happy, yet it possesses a little kick, some strength.

"It's purple," I say.

"Oh. *Almost Famous*. We could watch that today if you want."

Confused, I frown at her. "Huh?"

"Purple. Your aura is purple!" she says. "Come on, Hendrix, you've seen *Almost Famous*, haven't you?" Before I can respond, she goes on. "I worked with Alice to make this into a media room-slash-office. I hope the color is okay with you." She switches from excited to anxious in the space of a single breath.

"Darling." Scooping her into a bear hug, I stroke her hair. From the research I've done about neurodiversity, I know deep pressure can be calming. So far, it seems to work for her.

Anxiety and excitement light up all the same parts of the nervous system, so if she's really excited, yet something feels off, she can quickly slide into worrying territory.

"Don't worry, be happy." I smirk down at her. "Right? That's what we're doing today? Weed jokes, movies, snacks, snuggling?"

She smiles wide, but it's still a bit shaky.

She hugs me back harder than before and exhales. "I also went to the dispensary and picked up a few edibles, but you don't have to do anything you don't want to. I don't remember you ever smoking, but that was high school," she prattles on, "and in Denver, we didn't discuss whether it was a one-time thing for you. Plus, you said you were pretending to be someone else. So if it's beyond your comfort zone, that's okay. Personally, I think it's ridiculous that we've made alcohol legal cross country while holding on to these racist and xenophobic laws that lead to the mass incarceration of young men of color when someone who looks like me is just an adorable hippie for the same recreational activities..." She trails off, blinking up at me. "Did I do the side quest thing again?"

I nod and kiss her forehead. "Yes, but my favorite kind. Where you get worked up about how people should be treated well." Giving her another deep squeeze, I add, "You know what privileges you've had, of course, but you are so quick to care about hypothetical people you've never met. People you may never meet."

I lean forward to kiss her again, but she holds a hand over my mouth and *hmphs*. "They aren't *hypothetical*. These are real people. Maybe we don't know them, or we don't know them well, but—ugh... I'm doing it again." Groaning, she drops her hand.

I resume the tight hug and kiss her forehead.

This woman is full of so much love and kindness, even after her own struggles. It's dumbfounding that anyone could be anything less than awed by her.

I'm smiling like I've already had one of her gummies while I hold her in the middle of a room that absolutely is the color of grape Laffy Taffy, knowing I would give her the moon if I could.

"All right, darling," I say, "my point remains that your ability to care about so many people when the world has not always shown you that kindness in return has me in awe of you." I grin at her and squeeze her upper arms. "Can we move to the ridiculously comfortable couch I see over there? Is that velvet? With a million pillows and a TV on the wall across from it? I believe you have plans for us today, correct?"

The room she designed is a perfect metaphor for her: tough as steel and yet so much gentle softness. A velvet couch in dusty blue with gray and white blankets surrounded by sturdy wood and iron fixtures and tables.

The movie and snack marathon, the snuggles, the periodic breaks to stretch and walk Pete, or to christen the new couch, are perfect.

I was right. This wasn't the right day. But I'll tell her soon.

forty-one

Lily

JIM KELLY and Anna Lucia Salvatore stand on the dais in the town square, along with two peacocks. When Jim bangs a gavel, I realize that I have somehow made my way into a town meeting. I'm ushered by my friends toward a single open folding chair as a chorus of townsfolk shush us.

My stomach twists as I sit, and I break into a cold sweat when my friends tiptoe away. Is this a planned meeting or an ambush?

Jim's first order of business is the annual peacock auction, where one lucky donor is allowed to name the pair of peacocks in attendance today.

Knocking the gavel against the podium for emphasis, he shouts for bids. "Do I have twenty-five dollars to open the bidding? Twenty-five American dollars?"

Pointing with the end of the gavel's handle like he's a wizard with a magic wand or a conductor leading a symphony, Jim brings the bids from twenty-five dollars to two hundred and fifty. Sold to Seth.

Never one to miss an opportunity to provide a lesson to the people in his vicinity, he steps up to the microphone and in his grumbling tone says, "Pages Bookstore wants to thank you for continuing to support the American dream by introducing Daisy and Gatsby the peacocks. I hope the glitz and the glamour we set on the loose today will bring prosperity and not wreak havoc on this town like Sid and Nancy did last year. Truly, that was the mistake of the collection of us small-business owners with an appreciation for punk rock."

Jim appears at his side and nods. "That was, well…" He grasps the sides of the podium and nods once. "Thanks, and welcome to Daisy and Gatsby."

The crowd claps and Jim encourages them to cheer louder.

"I would like to bring to the floor a recent re-addition to our town," Jim says, his tone businesslike. "We'd like to welcome back Miss Lily Long, formerly Mrs. Lily Morgan. Can we have a round of applause for this wonderful opportunity?"

The crowd claps politely but far less enthusiastically than it did for the peacock couple, many faces around me hardening.

"Lily was a wonderful member of our community for a number of years. Her parents are upstanding members of the community, but Belinda and Neal apologized in advance for not being here today. They have sent in their information by proxy, and Anna Lucia Salvatore will be reading their statements when this portion of the proceedings arrive."

Heart in my throat, I search the square for a friendly face, but Seth has disappeared, and Nessa, Stef, and Delia are across the lawn working on decor for later this weekend inside the gazebo, while doing a poor job of pretending they aren't listening and avoiding my gaze.

I haven't seen Lee at all. Is he out of town this weekend?

And where the hell is River? He would have warned me.

Shouldn't he have warned me?

Blood whooshes in my ears, and my head spins, though when a hand clasps mine and squeezes tight, my panic ebbs just a little.

River. Spots dance in my vision, though the settle, merging into the familiar T-shirt logo.

"River," I whisper, voice shaky.

"Darling, I'm here," he assures me.

He holds me, squeezing me tighter as one person after another stands at the podium and gives statements about me.

I was a teen bride, I want to shout. *My parents coerced me into getting married and skipping college. Then I was cheated on.*

Citizens continue speaking on the topic, but all I hear is a ringing noise. Anger, shame, and embarrassment grow into resentment, and the confidence that I'm worthy of a little bit of kindness rises inside me.

I jump to my feet and throw up my hands, my heart pounding and my blood boiling. "Enough."

With a grunt, I yank River to his feet. Then, with my hand in his, I storm to the dais. When I release his hand, he slinks back to the front row, where Seth was sitting.

Ten years of pent-up disappointment releases. "This is enough. Please, I beg you. I know what was said all those years ago. And not one of you stood up for me. Not my parents, my so-called husband, and none of you. You watched from the wings as I was pushed into something I couldn't understand at such a young age. Then you watched me disappear without a concern."

Hands fisted at my sides, I force myself to take a deep breath.

"Too many times I've wondered what would happen if I came home. If I wanted to stay. I put my future in your hands no more. I'm taking back control." I turn to face Jim, whose eyes are wide. "Here is what's going to happen. I'll discuss everything with the counsel, privately, but this isn't happening here. Not like this. Give Stef back her time to set up. This is unnecessary."

Leaning into what River said about my impassioned speeches

and the kindness I give others, I barrel on and point at Stef. She and Lee deserve to be the center of the town's attention. Not me.

"She," I say, pointing at my friends in the gazebo, "is the best thing that's ever happened to most of your children. Stef dedicated years to learning how to make education accessible to every kid. This can't be a town where everyone loves quirkiness without loving your quirkiest kids, and you do."

Jaw set, I force myself to scan the crowd.

"Do you know why you do it so well? Because of her work for your schools. So can we *please* put this conversation on hold until after she's had her day? You may think of me as the Wicked Witch of the West in Grant and Landan's story, but that does *not* mean that I don't have feelings. I'm not the bad guy in every story, and I definitely don't want that role in Stef's. So please. Let her have the attention she's earned."

I step away, and River hops to his feet and pulls me into a huge hug. His hold gets tighter again and again as Stef, Nessa, and Delia pile on. Seth and Lee join in too, nearly knocking us over in the process.

The group fans out with arms linked, like we're playing Red Rover. Like this, we're strong. Each of us a link in a chain. My friends have rallied around me.

I want to stay with them. Here. And frankly, they don't deserve my repeat disappearance.

Pride and determination bounce through me, along with fear.

When a soft and familiar voice takes the microphone, I extract my hands from River's and Stef's and turn to face Prudence, who's wearing a black dress, her hair wrapped in a colorful scarf.

"Lily Jayne Long, I want to say something that hasn't been mentioned enough around these parts. And this town needs to hear it as much as you do." She lifts her chin. "You are focused on others. You create opportunities to make others better. We see it in the way River is changing the Featherweight: he is caring for tourism and the planet. We see it in how impassioned you are about your friends."

The deep ruby shade of Pru's lipstick emphasizes the power behind her words, and yet she doesn't sound angry.

"You were hurt," she continues, her eyes flashing with sympathy. "And no one ever gave you the apology you deserve. You were not shown a fragment of the kindness and care you've given others. Carmine." She scans the audience, stopping when she finds the patriarch of the Salvatore family. "During the few months that Lily and Grant were married, how many times did she come in to buy the same ingredients over and over to make Grant's favorite dish? A dish that we all know Landan just pays someone to make for him? Hmm?" Prudence narrows her eyes with a fierceness.

The butcher who has personally taken apart livestock for over thirty-five years cowers in his chair.

"How about you, Albert?" she asks, brows arched. "Hmm? When you broke your leg, Lily was there week after week, shelving books for you. Not for pay but out of the goodness of her heart. She was there so consistently we asked you to add her to the payroll behind Belinda's back. And what did you do? You agreed with Belinda to hold her to a fine for a single book you still have no less than eight copies of on shelves."

The whole crowd is silent, expressions nervous as if they're worried she'll call on them next.

"Lily," she says, her tone gentler. "I paid that stupid fine, by the way. It's gone."

Albert shrinks in his seat, muttering about his hope of being abducted by aliens. Although, to be fair, he's often mentioned that he'd be delighted for that to happen. It's why the library owns eight copies of his favorite alien conspiracy theory novel.

Next, she turns toward Miss Nicole. "For years, Lily was your star student. Then when she knew she wouldn't dance professionally, she became your assistant. She volunteered to teach toddler classes for you. She got on hands and knees and scrubbed the wooden planks of that studio floor so that when your older students arrived there was never a hint of the inevitable urine accidents those babies left you. She hand-washed costumes and sewed the sparkles onto the accents. She showed up every Tuesday morning without fail, did she not?"

With a firm nod, Miss Nicole agrees. "And she makes a mean cup of coffee. And she'd heat up my lavender rice packs and get things nice and cozy so I could rest my bum knee. And she'd take over movement examples when I needed for advanced classes. Never failed to arrive when asked."

She taps her cane against the dance floor that's already been set up for tomorrow's party and meets the angry eyes of Mayor Kelly with a shrug. "What, Jimmy? It's just facts. The girl worked her ass off. She understood how to demonstrate movement, and she's built a damn good following teaching others to use their bodies at any age. She'd be a great addition to our community. Her internet fame could pull in college students from nearby towns and increase our revenue. I'm not going to lie because you have a bone to pick."

My heart thuds loudly. Prudence is roundly eviscerating the town's lead businesses in an effort to protect *me*.

"Lily, you are a good woman. We will revisit this conversation when the time is appropriate. And I expect," she says, once again glaring at the crowd, "these stories will be kept in mind next time. If Belinda balks, then she can bring it up with me. Don't think I do not know how to find any of you. Ask Landan." Her eyes narrow on a willowy figure trying to blend in, face hidden under a floppy hat, long limbs covered by a black hoodie and leggings, hair in an uncharacteristic ponytail. "Landan's surely heard from Grant about our little run-in on NJ Transit a few months ago, no?"

———

ONCE THE TOWN MEETING ENDED, Daisy and Gatsby were, thankfully, returned to their pondside home rather than given free rein of the park. This should have been the moment we're reminded that the birds are never well behaved. Instead, the whole town was fixated on the gossip surrounding me.

Delia, Nessa, and I covered the buffet tables with intricately woven white tablecloths, then set up the silver chafing dishes borrowed from the team at Coffee Crumbs. The needed items to grab oneself a plate on the front end were boxed and under the tables.

"Don't forget there is fire," Nessa cautions.

"Ness." Delia puts her hands on her hips. "What are you planning? You know Susan will skewer us if we cause a ruckus. This is not the day to create chaos. This is the formal bridal shower–slash–engagement party," she emphasizes. "The one with grandmothers and aunts present."

Nessa smiles sweetly. "How could you underestimate me so? Of course I know. That's why I am pointing out that the wind is going to blow your pretty ribbons into the flames if you don't space things out more."

After confirming the weather overnight and covering the tables with weights and tarps to protect the setup, we make our way toward the girls' home. Silently, I curse myself for not remembering that Nessa has a serious fear of fire.

I clear my throat, readying to apologize for putting her back in the role of the pot stirrer, but before I can, she says, "You assume that because I am the prankster of the group, I'm bound to regress into that role. That's resoundingly unfair with my doctorate and thriving businesses. Yes, I'll always start some shit, because life is boring without the chaos. But thankfully, there are *two* peacocks in the square. I do not need to be the one who causes chaos. They will. Guarantee it."

forty-two
Lily

LUCKILY, the weather held overnight. The tarps are still perfectly in place, and the bins of supplies that still need to be set up are as we left them, meaning we're just about ready for the catering and bartending teams to set up their portions. River's expanded team for events is here hauling dishwasher racks of glassware from the building.

Susan hired the Featherweight *and* Manila Cuisine from Bergen County to work together. Over in one corner, Carmine is chatting with the other team's head chef as he prepares the whole pig he's roasting on-site. He's animatedly discussing the process as the two of them compare notes on chef's blades. Carmine looks like a tiny balding man with a beer belly covered in a stained apron holding a cleaver near an elderly Filipino grandpa's face. Carmine is the ultimate source of his own mafia rumors.

In another corner, Miss Nicole is wrangling a slew of tiny ballerinas in white leotards and sparkly tutus. They're practicing their performance for later. One of her students, a little girl, is doing the shifting from foot-to-foot peepee dance during her teacher's explanation. Frowning, she darts away, headed for the nearest store, a woman with a backpack scurrying after her. When they return, the little girl's white leotard has been replaced with a black one, and she's sans tights.

The woman with her is carrying a large plastic bag. "Going to run these to wash now, Miss Nicole. She'll stay here for practice. No more juice boxes, kid," she says to the little girl. "Hear me?"

I giggle. That's exactly what I would have said if I were the one in charge. Some things never change, the realization that I like this familiarity warms me.

The square has changed little since yesterday, but it's so much brighter today.

Helps when you aren't lost in your own head, doesn't it? Dorothea's wisdom echoes in my head.

I survey the Featherweight with a smile, thinking about River. About how natural it feels waking up in the rose room each morning. About the violet media room antics. About the gorgeous, thriving living wall he gifted me. The flower boxes he and Rosie filled outside our cottage.

Every time I see those buds taking shape, my heart skips a beat. This is Taylor Swift-Cottagecore-Instagram-worthy stuff. The aesthetic my livelihood depends on. A line of work that, if I'm being honest, has lost its shine.

I find myself staring wistfully at Miss Nicole and the tiny dancers, then scanning the square decorated for Stef's shower, and a question comes to mind. *Would I want to have this sort of event ever again? Could I have it?*

As I do a quick round, checking that each detail is perfect, I try to visualize a reality in which the answer is yes.

Lingering walks with Pete while holding hands with River. Picnics with Stef and Lee. Farther in the future, a large blanket spread on the lawn, their children each holding a little snack cup. Seth looking as surly as ever, though he never says no to reading to the little nieces and nephews they give us. Nessa writes in a notebook while Delia perfectly reapplies her lipstick.

Pushing my thoughts out even farther, I consider being here with them. The kids now in school, me wearing River's ring.

Could one of those small humans be mine?

Would I mess them up? Or repeat the mistakes made with me?

That single thought sends me from dreaming of a different future into an anxiety spiral.

Thankfully, before I totally slip, two strong arms wrap around me from behind, grounding me. Giving me enough wherewithal to focus on my surroundings. I zero in on the paint-chipped gazebo. Focus on the scent of smoke in the air from the pig roast. The sound of River's voice in my ear.

"Darling." He turns me to face him, and as he plants a soft kiss on my mouth, he gives me the last two senses I need to ground myself. The soft warmth of his lips and the taste of the cinnamon and whiskey of the craft cocktail he prepped for today.

Like he knew I needed him, he's here, comforting me. So I take advantage and breathe him in.

I lean back, peering up into the pine and sky eyes that have made my weeks here feel less like being lost in the woods and more like Christmas morning. Once again, I'm awestruck by the ease we share. He drops something in my hand with a smile.

My pill bottle. The one I leave on the counter in the kitchen.

"Good thing my sundress has pockets," I say, pushing the orange container into one and my fist into the other. The delicate floral T-shirt dress with a swinging skirt flows with me as I move from side to side.

With a gentle forehead kiss he says, "I thought you might be too busy to pop home, and I know parties like this can be overwhelming. I wanted you to have the opportunity to take your afternoon dose if you want to. I can put it away if you want me to, but I saw it was on the counter and thought I'd check. It's your call."

For a moment I want to balk. I want to be frustrated that he's stepping in, as if I can't take care of myself. But then my brain catches up with my ears and my frustration evaporates. Because he isn't taking over. He's giving me an option. Using that one important and empowering word. *If.*

He didn't tell me I must or tell me that I was forgetful. That should have set a timer or that I would be wrong if I didn't want to take optional medicines.

Instead his message is: *if this would help me, he didn't want access to it to be an obstacle.*

I jump and loop my arms around his neck, feet kicking into the air, forcing him to lift me slightly.

"Thank you." I kiss his jaw, realizing in this moment that I am in love with him.

And that truth has my already frazzled nerves working overtime. This man has the ability to make me believe that I could be someone's chosen person. That he could be the one who sticks around. I cannot help but soak him in.

I'm so lost in my own thoughts that I'm startled when Mateo Santos Manolo shouts, "What's up, girl?" across the lawn, his impression of Jason from *The Good Place* as perfect as ever.

"Not a girl," I respond, breaking into a smile.

We easily fall into the bit, the silly greeting between Jason Mendoza and The Good Janet, when we ran into each other at a Halloween party a bunch of years ago.

I was working as a cocktail waitress at a resort, dressed as Janet. He arrived wrapped up poorly in bed sheets, a sad imitation of Jason's red and gold Buddhist monk robes.

Mateo kept his team on their best behavior that night and then left a hefty tip. Whatever he does in real estate is clearly going well for him. Yet I can't help but think that his always happy, easygoing personality is a façade. Behind his eyes, I swear he looks bored and confused. He seems like a lost puppy, searching for someone and something familiar.

"Hey there, co-best man." River breaks away to greet Mateo.

Mateo saunters over like a movie star, giving River a nod and removing his sunglasses. In my periphery, I'm pretty sure Delia snaps Nessa's jaw closed.

I'll need to poke Ness about that later.

Stef's brother is wearing a slim-fit maroon suit, and as he makes the rounds, cracking jokes and doling out high fives and hugs to every business owner, one would think he's Mr. Peacock Springs.

River drops a quick kiss and says goodbye, then doubles back for a few more. He pecks at my cheeks, forehead, and nose in adorably rapid succession.

His playfulness warms me more than the spring sunshine. The charcoal gray suit pants are just tight enough to hug his behind, and the black button-down is neatly fitted to his broad shoulders.

It's hard not to let bliss take over as I stand here in the middle of town. For the first time, I understand the appeal of being here.

Maybe I could do it for real this time. Even with yesterday's ambush at the town meeting. The only thing that could keep me from making this my home again is me. Not Grant's behavior or the rude comments about the state of my life. Not Landan's ongoing unapologetic stance or Belinda's disapproval. None of that is important.

The work we've completed around the square matters. The love we're pouring into Stef and Lee today.

Nessa is primping floral centerpieces and obsessively tucking ribbons and setting up Sternos for the buffet. Delia is sitting with Stef, who looks like the picture-perfect bride-to-be as sunlight streams across her face. Eyes closed, she holds still so Delia can touch up her makeup.

"Oh my god, Nessa. Just move the jars," Stef shouts, eyes still closed. "I do not need you having a panic attack today."

She's clearly been in education for too long if she can tell what's going on around her without looking.

"How did you…" Nessa trails off mid-question.

"I've known you since we were three. I just knew. Move the damn flowers. I don't care what Susan says."

A throat clears nearby, then a posh voice says, "I believe that is Nanay or Mother to you, Stefanie. Delia," Susan says, "stop fussing. She looks beautiful."

Delia backs up and Susan inspects Stef from head to toe. She fixes invisible issues with her hair and her dress placement, then looks at her from bottom to top once more.

"You'll be wearing a proper heel when guests arrive, correct?"

With a heavy swallow, Stef nods.

"Nessa," Susan snaps, "Don't stress about the centerpieces. Move the extras over to the gift table." She then turns on her heel and walks across to Coffee Crumbs, where she meets the other ladies from her church for coffees and gossip until the party is set to begin.

———

EVERY IMPORTANT FAMILY in Peacock Springs is in attendance when the party begins. The bars are tended by the Featherweights staff, the pig has been roasted and served. Prudence is running the DJ booth, her playlist full of girl power pop music that has our group enjoying ourselves thoroughly between snacks and games. It's almost time for presents when it dawns on me that this is a very formal event.

Pulling Nessa aside, I whisper my anxiety about my gift.

"Did you watch *How I Met Your Mother*?"

"Do you mean *How I Met Your Father* with Hillary Duff? Because Oh my god, I love her. I think I sort of look like her, right? If I cut my hair, but I'd never…"

"No," I say, squeezing her arm. "Mother. With the dad from *Full House* narrating even though he's played by someone else? The one that would never ever get made now because every sentence out of Neil Patrick Harris's mouth would get the show canceled? Shit. Never mind."

I run over to Delia and ask her the same question. She cuts me off, saying, "I love when you have these random thoughts mid-event, but I have to focus on keeping things running. River trusted me with the staff so he can join the guys for whatever they're doing."

"I think it's batting cages, but Mateo was in a suit, so maybe not," I jump in.

"Of course he was." She laughs. "Either way, we have to prep the gifts to be opened and I need a hand. Can you get the iPad from Kirk behind the bar so I can make a list of gifts for Stef? Also grab two trash bags, and ooh. You're creative. Can you make her a paper plate hat with the wrappers and ribbons? I wanted to do a bouquet, but Susan insisted it must be a hat."

Disappointment threads through me. Why can't I spit out what I need to say? Does nobody catch my reference? Sometimes my brain explains things perfectly. But only to me. Everyone else is staring like I have snakes for hair.

Since I can't get my words out, I turn and stride to the bar to round up the requested supplies. I also snag a pair of scissors and a roll of scotch tape. There was an important reason for trying to get the girls' attention, but now that I'm focused on this task, I can't remember what it was. Whatever. I'll figure it out later. These new tasks have absorbed my limited remaining focus.

Take the pills that River brought you," a voice says. *"Holding them isn't the same as taking them.*

It isn't until she picks up the gift I brought that I remember what's in it, and panic washes over me. "Wait. Stef, don't open this one."

I thought this was more of a gag gift situation, so I went with a sex toy, and I really do not need to go from being a fire starter to a sexual deviant in one fell swoop. Naturally this would happen within an hour of really considering sticking around.

She holds the gift up, pinching a piece of wrapping paper she's mostly torn off the corner. "This one?"

In slow motion, the paper tears, the weight of the box doing the work for Stef. The white package with bright silver letters comes into view, along with the extremely phallic hot pink image printed on it.

Mortification sweeps through me. Dammit. The last thing I need is another town-wide scandal.

Nessa, the goddess, my savior, shouts, "That's from me. You know, sex therapist… marital pleasure. Blah, blah… you can put me on your *longest*"—she winks ridiculously—"thank you list. Anyone else in the crowd who needs to reacquaint themselves or their partner's desires can always submit their questions to *Flicking the Bean with Rabin* anonymously. I see you looking, Mrs. Bell."

She gives a tip of an invisible cap and then scoops up the gift and adds it to the pile of open items, then elbows me.

"Ouch." I complain, rubbing my arm.

"Keep. Your. Shit. Together. Long," she whispers through gritted teeth. "Or you will give yourself away."

The final few presents are far more fitting of the upscale event. A set of dishes here, a set of towels there. All the supplies a couple needs to start their new life.

A loud bird-born scream akin to the meow of an angry cat cuts through the square and everyone freezes. Daisy the peacock angrily mews, sending the grandmothers in attendance, including Ava Marie and Miss Nicole, into a fit of cackles that make me wonder if they really are a coven of witches.

Susan, Anna Lucia, Janet, and the late-middle-aged mom squad eye us, fury in their expressions. I don't understand why until a woman several feet away whispers to her friend, pointing at the gift table. It seems Miss Nicole and Prudence opened the sex toy box and left it on a table.

The peacock is also on the table, clamping the vibrator in its beak. She takes off, blue, green, and gold whizzing by, along with the dual-stimulation toy.

The toy, ridiculously, has been activated and is wiggling to and fro like an insect.

The outburst is so absurd that my filter is decimated.

"Peacock with an extra cock on the loose. Watch yourselves, ladies," I say with more earnestness than deserved.

Nessa laughs so hard she would have fallen off her chair if Delia hadn't caught her by the arm. Stef has her face in her hands, likely plotting my slow demise.

Seth, Lee, Mateo, and River are striding our way, having returned to load gifts into the cars. Lined up like this, they look as though they're about to break into song like a nineties boy band.

Peacocks spend less than 2 percent of their time flying, yet Daisy takes off, soaring upward, and when she's floating over the men, she drops the vibrator. The head of the silicone phallus smacks Seth in the face. Hard. Leaving a red mark that may bruise.

The guys, as expected, double over in laughter, putting Nessa's giggle fit to shame.

The sound of River's laughter is like honey to my ears. It reminds me of Denver, of childhood, and playing pretend in the woods. Joy radiates from him. Underneath his bearded face and muscular exterior, he's still that young, unburdened boy. Hands planted on his knees, he guffaws. Then he straightens, tugging at the collar of his shirt like he's overheated.

We're all gasping for air. Except Seth, who's looking more frustrated by the second. And the more frustrated Seth looks, the harder the group laughs.

Finally, he picks up the vibrator, shuts it off, pockets it, and flips off the group of men. He gruffly stomps to the gift table where he haphazardly grabs a large armload of items and heads to the car.

Adrenaline courses through my veins, the air suddenly

intoxicating. There's no containing the exhilaration. My feet move of their own accord, leading me straight to River. I jump into his arms, hugging him like a koala to a tree.

I'm finally able to exist in the moment without the burdens of the past hanging over me. Without concern for how I'm perceived. I'm left with the kind of weightlessness I've spent years searching high and low for. While traveling *almost* provided it, it was never there. It was always here.

———

"THOSE DAMN PEACOCKS are never anything but trouble." River interlaces our fingers and pulls me closer for a kiss.

I giggle. "The Kelly family would rather have someone hit with a silicone dick annually than adjust tradition."

He shakes his head, his hair flopping across his brow. "Don't let them hear that, or it will be added to future years."

My earlier hopeful heart has only grown closer to bursting since we left the square. Because I'm certain now that I belong here. The best parts of small-town life are why we put up with the challenges. The knowledge is immediate but not impulsively decided. I need to be here.

Squeezing his hand harder, I pull him to a stop at the gates of the Featherweight, rose vines woven over our heads. The same spot we stood in on that dark night in September.

I grin up at him. "I'm going to do it."

He nods, though confusion flashes in his eyes. "Great. What exactly are you doing?"

"I'm going to suck it up and serve my stupid time in the stocks. They only use those ankle things, right? Sports teams have used it during festivals to entertain tourists. You've done it before. It's not so bad, right? I'll bring a book. Maybe I can convince them to shorten my sentence. Add bathroom and meal breaks." Words escape me at a million miles per minute and my face hurts from smiling, but I'm filled with confidence. "I'll suck it up. Then stay. I want the peacock silliness. I want to see and hear you laugh like you did today. I'd be a fool to miss out. I've missed too much as it is, and I love that sound."

Filled with excitement, I jump, my mouth aimed for his, but miss full-on kissing him, instead finding the corner of his mouth.

"I love you. I think I've said it, but I can't remember and I will say it as many times as you want to hear."

With a sharp intake of breath, he takes off toward the cottage, dragging me with him. Past the new boxes of the vegetable gardens, herbs, and blooming florals. Across the paver stone walkways that now dissect the grass into additional regions, and up to our front door. *Ours.* For weeks, River worked to make this place feel truly like mine.

I've never experienced that before. Not even my childhood bedroom felt as though it belonged to me. As hard as I tried, I didn't feel rooted anywhere.

But when I'm with River, I am home. That future I pictured earlier becomes more clear. I know if I let this go it would be the biggest regret of my life.

As we step inside, Pete barks from his crate in the living room.

"Not now, dude," River tells him.

I am excited for everything life together with him will give me. Will give us. I need him to feel my love, to feel that all of this change happened because of him.

Heart racing, I lead him into the purple room, and when I turn to him, I find that the buttons of his fitted black shirt are mostly undone, leaving his broad chest with a smattering of dark hair showing.

I nudge him backward and he lands in a huff on the pile of clothes I left on the couch while getting ready this morning. Shoving them toward the desk with one hand, I pull the zipper of his pants lower with the other, rushing like we're going to be caught.

Maybe I am a little afraid of that. Being caught by life. Broken apart and snapped back to reality. To the world where people cannot be together forever, and there's no time but this moment for me. I open the button at the top of the fly and he raises his hips to help me remove his pants. His dark blue boxer briefs are stretched tight around his growing erection, so I cautiously bring my fingers to the waistband in an effort to free him. Softly dipping my hand into the elastic, I graze along his ass and work the fabric caging him in lower.

As he springs free, his crown thumps against his abs, standing tall and proud. His breath hitches, his eyes on me like he's waiting to see what my next move will be, and for a moment I'm scared that I went too far too fast despite how many times we've done this all.

"This is still okay, right?" I run my hands up his strong thighs.

"I need you to touch me," he grits out. "Or I will take over and show you what this torture is like."

Leaning into the mischievousness, I run my hands up and down his legs, moving closer and closer to his quivering member.

Using one hand, I fist the base of his cock. Then I take a tiny soft taste with my tongue. He's already dripping precum, the salty taste encouraging me to continue my teasing.

As I place soft kisses and light licks over him, he groans, his patience thinning.

I work his length with my fist while keeping my mouth motions soft. Then, when I'm back at the tip, I hollow my cheeks, taking him as deep as I can and hum, letting the vibrations of my throat massage his head.

"Fuck." He heaves out a long breath, providing me the encouragement I need to keep going.

I move him in and out of my mouth and swirl my tongue around the ridge at the top.

His hands gently sift through my loose curls, gathering the

strands at the back of my head gently. His kindness shines through, even when I'm torturing him.

Though his face is etched in restraint, I push him a bit further. "Darling, relax. Let go. This is a moment for you. Be a good boy and give me everything you have."

With a guttural groan, he tenses, moving toward the finish line. When I slide my hand from his base to his balls, he comes undone and pulls himself back mid-orgasm, painting his stomach with sticky release. I grab his boxers off the floor and kiss my way up his lower stomach, slowly wiping him clean.

He yanks me up toward him for a deep kiss, with tongue, gentle hair pulling, and a plethora of passionate energy reverberating from him.

"I swear to god, I didn't think I could love you more than I do, but then you go and…"

He grasps the hem of my dress, but I palm his chest firmly.

"I'm not a period sex person. I wanted to show you how I feel about you, and I wanted this moment to be big because I know what telling you I want to stay means to you. Girls make grand gestures too, you know."

We lie on the couch, holding one another, and before long, his breathing gets heavier, signaling he's falling asleep. Before he can doze off completely, I rouse him and we make our way to our bed. This is exactly the sort of home I've always wanted.

Once his breathing is deep and rhythmic again, I whisper, "I promise to choose to love you every day. I promise to love you more and more over time."

With a hint of a smile, he pulls me close and we drift off together.

forty-three
River

SUVS LINE the Featherweight's parking lot as we all load our duffels and small suitcases into vehicles.

Nessa and Seth both check through a bunch of bags, which can only be trouble.

"River of Dreams," Mateo shouts as he heads over to give me a high five. "What is up, co-best? Have a moment to show me your latest improvements?" He nods toward the back of the building.

I find Lily and hitch a thumb over my shoulder, letting her know that I'm going inside.

"What's the plan for the weekend? I swear Nessa and Seth had shit that looked like body parts in their bags. And as much as I love to see some boobies," he snickers, "I really, really cannot go to a strip club with my baby sister. Please tell me the guys and women are splitting up a bit. I know it could be fun for you and Lily to be someplace so horny together, but you've got my back, right?"

A huff of a laugh escapes me. "No plans for joint visits to strip clubs. We've got to set up the suites first. Nessa said she is decorating. She insisted guys do this wrong and purchased a bunch of stuff like 'last fling before the ring' for our suite too. Tonight we're having dinner at one of the best steakhouses in the area. Then it's either poker, blackjack, or dancing at the club."

So far Mateo is on board. Good, I was worried the not-so-involved co-best man would show up and stir up trouble.

"Tomorrow, we have a Lee-focused morning," I continue. "Brunch in the two connecting suites with a bacon bar, followed by some sort of painting class the girls organized. I'm pretty sure anyone who doesn't want to paint will be welcome to head to the pool or nap or whatever.

"The second night will be more of the same: dinner out, gamble, dance, drink. Lee doesn't really want to do strippers, so unless there's a big demand…" I hedge.

"Good, I barely want to think about him with my baby sister," Mateo says, shuddering.

Lightly punching at his bicep, I remind him, "Stef's a grown-ass woman. Lee is a good match for her, and she's giving you a brother. Focus on making the weekend fun for him."

"Cool, cool, cool. Then we head back?" A hint of embarrassment flashes across his face, like he didn't know who I expected him to be or which version of himself he wanted to be here.

"Yeah, sleep in, grab food, and head home. You going back to the city? Need us to drop you at the train station?"

Spinning car keys around his finger, he says, "Susan Santos Manolo will expect me to be present for Sunday dinner, so I'm with the crew for the duration." With a glance over his shoulder, he leans in. "What's everyone else's deal? Delia? Nessa? Seth? Who is seeing someone? Who is going to bed early and who is down to drink all night? Any good wingmen or wingwomen other than you in this crowd?" He breaks into the grin that somehow makes him charming when asking these sorts of questions.

"We all know Nessa is always down for just about anything, so she'll probably wingwoman you, no problem. Seth will likely dip out and read or he'll be super drunk and lecture us all. That one is a jump ball. I'm not sure what's going on with Delia. Something has been a bit different since her time in London, so your guess is as good as mine. The rest of the party consists of your cousins. So you tell me."

With an airy grin and a laugh that make me think he understands while knowing nothing at the same time, he says, "Cool. Good tips."

———

NESSA IS COVERING the common spaces with boobs and dicks. She's got sparkling nipple tassels and pin the nipple on the tit, the body parts in every color.

Delia and I were tasked with running meals and in-room drinks. Harry, Mom's favorite distributor, even tossed in some extras for free.

After the bars and decor are set up, we lounge with sports and movies on and graze on snacks. Once the guests of honor arrive, dinner and gambling go smoothly. I wish I had bet Mateo on Seth's choice of activity, because he digs into his jeans pocket and produces a thin novel. We lose him, then find him again, sipping free beers while reading at a slot machine. To keep the free drinks coming, he'll drop in a coin every so often.

The women went to a club nearby to dance. As much as I want to go find Lily and be the one she's grinding against, I'm exhausted from trying to run point across all these moving parts.

My chip pile is shrinking as Mateo, Lee, and I sit at this poker table. "Folding," I say, tossing my cards down. "Gotta cash out for tonight, boys." I clap Mateo on the shoulder and nod to Lee.

When I check on Seth, he's happy to dip out with me. "It's

probably good for the future brothers-in-law to bond a little, you know?"

Seth's probably right. I just hope Mateo remembers his sister and her fiancé are public school employees. I grab my phone and shoot a quick text.

GROOMSMEN

RIVER:

Mateo, cover some of Lee's bets. He's a middle school teacher

MATEO:

<salute emoji>

I MAKE a mental note to check in with him tomorrow as we head up to the suite.

A few hours later, the faint smell of cigarettes and a pungent citrus and smoke aroma wake me.

Ugh, tequila drunk.

I roll over, finding Lily sprawled out beside me, her back damp with cooled sweat. I nudge her toward the glass of water on her nightstand and encourage her to drink it. Once she's sleeping safely, I drift in and out of restless sleep. I really hate bachelor parties.

Also, I still haven't told her about the night of Grant's bachelor party.

That thought haunts my dreams all night long.

———

"RISE AND SHINE, SWEETHEART," I whisper, holding an electrolyte drink, ibuprofen, and prescription bottles.

Lily groans, rubbing the sleep from her eyes. "I never drink like this. I didn't feel it… why?"

"Side effects." I shrug and shake the orange bottle at her.

Her eyes go wide, like she had no idea.

"Your medicine," I tell her. "It makes it harder to feel drunk, and it'll make you feel a bit better this morning. Drink the full glass too, darling." I give her a kiss and a wink. "I'm gonna handle the food. Come eat soon, okay?"

Slowly, folks trickle through the adjoining suite doors into the open common space, where I've set out coffee, mimosas, and a few random extras. Delia has really outdone herself next door. Pancake trays. *Plural.* Scrambled eggs with shredded cheese. All being kept warm by the Sternos. The place smells like bacon and Taylor Ham, making my mouth water. Some pieces are done, laid out on layers of paper towels, ready to be eaten, and even more wait for their turn on the electric skillet she's using.

It's a mystery how she pulled off the full spread after last night. She's even got berries and mint and yogurts arranged in a tray of ice.

"Boss," she says, causing me to look up from the smorgasbord. "You act like you haven't seen catering pre-work done before. What is going on with you?"

Taking a long, hearty sip from my mug, I scoff. "It's called a hangover, Shane. You heard of it? But seriously, nice prep work. I'm thoroughly impressed."

This suite is decorated with rainbow tits and rainbow sparkly dicks as well. There is even a large glittery banner that reads *Same Penis Forever* on the wall. By the look of my friend group, we're all in a similar boat when it comes to hangovers. Except for Nessa.

I need to keep an eye out tonight. What is her deal?

She lets out a clap and a shriek that are way too loud and energetic, then hurries Lee and Stef into a pair of chairs set up back to back.

"Welcome to our first game of the weekend. I've handed our

lovely couple each a pair of boxers and a piece of lingerie." She gestures wildly toward them as if we can't tell. "I'll ask a question like *Who is better at school?* Then they'll both hold up Stef's panties, since we all know it's her. Since they are back to back, we can see how they answer but they can't." She lets out a laugh that teeters between evil and self-entertaining. Affecting a gameshow host voice, she wraps up with, "Now, let's see if they're truly on the same page. Our perfect couple, Stef and Lee."

The room fills with groans and half-hearted *yay*s as we fill our plates and circle the couple.

Lily sits on the floor between my legs with her back against the firm base of the couch, quickly downing a cup of coffee. Spearing strawberries and pancakes onto her fork, she eats the giant bite and turns toward me with a grin before resting her head on my knee.

"Okay, people," our master of ceremonies commands.

Mateo enters, sees his sister holding a lace bodysuit, and groans into his coffee. "Isn't this supposed to be done with, like, shoes or signs? Do I have to look at her holding that?"

In response to the complaint, Lee swings the tiny black leather thong Nessa handed him overhead like a lasso.

Mateo chokes on his coffee and grumbles as he heads for the breakfast spread.

"I didn't take you for the kind of man who'd care about his sister's relationships like this," Delia shouts. "I'm sure all those chicks you pick up in the city have their own big brothers, uncles, and dads who feel like that about you too."

He shakes his head again and chugs more coffee, then tosses blueberries in the air and catches them in his mouth. "Whatever," he replies with a little less feeling than expected for the brother bear act he just had going.

"All right. I'm going to keep this one simple to start. Who has the bigger family?" Emcee Nessa begins.

Both raise the lingerie, and Mateo raises his glass in a toast to Stef.

"Next. Who studied harder in school?"

Again, they twirl the lingerie.

"To be fair," Lee interjects, "more of my classes involved creating something than studying, so she was going to win. I think I worked a lot more. Painting on a time crunch is not easy."

"Great advice for later, Lee. Back to our questions," Nessa dismisses. "Who," she asks in a suggestive tone, "is more adventurous?"

Mateo puts a hand on my shoulder and whispers that he's headed back to bed for a bit. He rolls a pancake into a tiny spiral and shoves the whole thing into his mouth before slinking back to our side and closing the door behind him.

Nessa laughs as Stef and Lee each choose their partner for this one. "Lightning round," she says, eyes dancing. "Going to go faster now. Who kissed who first? Who is the better kisser? Who made the first move past kissing? Who is kinkier? Who is usually on—"

A loud knock on the door interrupts her.

"Oh, they're here. Yay."

She darts to the door and opens it. Three people step in, bringing with them a slew of art supplies.

"Amazing. Welcome, welcome. You must be Seraphine," Nessa says to the woman with blue- and pink-tipped hair.

"I am. Are you Nessa? And is there a dedicated space for us?"

As Nessa leads them through the door to our suite, Stef giggles and blushes a little. Lee collects garments from her and takes them all to the king room they're sharing.

The group spends the next half hour lounging and snacking.

Seth goes back to his book, the cousins head to their rooms for naps, and Delia is wiping down counters in the kitchenette.

Lily is asleep, her head on my thigh and her jaw slack.

It's hard to not find her both adorable and incredibly sexy. Scooping her up, I pull her close. With one hand smoothing her hair back toward her messy bun, I settle her on my lap and guide her head to my chest. I would hold her like this, surrounded by all our favorite people, forever.

The peace I've settled into is disrupted quickly by the nagging voice in the back of my head. The one reminding me that I owe her the truth about that other bachelor party.

But when she nuzzles farther into my chest and lets out a soft sigh, I think *when we get home from this trip.*

forty-four
Lily

I LAUGH into my champagne flute. This blob looks nothing like our "marital bliss" nude models.

Leave it to Nessa to set up a scandalous paint and sip class with live talent. The couple is lying on a chaise lounge, both wearing sleepy neutral looks.

Honestly, I wouldn't be surprised if they did fall asleep. It has to be boring to lie there mostly naked for a few hours.

"That cannot possibly be comfortable," I whisper hiss to Delia.

"Huh?"

"He's only wearing one sock." I nod at the male model.

She snorts. "How did you notice the sock when his dangling bits are out and practically stuck to his leg like that?"

Nessa rings a bell and gives us the stink-eye.

Delia leans in. "Where did that come from?"

Our giggle fit takes over, and heads turn our way.

"Ladies, please. Show some maturity." Nessa tries to affect a haughty tone, but the façade crumbles quickly. "Oh fuck it. Lunchtime, people."

"Let's go back to Titsville." I loop an arm through Delia's and haul her up with me.

"Yeah, Penis Palace is too crowded," she agrees as we wander through the connecting door.

The moment we're near the kitchen, she snags a dish towel and slings it over her shoulder.

"Absolutely not, Deals," I tell her, swiping it away. "You keep acting like you are working. Take a legit break. You look like you could go on a murder spree." I deftly swipe the towel from her.

Huffing, she walks off. Shortly after, the shower starts.

Good. I swear she's been off since she got home from London. If I can feel this, can everyone? I want to tell her to talk to me, but I know she'll talk when she's ready.

My mind is busy running through all my concerns about her as I move around the kitchen, yet somehow I manage to pull the sandwich trays and condiments out and get them set up.

———

"I'M JUSS NA'T VERY GOOD," Mateo grumbles around a bite of food, "with these kinds of things." He swallows audibly. "I wouldn't worry about yours. Seriously, you should look at what I have. Calling them stick figures would be generous."

The guys bark out laughs, having a good time picking apart how little skill they have.

"It's like a Rorschach test," Seth says with a laugh.

Seth. Laughing. To think I could have missed this.

My pulse beats slow and steady, my chest lighter than it has been in a decade. I exhale, and more of the tension falls away. It doesn't matter that I had a failed marriage, that my parents disowned me. Those concerns have melted away like snow on the first day of spring. It's peaceful. I just want to capture it, hold it close forever.

How did I let anyone take this away from me?

———

WE FINISH our lunches and paintings, then split up. As Stef and I stroll side by side on the boardwalk, I pull her into a firm side hug, squealing, "I can't believe how little I've seen you despite finally living in the same town after all these years."

She leans into the hug, and we take turns apologizing, me for making her feel bad and more stressed and her for being hard to reach.

"Seriously," I say, looping my arm through hers, "I haven't been the best maid of honor."

"I'm sorry I haven't been around. I want to know more about you and River. Things are better than they were in January, right?"

"This weekend's about you, not me," I deflect.

"It's about you a little bit," she replies. "If I'm being honest..." She trails off. "Well, the whole wedding thing didn't appeal at first. Not after—"

"Not after my marriage imploded and then I went cuckoo bananas?" I offer.

"After you were gone. The party felt like it wouldn't be worth it. It was incomplete without you. I couldn't do this if you weren't part of it. But I didn't think I could ask you to be part of it when things were so bad. Lee's been my person for a long time and our lives pre- and post-party aren't changing." Her stare is firm but loving. God, she must scare the kids who misbehave.

From wedding talk, we move on to making plans to spend more time together, including in-person meals and hanging out at her house rather than video calls.

"Okay, I've let it slide long enough. I need to hear the details about you and River, stat," she eventually says. "Also, tell me you're staying for good again. Please. I still don't believe it."

It's a nudge, but rather than pressure, I only feel loved.

Her eyes are bright with curiosity and joy while she waits for my response.

Truly, this weekend and the joy that comes with spending time with my friends have been a balm to my soul.

"I'll tell you if…" I hedge, rocking back on my heels and eyeing the Skee Ball machines nearby.

"Oh hell yes. I will school your ass. Then you will tell me everything twice."

Laughing, we race into the arcade. Once I've secured our game cards, I find Stef guarding two Skee Ball alleys from a group of skateboarders in band T-shirts.

As we swipe the plastic cards over the token reader machines, the familiar noise of the wooden balls being dispensed comes down the alley. They knock against each other and the sides of the chute as they roll toward the end in a line.

The little things, like being here with one of my best friends ahead of her wedding, playing a favorite childhood game, are precisely why I can't let anyone run me out of town again.

I roll my first ball, and it connects to the alley with a hearty clunk, followed by familiar sounds. It hops over the gutter and sinks into the middle ring of the bulls-eye, giving me thirty points.

Beside me, Stef is two balls in and also at thirty points.

With a deep breath in, I get into the zone.

At the end of the first game, I'm up by ten points, so I use my winner's status to get a question of my own in.

"You've barely said a word about how wedding planning with Susan has been. Are you really doing okay? She can be a bit…" I trail off, being mindful of the mixture of irritation and reverent respect Stef has for her mom.

"Militant? Demanding? Unaware that this is 2024 and that Lee's parents should have a say as well? Yes, she's been all of that," she tells me. "But what does complaining about her get me? I love you girls. Your advice is well intended, but I don't have a white mom. I have brown immigrant parents. It's different. So I bitch to Mateo or my cousins when I need to vent, or I blast music and dance in the kitchen. Once, I was so mad, I took an ice-cold shower so I could scream without being heard. I kind of scared Lee that time, so I haven't done that again, but seriously, it's fine." She straightens, crossing her arms. "Now I get an easy one since we were basically tied." With her brows arched, she silently dares me to argue.

So with a resigned sigh, I nod.

"Are you *really* going to stay?" Her expression is half hope, half resignation.

The resignation confuses me. She knows how badly I want to. Doesn't she?

I beam. "Damn straight I am. Then I can kick your ass at Skee Ball any time I want." I slap the token card against the starter and the rolling sounds fill the lane again.

Stef wins the round and pointedly asks, "Why didn't you show up in March like River and Delia expected?"

My chest constricts. "Right for the jugular. That's too far. Dial it back," I plead.

"Okay." She stretches out the word. "Then what's going on with you and River?"

"We're good. Really good," I tell her. "In December, I guess he finally decided it was time to shoot his shot. But it's more than that. He, um. I didn't take you two back to my room in Denver. It was a shithole. I think he saw the cracks in my façade while he was there." Relief threads through me as I admit this next part. "I'm tired of moving from place to place, pretending to have fun with shallow faux friends. I'm tired of keeping up with multiple versions of myself. The Lily people follow on social media, the

Lily Grant approved of, the one Belinda expected. River saw the messy beneath it all."

"Literally," she teases.

"Yes, but also, he let me take my time. I know Delia is mad about March." I stare at my toe as I draw lines on the floor.

"It's kind of fair, right?" she asks, her tone soft.

"I figured that it would be another short-term thing. Like if I took a leap of faith and came back sooner, you'd all be sick of me sooner," I confess. "Over and over, I've dated, only for the person I'm with to eventually outgrow me. They move on to find their forever person. I just…" I pause and take a few deep breaths. "I… didn't realize. It went right over my head that River… truly loves me. I just didn't want to lose that before we got here. If I came then and things didn't work out, I worried I'd be too afraid to stick around for the weeks you needed me."

My gaze goes from my shoes to the ceiling and then an influx of tears blurs my focus. I squeeze my eyelids shut, pressing against the corners, willing myself not to cry. My head pounds from the sounds bouncing out of every game and excited child.

"I don't think he's going to get sick of you."

The sincerity is too much. This has to stop or I'll be tempted to run and hide. I deflect by saying, "Well, I think time's up. Play ball, Mrs. Carter." I start another round for both of us using my token card.

Using her teacher voice, she chides, "That's *Future* Mrs. Carter, Former Mrs. Morgan."

Groaning, I beg, "Never ever call me that again, please." I swipe a ball from her lane and aim it at the gutter, earning her zero points. "Serves you right."

She retaliates by trying to do the same but ends up scoring twenty points for me instead.

We settle into the game properly, and when we're done, she's determined to subtract that twenty points from me to make it a draw.

"Okay," I say. "My last question for you is: Are you happy?"

Looking at me with an easy smile, she sighs. "I'm really happy, Lils. Are you happy?"

Hugging her close, I confirm, "Yes, I am the happiest I have been in a long time. But time to go, bride-to-be. Tonight is our girls' night out, and that means Delia is waiting to show off her new skills and make us all even more beautiful." I link my arm with hers, and we make our way back to the hotel.

"She's such a contradiction, right?" Stef asks. "She's the most hyper feminine of us and also the most feminist."

"It makes sense," I say. "Despite some of the ways femininity is meant to attract a mate—a male mate, generally—it's also about being playful, feeling beautiful, and, most importantly, feeling powerful. Cordelia Shane is absolutely a femme fatale in that respect."

Back at the hotel, we close the door between the suites and put on our favorite pop songs from middle school. Dancing around, snacking, and taking turns in Delia's chair, we get glammed up for a night of sushi, drinks, dancing, and more drinks.

We've specifically asked the guys to keep their plans to themselves after overhearing Mateo lobbying to switch it to a strip club. It was hilarious when he tried to get Seth on his team, forgetting his audience.

"No fucking way am I going into a strip club and sitting down, bro." He accents the final word sarcastically.

"Why not? It's not really a bachelor party if we don't take the groom for a lap dance, right?"

"No sitting, no lap. No lap means no place to dance."

forty-five
River

NOPE. No way. Not again. I do not have a great history with drunk grooms. With this group, lord only knows what Lee will spit out.

As we wind our way through the casino to head back to the hotel suite, Mateo and

Seth veer off, searching for a luggage cart. There's zero chance we're getting Lee to bed any other way. He sat down and can barely keep his eyes open at this point.

God, this is my nightmare. At the Featherweight, I'm always watching, cutting folks off before they get this bad. He's going to be so sick tomorrow.

Where are they?

Before I see them, I hear them. So do all the people around us. Arriving like Tony Hawk and the queen have birthed a Filipino male model, Mateo sails down the hallway on the back of a luggage cart, giving a dainty wave. Every few feet, he kicks off with one foot to keep the momentum going.

Meanwhile, Seth is sitting in the middle of the cart, cradling an armful of liquor bottles like they are his babies. I have to assume he lost a bet to Mateo. *Is Seth singing?* For a second, I worry someone slipped something into his drink.

Seth's "baby" liquor bottles are semi-full, and I swear they better have paid for them. The last thing I need to deal with is security showing up to "assist" with the situation. There's little doubt in my mind their behavior would get us tossed into the parking lot, and not one of us is in any state to drive home.

Which means we'd have to sober up in the car or pace the boardwalk.

Ooh, but that would mean we could have pizza. Do we have pizza upstairs?

As they get closer, Seth's words register. He's singing a Backstreet Boys song. Yeah, Mateo definitely roped him into something. After they finish their off-key rendition of "I Want it That Way," we work together to lift a now half-asleep Lee onto the cart.

As we roll him to the suites, Lee tells an incoherent story, every word slurred. I just want to get back to the room and go the fuck to sleep. Don't think I could handle listening to another drunk groom spill his guts.

He rolls to his side, grasping the golden bars of the cart, his voice louder, his words clearer, begging us to stop. Concerned the motion is going to trigger his upchuck reflexes, we obey.

We're just outside the girls' suite. Shit. If he says anything weird and they hear it, he's doomed. I just want to get him inside without saying something he'll regret tomorrow.

"Guys. Seriously, listen," he demands. "You are the best friends anyone could ask for. Matty! My brother, I've always wanted a big brother," he coos. "I love you guys, which is going to make what I have to tell you so much harder, but shh." His shushing is more like a scream, making my head pound. Then, in a childlike tone, he says, "Because it's a secret."

I've had just enough to drink that I've crossed over from fun-drunk to stern bar owner. I get loud, cutting Lee off with a confession ten years in the making.

"Absolutely fucking not, Lee Samuel Carter. I swear to god, being a best man in this town does *not* mean being the keeper of secrets from wives. You better not say some stupid shit like Grant did when he confessed his love for Landan the night before he married Lily. I will not watch another train wreck."

Their eyes all go wide, the hallway going silent. Probably from shock, since I rarely yell.

You have been with Stef for how long?" I ask, undeterred by their surprise. "If you admit to something that fucked-up, I can't let you marry her. I won't live with this guilt anymore. If I had been older, or if I'd had more of a backbone, I could have prevented Lily from getting hurt. It's all my fault." My vision goes blurry and a tear rolls down my face, yet my friends are all still frozen in place.

What is wrong with these guys?

A door creaks open, snagging my attention, and the girls appear at the threshold.

Standing at the front of the huddle with a look of devastation on her face is the last person I wanted to hear this. Her messy waves cascade down her back and her eyes are rimmed red and swelling as tears threaten to spill over her lashes and take her mascara with them. She's shaking, her shoulders rounded as if her body is turning in on itself.

"What did you say?" Lily chokes out, her voice wavering, the tears now rolling down her face in silent streaks. "What. The fuck. Did you just say, George River Hendrix?" she asks again, her voice laced with venom.

She's probably done with me, and I fucking deserve it. My feet feel like blocks of cement, making it difficult to face her. But I do it. Though I only make it halfway before my body seizes up, leaving the doorway to my left and the guys to my right. Like this, I'm a caged man. There's nowhere to run now.

"The hell, dude?" Delia shouts.

Nessa shrinks back. She's usually good for a one-to-one conversation about these kinds of topics, but in a group, not so much.

Stef, who's holding Lily up, glares at Lee, then me, just long enough that I know I should be fully frightened of what comes next.

My beautiful flower wilts in her friend's arms. The sight is like a knife to my chest. Like my heart is breaking in a literal way, not just a metaphorical one, my entire being crumpling in on itself.

Lee is coherent enough to stand and stumble past me to Stef and Lily. "But babe," he complains as he pulls up short in front of his fiancée. "Babe, I'm going to miss these guys. I didn't have guy friends like this growing up, and I'm going to *miss them*." The last two words are spoken in a high-pitched whine more fitting for a little boy than a grown man.

"You need to remember what a secret is," Stef chides him. "But more importantly..." She zeroes in on me again. I now fully understand the phrase *if looks could kill*. Because if they could, I would be dead, cremated, spread across all seven continents. She'd come back to stomp on the ashes, and even that would not be enough of a punishment.

Using her teacher voice, she demands we get in their suite now.

We file in like the naughty boys we've been. Lee makes it four steps before flinging himself onto the floor near the island in the kitchen area. Seth and Mateo drag him to his feet and toss him onto the couch.

With a moment of sibling bond compassion, Stef addresses Mateo. "Big brother, I'm about to say a bunch of things you may not want to hear. Mostly because you'll have to keep it from Nanay and I don't want to drag you into my shit if you don't want to be." She lifts her chin, signaling for the door to our suite. "You want to get out of here, go for it."

Mateo eyes each of us. Lee has possibly fallen asleep again. Seth is chugging mini water bottles like he's in the desert. Nessa is settled in a chair, scrolling on her phone. Delia is glaring at me like she's wishing she could burn me at the stake. Lily has not stopped crying, and Stef has her teacher face on.

Winking at Nessa, Mateo says, "This should be interesting. Perfect Princess saying something I shouldn't know? I'm going nowhere." He hops up onto the faux marble countertop, grabs an apple from the bowl, and sinks his teeth into it with a loud crunch. He swings his legs like a little kid about to watch a PG-13 movie.

"Our secret is nothing like Grant's apparent drunken confession," she says, giving me a death glare again. "But we will get back to that in a moment."

Lee groans. "Babe, no. We said no telling until the speech at the wedding."

Laughing, Stef strokes his shaggy blond hair. Then she kisses his forehead. "You fool. You are the reason we're in this mess. Let's just spill since it's such a small thing compared to..." She huffs out a disappointed sigh. "Compared to the other secret just confessed."

Stef softens, her eyes going shiny, her body suddenly full of nervous excitement.

She's been drinking all weekend, so I don't think this is that sort of secret, but I can't imagine what else it could be. They already have an adorable bungalow in a residential section of town, they both have amazing jobs in the school district, and Lee has been painting in their home art studio and selling his work for a while.

"Our big secret is that I'm getting my PhD. At Columbia Teacher College," she says. "That means we need to move to New York City for the next few years so I can complete the coursework." She bounces on her toes, clapping, her tipsy excitement for this professional milestone abundantly clear. "Getting into an Ivy League program like this is a big deal, and at first, we didn't know if we could afford it. But we just found out that I'm getting a scholarship so I can do this for real–for real..." She trails off, her expression falling, like she's remembering how this reveal came to be. "Which, honestly," she says, "is absolutely insignificant compared to your revelation, River. So before Nessa buries herself in the chair cushions and disappears so completely that we have to use the jaws of life to free her—"

"I'm good, babe," Nessa says without looking up. "Keep going."

"Okay, then before Delia skins you alive or Lily disappears on me for another decade, talk. What exactly did Grant say before the wedding? *And* why is this the first we're hearing about it?"

Every pair of eyes in the room turns toward me except the one set that matters. I just want to look into those chocolate brown irises and take in that dusting of freckles over her pert nose and sweet lips. Hers is the prettiest face I've ever beheld. Her hair has gone from down in those gorgeous, messy waves to gathered in a knot on her head. With tissues in hand, she wipes at her running makeup.

The ache in my chest comes back. Dammit. I caused this. I have gotten everything I ever hoped for over the last few weeks. Her watery, red-rimmed eyes are the same ones I've been lucky enough to make roll back in her head with pleasure, finally after all these years. And rather than focusing on me, they're set on her fingers while she fidgets with the box of tissues.

Sighing, I garner all the nerve I can. I have no choice but to get it all out there.

Trying not to cry, I take the group back ten years. "Lily, please, please trust me that I've been searching every day we've been together for the right moment to tell you this because I knew if I didn't, the guilt would always eat at me. I didn't plan to let it go on for this long, but in December we were having so much fun and I was in shock that you finally saw me too."

I move closer to her, resting against the coffee table across from her.

"I just wanted to make everything perfect for you. For us. I want there to be an us still. Tonight. Tomorrow. Forever. You're the only person I've ever wanted like this."

I reach for her but hesitate with my hand inches from her knee, thinking twice about it, and retreat.

"You came to all our junior hockey games, and that made me feel like I had won the lottery. But I was too chicken to make a move. When Grant and Landan broke up, and he decided to pursue you, I was mad. Not at you; at him. Hell, I was mad at everyone here. You all knew how shy I was, so if you all knew how much I liked her, how come nobody ever set us up? Why didn't I get a wingman?"

My anger rising, I stand and pace the length of the sitting area.

"Ugh, no. The point is that the night before the wedding while you ladies were having a girls' night in, Grant and I got alcohol from the bar cellar and drank too much." I turn and point at our most introverted friend. "Seth was with us too, but he'd wandered farther down the riverbank by then. He couldn't have known, and I didn't tell him. Grant got drunk. So drunk that it makes Lee look sober, honestly. Anyhow, that grease ball started to murmur Landan's name to himself. He was despondent, confused about why she didn't love him. He prattled on until his word vomit turned into actual vomit."

Seth tilts his head thoughtfully, holding his water bottle in midair. "I do recall him recreating the exorcist on the lawn that night." With that, he goes back to sipping, clearly waiting for me to continue.

"Right." I blow out a breath. "Once the remake of the exorcist began, I shouted for Seth and we got him home to bed. The next day, you were married, and I hadn't found a moment to ask him about what he'd said. I had always heard that drunk words were sober thoughts, and I wanted to confront him so badly. There just was never a good time. Ugh, that's always the problem. I never know when to do this, to have the impossible conversation with someone. So when you and Grant split, I felt compelled to help you however I could. That's why I told you about the stupid town council things I overheard. I wanted to make it right by tipping you off. Getting you out to Stef at school was the easiest way to do it without sacrificing my chance of running the Featherweight."

I stop in front of her and crouch, hands pressed together. "Please, please, Lily. Please. You have got to believe me."

Nessa stands and hip checks Delia. "Well, gentlemen, thank you so much for this riveting end to our night. I'm going to borrow these two. Stef, if you want to join us for a slumber party, you are always welcome. Good night my dudes, and Mateo, seriously, stop grinning. This isn't some television show. It's not for your entertainment. Grow the fuck up." On that firm note, she and Delia help Lily up and guide her into their room, slamming the door behind them.

Fuck, I need to fix this.

forty-six
River

SUNDAY MORNING

I **WOKE** up to no sign of Delia, Nessa, or Lily. And with a killer hangover. Alcohol, emotions, the full spectrum. On the drive back, my phone pings.

GROUP CHAT: [DELIA SHANE, NESSA RABIN, RIVER HENDRIX]

DELIA:

Taking Lily to grab some stuff. She's going to stay with us tonight.

RIVER:

Tell her I will go to the apartment. The cottage is hers

DELIA:

With all due respect "boss"

Ya fucked up

Ya fucked up big time

RIVER:

Thanks, I had no idea

DELIA:

Happy to be of service. If you need help fixing this, ask someone else

NESSA:

I'd normally send you a bunch of romance novels I love but...

<sends link for Taylor Swift's "You're On Your Own Kid">

Play this

RIVER:

Please make sure she's ok. Delia, I'll handle the bar deliveries

DELIA:

You're damn right

277

forty-seven
Lily

"YOU WANT TO GO, don't you?" Nessa whispers in the early morning hours.

"So fucking badly," I admit.

"Too many lights, noises, people?" she pokes.

"It's fun," I deflect, knowing that this was all supposed to be fun and not overstimulating.

"Permission to put my professional hat on?" she asks, her tone turning serious and her gaze hard.

"Fine," I groan, even as nervousness stirs to life inside me. I don't know if I really want to hear this.

"First of all, you've been running from your problems for as long as I can remember. You always take off when it's scary. Do you remember the big argument Landan and Delia had in eighth grade?"

Confusion stirs in my mind. "No."

"Of course not, because you didn't like confrontation then either,

278

so you magically avoided getting involved by helping River study for a test in the library. We all knew they were going to get into it in the lunchroom, but you skipped, and in turn, you didn't have her back."

"Can we not, please?" Delia moans from where she's packing her things.

"Moving on," Nessa says. "You've always done everything you can to come across as perfectly put together. I'm guessing the external pressure kept you on task? Belinda isn't exactly the warm and fuzzy type, so angling to please her added a level of stress you needed to stay motivated. Focusing on schoolwork and on tutoring River externalized it. These are all classic behaviors we're discovering help girls mask ADHD." She shrugs.

Changing her tune from her house a month ago, Delia adds, "Dude, you know we don't care about the label, right? We just care about you."

"What?" I'm shaken. "You said I was making excuses not too long ago…"

"I did. But I've been thinking about it and started connecting dots. You can't sit still for long, you overthink, and you over-share, or at least it seemed like you did. It was a version of sharing everything with everyone." She gives me a sheepish smile. "I was the one who pushed River to pursue more after the two of you got along so well in September. It seemed like if you'd let anyone catch you while you ran, it would be him."

Nessa adds, "I've been worried for a while that you were hiding something, and now it all adds up. Now that you are learning how your brain is wired, does it feel easier to be around us? To be home?"

"Sometimes yes, sometimes no," I admit.

"Keys." She holds open her palm to me. "I'm driving. And you…" She glares at Delia. "You gotta rest too. I've been taking it slow all weekend. I had a feeling someone would need to have all their wits about them."

Delia glares back. "You might be the oldest of your siblings, but we're your friends. You get a night off too sometimes."

"I promise to relax the weekend of the wedding, okay?"

———

I REST my head against the passenger side window of my car, the car I escaped in and used to try and outrun my feelings at every turn. Thoughts of Belinda, Grant, Landan, all the small ways I've been told that I'm not good enough, make me want to curl into a little ball and sleep under a weighted blanket or seven. It's tempting to disappear into the darkness by turning off all of my socials and my cell phone, or even just throwing it in the fucking river.

River. God dammit, River.

I don't want to think about him.

He didn't set out to deceive me or hurt me. His guilt and anguish were written all over his face as he explained. The darting glances, the haunted look in his eyes, and his frantic movements made my heart ache. Then finally, his body practically crumpled in on itself as his shoulders turned inward. The look of disbelief as he realized that his mouth betrayed him was life a knife to the chest, yet a relief too. Because it was obvious that holding on to this alone for so long had hurt him.

I wished so badly in that moment that I could feel something. Anger at him for keeping it from me, concern for how burdened he's been by this secret, resentment that Grant went through with our marriage knowing it was a sham. I wanted to muster up a wave of disgust. Fury for everyone who blamed me. This revelation turned the cheating into an inevitably. No matter what I've done or will ever do, I will always be me.

Instead, it became too much scrutiny. Too much focus was directed my way. Truly, Nessa was the only person not watching.

It felt like my friends were taking a bit of pleasure in my suffering. Meanwhile I went fully numb.

———

I MUST HAVE DRIFTED off because we wake up in Philadelphia instead of New Jersey. In front of a building with a bright sign with an animated crown on it. The violet letters read Condom Kingdom.

Nessa puffs out her chest with a self-satisfied look. "I have to pick up a few things on the way home. Plus, my college roommate always said the cheesesteaks over there," she points to a black and chrome building catty-corner to this one, "are the best in the city. I figured the grease is good for the hangovers. The stuff here," she points a thumb over her shoulder like a cartoon hitchhiker, "is literally ready for pickup, so it'll take no time at all, unless you want to look around." She wiggles her eyebrows suggestively.

Outside the Jeep, Delia playfully shoves Nessa toward the door and squeezes my hand once quietly. Inside, the ceiling is covered in plastic pink and blue sperm figurines. It's ridiculous. Delia and I giggle and whisper like schoolgirls while Nessa strolls over to the employee to collect her order.

Delia stops and plucks a pair of hot pink fuzzy cuffs off a rack and swings them. "You're still getting that bullshit over with when we get home. I'm not prepared for the emotional fallout that would come if you ran again."

Deflecting, I pick up a large bundle of corded black bondage ropes and cock an eyebrow. "Planning to hog tie me and deliver me personally?"

"Don't be silly," she quips. She picks up a rainbow dildo and a pair of socks with pot leaves and the words *best buds* printed on them, then slides the sock onto the silicone cock and hands them to me. "You'll swallow your pride and go talk to your *best bud*, Jim, yourself," she confirms.

Turning around, I pick up a mesh bodystocking and a pair of hot pink leopard pasties and up the ante. "While wearing this lovely fishnet catsuit? But of course."

We dissolve into a fit of laughter.

The door opens and the voices of high school boys echo through the room. They toss a plush stuffed mushroom between them, nailing one of them in the head.

Turning to look at the commotion, Nessa surveys them. One of the boys freezes, his eyes going wide.

"Joshua Rabin, what the hell are you doing here?" Nessa growls at her youngest sibling.

"I was—I was just at a camp friend's house. We were going to get cheesesteaks and saw the sign and it was funny, and…" he sputters.

Seeing Nessa's little brother further stirs the messy emotional soup inside me.

"Shua." I shout, stepping toward her brother.

"Silly?" He breaks into a grin.

The last time I saw him, he was five, so that would make him fifteen, I guess. He's nearly six feet tall and gangly in that pubescent sort of way, but damn, does he look like his dad.

I lead the boys to the door and point. "Your sister said that place has the best cheesesteaks, and I'm buying if I just so happen to bump into you getting food and not here. So"—I push the door open, making the bells above it chime—"see you over there in ten?" Peering back at Nessa who looks like an actress trying not to break, I add, "If the tables are clean, I'll throw in a soda. Bye."

I pull the door shut in their faces, and a group of three women nearby howl with amusement.

I curtsey and hold a nearby personal massaging wand as a microphone, announcing, "It has come to my attention that I have allowed others to dick-tate—" I laugh, picking up the stuffed mushroom and placing it back in its bin. "Ha, dick. Get it?" I scoop the supplies out of Delia's hands and put them back one by one. "I've allowed others to dictate things for me for too long. I have to get Pete from the vet clinic, anyway, so yes. I'll talk to Jim." I sigh dramatically. "Because of course the mayor is also the vet. But not with the peace offering you chose. Sorry, Deals. I, Lily Jayne Long, will not allow us to be separated because of any other dicks, I promise." I cross my heart like we did when we were little girls. "So, my dears," I declare, grandstanding now, "seeing that teenager walk through that door is another reminder that I've let a lot of time pass. He is going to eat a grease ball with me because when we get back to Peacock Springs, New Jersey, I need to see a man about a weird town requirement."

forty-eight
River

AFTER GRABBING A FEW ESSENTIALS, I head to my parents' house. The weather is nice, and I find Mom sitting on the porch, a wineglass in one hand and her Kindle in the other.

Like she can read me from miles away, she stands and heads inside as I'm walking up the block. By the time I reach the oversized wicker two-seater she was on, she's back with an extra glass, except that one is filled with orange liquid.

"Gatorade. You look like the sun is trying to murder you, sweetheart," Mom says as she shoves the glass into my hand.

I take a sip and wince when it burns a little on the way down.

"Okay, it's a Gator-odka," she says, waving a hand. "But it was only half of a shot for some hair of the dog. I'll grab water and the ibuprofen for you when you finish this. Looks like you had a fun weekend." She sits and pats the cushion beside her, beckoning me to join her. I obey and continue drinking the orange-and-gasoline concoction. I have no choice now but to pay the piper, first by chugging this disgusting drink and then by confessing everything to her.

In true Elizabeth Hendrix fashion, she quietly listens as I recount the good parts of the weekend.

"Uh-huh," she draws out, waving a hand in a motion that suggests I move on. "River, since I discovered I wasn't just bloated and exhausted but pregnant, I've known you, so spit it out. Yours is not the face of someone who just had a lot of fun with his friends. Did you lose a lot of money gambling?"

I frown. "No. You know I don't gamble much. I'd rather not just hand all my cash to the casino."

Nodding, she prods me further. "No argument here. So what happened? Did you shoot a man just to watch him die?" she teases.

"Yes, how did you know?" I dryly reply.

She taps me lightly upside the head, making sure her ring makes firm contact with my crown. Rubbing the spot, I exhale. Then I give her the play-by-play, starting with Grant's bachelor party and ending with last night's fuckup.

With a mix of amusement and exhaustion, she shakes her head. "I thought you were my smart son, George River Hendrix." She puts her arm around me and I lean my head on her shoulder.

I exhale again and let the heaviness take over. "I thought Robert was the smart one," I snark back, but the attempt falls flat.

"Sweetheart, there are lots of kinds of smart. He's serious in ways your dad would have gone after if he was allowed to. You always had Grandpa's passion for the bar, the town. You're your own kind of smart."

I huff. "That sounds like an insult, you know."

"Stop it. Listen to me."

Defeat has wound itself into every cell in my body. My head is foggy and my limbs feel awkward and cumbersome when I try to move. So instead, I give in. I sink into the hug she's offering.

She rubs my arm with a few quick, firm strokes that warm the area before removing her arm and clapping once. "We can wallow here, or you can do something about it. What'll it be, kid? Do you plan to let her walk away again or are you going to fight for what matters to you?"

<hr>

I OPEN the door to Curl Up & Dye and brace myself to be confronted by one of the icy Salvatore women. Chiara and Tina are arguing, and as I approach, the women turn to me, demanding I settle the dispute. I've been so lost in my rehearsed speech recitation that I missed the topic of the argument.

"Huh? I just, I need to talk to your mom or nonna. One of them here?"

Laughing, Tina yells for her mom, who replies with a dismissive and irritated "Basta! Enough! Figure out your own drama, girls." In the same breath, Ava Marie beckons me. "You." She waves me deeper into the shop.

I find myself sitting at the wood and gold cafe table with a navy ceramic cup in front of me, along with a saucer and engraved gold spoon. The place smells like the coffee and ammonia, along with hints of shampoo and bleach. The combination is overwhelming, making me a bit lightheaded.

"*Cin, cin.* Drink up. From what we hear, you have had quite the weekend," Ava Marie coos as she and Anna Lucia smirk.

With a deep breath, I open my phone's notes app. I can't mess up, so I need to reference my list. As much as my palms are sweating, this is my only chance at redemption, so I have to take it.

I need to grovel and sweep her off her feet, like Lloyd Dobler with his giant boombox. So I adjust the brightness, ignoring their scowls. I'm mad at myself already. The angrier I am about my inability to spit it out, the harder it is to speak. My brain is preparing to take off in a million circles when Sofia walks by and plucks my phone from my hands.

She locks the device and puts it screen-side down on the table. Then, with her hands on her hips, she goads me. "We all know this is about your love for the pyromaniac, so spit it out."

"Wow, okay, Sof. That makes me regret all the times I didn't rat you out for trying to extend your time with the TV while I babysat. Or for the extra scoops of ice cream or the hundreds of questions you asked about boys before you were allowed to date." I try to mirror her smug but charming smile. Faking the self-assurance helps calm my nerves. "Do you want me to go on, Sofia Giovanna Marie Salvatore?"

She eyes her mother. "He's lyin'. Don't worry."

To Anna Lucia's credit, she waves a hand at her youngest daughter in dismissal. "We'll discuss later. Go upstairs to start the salon laundry. Let us handle this."

She says *this* like our conversation is the equivalent of a pile of radioactive waste.

When Sofia is out of earshot, Ava Marie turns to her daughter with a look of disbelief. "Really? You're going to hold a nineteen-year-old to something stupid she did at nine?"

Lips pursed, Anna Lucia stews in thought.

Ava Marie, however, smirks coyly, waiting patiently for the reply she knows will come.

"Ma, come on," Anna Lucia finally says. "You know I can't teach her a lesson if I just coddle her feelin's. She ain't just waltz'n' in here as if she didn't do something wrong. Wrong is wrong."

A smiling Ava locks eyes with me, and I silently pray the look means she's not interested in what another young woman did ten years ago.

"You're right. I'd like to explain, if you don't mind." Over the years, I've learned that some folks need to be given a false sense of control. The Salvatore women are used to calling the shots, so deference to their position will give me the best chances of succeeding.

I wait quietly for her permission to plead my case. Thankfully,

Ava Marie gives a curt nod while snapping a sugar-dusted pizzelle in half and dipping it into her cappuccino.

"Ten years ago, I helped cause the problems between Lily, Grant, and Landan," I admit. "I was too scared to tell anyone what I knew, so I withheld important information from the Long family and didn't stop the wedding. It isn't fair to punish Lily. For years, she's been hiding in embarrassment. I know our relationship makes me seem biased." I scratch the back of my neck. "But..." I sigh. "Lily was the town-wide scapegoat. If you think back and *really* reflect on how it all went down, you'll see that Lily was being hit from every direction. If we are being honest with ourselves and our maker, the fault lies with all of us. We abandoned her during a time when she needed us most."

Ava Marie's usual mask of indifference flickers, but she steels herself while Anna Lucia swipes her hair out of her eyes absently, as if distracting herself.

I wait in deafening silence, and when I can't handle the anticipation any longer, I fill the silence with the first words that come to mind. "I'll take her place. Six hours is what she owes, right? I'll do it. Provided I get meals and bathroom breaks. I can't make her forgive me, but I need to make this right. Punish me, not her."

Both women scrutinize me, stone-faced.

Heart thumping and stomach in knots, I smooth the fabric of my black T-shirt over and over. It takes all my willpower to stay put where I am. The urge to pace the room as they have a silent conversation is nearly impossible to suppress. Sweat beads on my brow and the back of my neck, then under my arms. If this takes much longer, I'll be nothing but a puddle to be mopped up.

Anna Lucia nibbles on the hard edge of her cookie, creating a sharp crunching sound. The sound of water running through pipes and mechanical humming begins, signaling that Sofia has started the washer.

An eternity goes by as I wait. My impatience grows with each ticking second. In fact, the seconds are literally ticking. Without music playing in the shop, the sound of the wall clock is deafening, and when combined with Anna Lucia chewing and the hissing noises of the appliances, it's enough to drive a man insane.

Finally, she nods. Fine, Ma, you win," she says. "Whatever you decide to do from here, I'll back you. But you know that James Kelly will have a fuckin' field day with this. He prides himself on being the first to know things. If I bring this to him, I'm gonna have to sit through another one of his long-winded diatribes. Which means you and Pop have to come to me for gravy one Sunday." She stands, drops a napkin onto the chair, and storms up the steps.

With Anna Lucia gone, Ava Marie smirks. "We'll be in touch with next steps. Pleasure as always doing business with the Hendrix family."

Knowing I still need more help, I head back to my parents with my tail between my legs.

forty-nine
Lily

A VET TECH greets me when I open the door, though Jim is at his desk, which can be seen through cutouts in the wall.

I take a deep breath and let it out slowly. "Can I get a few minutes with Mayor Kelly, please?"

The tech frowns, and I'm certain she'll deny me, but then a woman calls out from the back, requesting I join them.

The tech assures me that they'll prepare Pete to come home, but the uncomfortable pinch to her face worries me.

When I discover former Mayor James, Jim's dad, and Ava Marie Salvatore sitting in the guest chairs across from Jim, my stomach plummets. This is a much larger audience than I wanted, but there's no running now.

In a surprisingly polite gesture, Jim pushes his desk chair back and stands in greeting. Clearing his throat, James rises and excuses himself. "I will let you handle the town's affairs as you see fit, son. Just be sure to follow the code and do not feel bad for being the voice of reason."

He doesn't acknowledge Ava Marie or me before stomping out of the office and nearly tripping over the lead the vet tech has put on Pete.

Good. What an asshole.

Pete pulls on the leash, moving closer and stretching toward me, his tail wagging. I kneel and scratch at his head, then take the lead and turn back to the room.

"I hope he was good for you all this weekend," I say. "You know, for a stubborn Shiba with a tendency to run away." With a shrug and a small smirk, I add, "You know, like mother like son, which is what I wanted to discuss, and since your dad and Ava Marie are here, I assume you do too."

They both nod, and I swear Ava's mouth twitches in what could be a smile.

"Here's the deal." I try to keep my confidence but my legs shake. "Can I—" I gesture toward the chair because if I don't sit, I'm going to throw up or faint.

Another silent nod from them both.

Once I'm seated, I address the woman who has a hand in all town business, "Ava Marie, some of this is older than just the Grant stuff so I want to address that with Jim first."

She looks at me blankly, but I carry on, turning to the man on the other side of the desk. "Jim, I'm sorry we called you a narc for so long. I was upset that you ratted me out when I tried to throw that party. Do you know how much cajoling and begging it took from Stef and Nessa and me to convince our moms to let us have a sleepover at my place while our parents were out of town together? We couldn't understand the sabotage." I exhale, searching for every scrap of sincerity I possess. "But after hearing what your dad said as he left, I'm guessing you understand the pressure of being expected to be a perfect rule follower, too, don't you?"

The recognition in his eyes is a good sign.

"We're a lot alike, you and me. I was talked out of my dream of going to college with my bestie and shoved into a wedding gown. I ended up a stay-at-home wife in the wrong era. Outside of Carmine's cooking lessons, I was alone. I was friendless." I glance to Ava Marie, hoping to right that overdue acknowledgment. "Since I've been back, I've wanted to thank him, but I've been scared to approach him because then I'm approaching the whole family." Not that it makes it okay. "Please, let him know I've always been very appreciative of his kindness. I still suck at cooking."

I laugh, and Ava Marie's eyes twinkle just a little.

"Anyhow, do you know what really burned? And I'm not talking about the stupid hockey things. What hurt the most was the way everyone turned on me. It didn't matter that I had been cheated on and humiliated. I was labeled the problematic one, and that's why I left." My throat gets tight. "That first Christmas I called home, because I missed my family, and they made it clear they didn't want to hear from me."

My hands are shaking, my voice breaking, but I continue on.

"I realize now that being isolated like that was a far worse punishment than the stocks would have been. And this weekend, I discovered that Grant showed up to the wedding knowing he was in love with someone else. He should have never gone through with it. The lack of punishment for him is truly the most—" A sob threatens to escape me, but I choke it back and open my hand, reading the words Delia wrote in Sharpie on it. "It was patriarchal, misogynistic, and predictable, despite the claims that our town is a liberal and progressive place."

Hot tears prick at the backs of my eyes. I can't be tough much longer, so I accept this is my fate.

Pete, sensing my discomfort, scoot back and presses against me.

"Thinking back over the last eight or nine months," I go on, letting my thoughts flow as they come, "I can see that River showed me this. I'm doing this for him too. I meant it when I said

I love him. He meant it when he said he loved me. He just... messed up by not telling me. I know I can bend without breaking. I can be soft and strong at the same time." Self-consciousness hits hard. Maybe I should have kept those thoughts to myself. But it's too late now, so I go on. "Can we skip the festival-adjacent fanfare to get my punishment over with quietly? Consider a shorter amount of time since I was away for so long? And I insist I get breaks for meals and to use the bathroom."

Above Jim's head there's a standard graduation photo, where he's dressed in a cap and gown and flanked by his parents. Then there's his wedding a few years ago, and his firstborn. Vacations with family. A typical dude-bro photo where he's holding a giant fish in the air, his buddies clinking beer bottles together in the distance. He may not be a teenager anymore, but at thirty, this man is also not exactly the most sympathetic figure.

I'm not exactly sure the feminist rant I included will curry favor with him, but it's too late to change that now.

Tapping my thumb to each finger, I focus on breathing.

Finally Ava Marie breaks the silence. "Jim, stop messing with her. We've already discussed it." She eyes me. "Yes, Lily, we'll approve that. One of us will be in touch with the date and time, but I anticipate that it will be soon."

———

I KNEW they didn't want to put it off for fear that I'd changed my mind, but I didn't expect them to organize so quickly either. That conversation took place late Sunday afternoon, and by lunchtime on Monday, Pru had hand delivered instructions. In the canvas tote she handed me, I found a pink crystal rock, a satchel of loose-leaf tea with an infuser travel mug, and a pair of tall, thick socks with the high school logo on them.

The note included was in her ancient-looking scrawl:

Dearest Lily,

The Peacock Springs Council formally accepts your proposal and would like to complete your overdue community obligation this week. On Tuesday of this week, we request you appear at Curl Up & Dye promptly at 3:30 p.m. You will be escorted to town hall from there. Per your request, you will be allowed a break for dinner and the restroom at 6:30 p.m., and you'll complete the second half of your sentence afterward. Once you have completed the six-hour stay, you will be released. We will follow up with additional information on the subsequent six hours owed after this first set is completed.

Included here are a rose quartz crystal, the ingredients for an herbal tea I have customized for you, and socks that should help you avoid chafing. We ask that you prepare the tea to bring along and have the crystal with you.

Blessings,
Prudence Cleary

fifty
Lily

BY MONDAY NIGHT, I've practically melted into Delia and Nessa's couch, and I'm being a miserable oaf. The conversation I need to have with River will have to wait until after tomorrow's nonsense.

"I've got to do a little work in the office today. Do you need me to grab anything for you while I'm there?" Delia asks as she touches up her red lipstick in the mirror.

"I've got everything I need as far as I can tell, except for entertainment. Pretty sure I'll die of boredom if I'm forced to sit still for that long," I admit.

"I've got a plan for that." Nessa winks from her horizontal position across the armchair near me.

"Actually, maybe grab me a few things." I pick up my phone. "I'll text you a list."

After a while, I convince Nessa to take a walk to Pages with me. As we enter, Seth barely looks up from his current read.

"Yo, Seth. Customers," Nessa teases him.

He only grunts in response.

Here and there, signs that his sisters had input in decorating are obvious. There's a large seating area with a mix of plush chairs and two-seaters near a refurbished coffee table. There's lots of low lighting, and the shelves are a soft natural wood color, reminding me of a ballet studio floor.

When we arrived, I noticed there was a large *blooming again soon* sign in the window of the florist shop, which has been closed indefinitely.

"Any idea who is taking over for Rosie? I'm shocked that she retired."

His scowl deepens, but he doesn't respond, and before we can prod him further, the door chimes and a group of tourists wanders in. Seth does his best impression of a pleasant salesperson while we make our way through the rows of bookshelves. Once I've decided on an interesting-sounding memoir, I head back to the front to pay.

fifty-one
River

I'M ANXIOUSLY PACING the basement stockroom in an effort to work on inventory—code for *I want to be left alone*—when Delia walks in.

She stares me down with her arms crossed but says nothing.

"Get it over with. She's gone? It's my fault, right?" I scrub my face. "Fuck, I really screwed up." I go back to dusting bottles. The bottles I've already thoroughly dusted. As the silence stretches on, my jitters get more violent.

"I'm going to do her time in the stocks for her." I tug my phone out of my pocket and check the time. "Soon. I'm waiting for Anna Lucia. It might not fix things, but I need to do something." I fidget more as I continue. "I know it won't save us, but maybe it will take one obstacle away. Make it easier."

The silence stretches on, like Delia is letting me spin out.

I eat it up. "God dammit, I didn't want to hurt her, Deals. I didn't tell her because I couldn't find the right time," I say, my voice loud and deep as my anger surges.

The desire to prove something to Delia as a proxy for Lily grows with each statement.

"I tried, you know. I really, really tried. I was just afraid she'd run away. And I didn't want to hurt her."

"Telling her was going to hurt her no matter what," she interjects.

"Yeah," I sigh. "I know."

"You could have told one of us. Seth, Lee, Stef, Nessa. Your mom. Me. We would have helped." Delia matches my temper. "Ugh. Men, I swear. Why do we put up with you all?" She tosses her hands up. "Lily has already decided she's staying. She went to the elders just like you did. She's waiting for Prudence. Holy fuck. You said soon?"

She darts closer, nearly toppling a box of empty bottles for the next batch.

We catch it in the nick of time and recognition flashes between us. Lily and I will both be locked in. Together.

"Okay, boss, this is your chance. So you're gonna go up to the apartment and take a shower. And calm the fuck down. You look like hell. Listen to me," she demands. "No, dumbass, she isn't mad at you. She was shocked by the idea that it could have been prevented. She's angry that Grant didn't own up to his own shit. Does it suck that you didn't tell her? Sure. Fortunately for you, she's not running. So take this opportunity, because you won't have one like it again."

Jaw slack, I replay her words, my feet rooted to the spot.

"She told us she's done letting anyone—not her parents, not her ex, not the curmudgeons living here—keep her from the people who love her. The people she loves. That list of people includes you, but you already know that."

I nod and mumble *she loves me* like I haven't heard it before.

"Your anxiety is all kinds of misplaced, dude. Did you talk to your mom?"

I nod again, unable to get words past my dry throat.

"So Elizabeth helped you make a plan, and you went to the Salvatores? Looks like they went to the Kellys who were waiting for Lily to pick up Peter Pan from boarding. Prudence dropped off a bunch of very Pru things to Lily this morning, like soccer socks for padding," she says.

"Oh, that's smart. I should dig out mine," I interject.

"Go. Prep, because you'll both be trapped there all afternoon and evening. Maybe you can both come clean about any remaining secrets. It's obvious you're good for each other. She's slowing down, and you? Look at this place. Look at what you made. You've implemented so much since your visit to Denver. If I see it, then I bet Elizabeth does too."

She bores holes into me with her glare, and then in the next breath, she perks up, her face brightening. "Anyway, I came down to say I did the draft schedules for the coming month for you to review. Also, I did payroll and paid a few bills. We're still in the black. So really, there's only one thing left to do."

"Beg her for forgiveness?" I guess.

"Tell her the truth. The whole truth." She rolls her eyes. "Go get yourself locked in the stocks," she says. "God, why do they even want to use them? Ugh, this town is so fucking weird."

Shrugging, I say, "I don't know, but I love weird."

———

I RUN upstairs and take a quick shower, trim my beard, and apply deodorant and a light amount of cologne. I jump into a pair of jeans and a bar shirt, then add a pair of old soccer socks, just like Delia said Pru told Lily to do. Running shoes on and Mets hat pulled low, I grab my phone and wallet and walk toward the salon.

The entire Salvatore family is there. Looks like nobody wants to miss this show.

On Tina's iPad, and influencer is discussing the latest makeup trends and tips.

"Isn't that the school Delia went to in London?" Sofia says. "She learned about events and bridal. Could be good for one of us to learn too. Maybe?"

I'm curious to hear what they say about Delia, but now is not the time, so I jog upstairs to the office.

James Kelly is already here and so is—

"Mom?"

"Hi, honey. I was on the committee that year. Don't you remember? I'm here on official business. Let's get this over with," she says, her tone firm. "George River Hendrix, do you hereby swear to replace Lily Jayne Long in the stocks?"

I nod, confused, and Mom continues. "Do you hereby authorize the township of Peacock Springs to record this in public records for posterity?" Face softening, she uses an easier tone. "You need to say yes for it to count for her."

"All right." I nod once. "Yes."

She matches the gesture, then resumes her mothering tone. "Just say yes to all of this so we can get a move on. You want to be first there. Pru's doing this with her now too."

Blinking a few times, I nod. "Right, right. Yes. I agree to whatever else you have on there. As long as it includes bathroom breaks and food breaks. That's my condition."

The three officials laugh.

"What is with you two? Both of you keep questioning this. Do you really think we want to see you covered in your own mess? Text me if you need to go."

James and Ava Marie head downstairs while Mom takes me by the elbow and leads me to a second set of stairs at the side of the building.

This set leads to the dim alley between the salon and Pages. Ahead of us, the door to the bookstore opens and Seth appears, hauling trash bags toward the shared dumpster.

"Good luck." Smirking, he walks away.

Mom gives me a quick hug, then pulls back, her hands on my arms, and looks at me with a soft fondness that is usually reserved for graduations or big accomplishments.

"River, we have a minute before this kicks off, and I wanted to say…" She swallows thickly, her eyes going misty.

Based on her expression, one would think she was shipping me off to war and not to sit on my ass in the middle of town for three hours.

"You've really grown into your name. You go with the flow. You come and go as you need and don't fight nature, choosing to simply wind or bend around obstacles. Don't bend this time. You've stepped up for the bar, for our family, and for me. It's time to step up for yourself and for her. You don't want to lose her again." She squeezes my arms hard, almost shaking me.

"But how can I be sure she'll forgive me?"

"You can't ever be sure. But no one is perfect. Look at your dad and me. We're not always on the same page. But we don't let the hard things keep us from each other. Frankly, when you do that, you hurt yourself. You've been trying to prove yourself by doing it on your own, when asking for help was the biggest sign of your growth." She musses my hair, brushing it off my forehead.

"Mom." I swat her hand, but my tone is soft.

"Thank you for asking me for help," she says. "Belinda and Neal seem to have moved to their beach house temporarily. Between us, I think that's for the best. I'm trying, but she's not budging. You'll need to keep being Lily's advocate, but also her friend and her partner, which means telling her the truth even when it's hard. It means you'll need to hear the truth too. So if you are ready to commit to being the kind of man we raised you to be, then let's go."

She places a hand on my cheek, giving me the same kind of look Lee's mom gave him when they got engaged. She's releasing me fully to someone else's care.

I can't get my words out, so I nod, then let her guide me into the sunlight.

Arm in arm, we approach the back of the square across from town hall, where the two cement pillars stand on either side of the wood plank. It's unlocked, and James and Miss Nicole are holding the top half so I have access to rest my ankles in the wells made for them.

I sit on the cement bench and stretch my legs, getting situated.

From here the archway of the Featherweight is visible. The sidewalk where Lily crashed into me months ago and turned my life upside down winds its way through the grass before me. To my left is the florist, Seth and Gemma's businesses in their shared space, and the salon. Over my right shoulder is Coffee Crumbs and town hall. Then along the side of the park is the library, the fitness studio, the vet clinic, and the peacock pond and house. Over my left shoulder, Beagle's Bagels, Pru's tea and tarot shop, and the butcher shop are out of sight, but they're not far.

Everywhere I look, townsfolk gawk, pressing against windows and loitering on sidewalks.

The clock on my phone reads three fifteen when Lily and Nessa round the corner of the salon, Lily clutching a tote bag for dear life. Outside, Jim stands, wearing scrubs, along with Prudence.

After the last forty-eight hours, it is hard to not want to run over and hold her close.

She's wearing a pair of black leggings and a large white T-shirt covered by an open zip-up hooded sweatshirt in a deep teal. On her feet, she's wearing a pair of soccer socks with our high school logo on them: one purple, the other blue. She's come out in full force with our town colors, that's for certain.

Her outfit is completed by a pair of white fashion sneakers. She has her usually large wavy hair pulled into a ponytail through the loop of a baseball cap and dark sunglasses covering those beautiful coffee-colored eyes.

She shakes hands with Jim, then opens the bag and holds it out to Pru, who inspects its contents. When Lily pulls out a travel mug, Pru's smile widens.

Has she noticed yet? My heart thunders loudly as they make the short walk my way.

fifty-two
Lily

"LET'S GET THIS OVER WITH," I say to Pru, focus fixed on my shoes.

"Hand me the crystal, please," she replies.

"Why?" I ask as I dig it out of the tote she gave me.

Cackling like the witch folks believe her to be, she takes the quartz from me. "For someone who loves Peter Pan, I expected you to understand that magic comes from a little faith and trust. If all else fails, there's always pixie dust." She shakes her head at her own joke.

I give her a tight smile and follow as she leads me down the road. At the edge of the green, I finally work up the nerve to look at the stocks, only to find a man already sitting in one of the two seats.

"What the—" My heart lurches, then leaps. "River?"

He waves toward the second spot. "Nice of you to join me, darling. Please have a seat."

"Not my monkeys, not my circus. Sorry, sweetheart. Looks

like I'm not needed," Nessa says with a pat to my back. With a wave, she heads off.

Prudence bumps me forward.

Looks like it's time to pay the piper and hear him out. I would love nothing more than to turn on my heel and run. As one exit strategy after another forms in my mind, Pru bumps me again, urging me to take a sip of the warm concoction in the mug.

"What is this, anyway?" I ask as I bring it to my lips for another taste.

"Just an herbal tea that will help you stay calm, dear. It's nothing magical. The magic was always within you. Go be the bravest of us all."

Once I've lowered myself onto the bench, she takes the crystal from my hand and gives it to River. "Looks like you need this more than she does. I'm sure Lily won't mind sharing with you." On a wink, she takes off toward her shop.

Heart thumping, I meet his gaze. He looks as shy as I feel.

Neither of us speaks as James and Miss Nicole approach and fit the top half of the stocks into place and Ava Marie approaches with a heavy brass padlock.

She attempts to kneel so she can click it into place, but before she can lower herself to the ground, Jim jumps in. "Let me do this for you, so you don't hurt yourself." His polite anxiety suggests a mix of respect and fear, her favorite combination, and she acquiesces easily.

With a heavy metal clink, our sentence begins. We're locked in for three hours together with nowhere to go. The crowd disappears, as promised, making no public ceremony. No additional attention is given to these weird circumstances.

We sit silently as the looky-loos in every shop spy on us, the tension between us ratcheting up.

"We have three hours," River finally says, his tone light. "Come on, Lily. Let's take this on. As a team." He inches closer to me, and like he's done so many times before, he deftly laces our fingers together and gives a squeeze.

I want to be angry at him, but with the condo across the lawn and the willowy shadow watching from the window that was once my home, I realize I can't keep rejecting people with the hope that I won't get hurt again.

The silence stretches on this way, our hands clasped, eyes flickering from passersby to one another.

After a while, I finally relent. "Why?" I whisper, the word shaky. "Why do you want to be a team? I've never been anyone's first choice. I'm not a keeper. I'm temporary. A stopover on the way to adulthood, before real things. Why do you want to do this?" The confusion and self-loathing I've held for so many years spill out of my throat, my chest aching.

"Because, Lily, I love you," he says, squeezing my hand harder with each word. The third squeeze is so hard it almost hurts, but it grounds me in the moment. "I always have, darling. And I'm pretty confident I always will. If you run off again and want me to chase you, then that's what I'll do. Or I'll wait. I'll be here, hoping you show up and bump into me again. Hoping for a second, third, or fourth chance. As many as you'll give me."

I swallow thickly and take in his beautiful teal eyes and earnest expression. With him here, I can forget that I'm being scrutinized by at least a dozen people. I focus on his firm grasp and his rich baritone, and within seconds, my heart rate slows and a calm washes over me. It feels like a religious experience, like I'm bathing in his love.

"Mom walked me over here," he says, his tone soft and low. For me alone. "She said that an important part of being together is accepting that we're going to keep messing up and continuing to choose each other anyway. We have to be honest, no matter how hard it is. We can't run away from talking to each other. I hate that I kept this secret from you."

Silent tears track down my cheeks as his words sink in.

"This has been destroying me since the moment I saw you in that white gown. Tipping you off about the meeting in the bar was selfish. I was trying to alleviate my own guilt. Yes, we talked here and there after that, but our friendship faded because every time we'd talk, I would consider confessing and then get scared. I never wanted to hurt you." His eyes are teary now too. "And getting to really know you again only made it worse. When I visited you in Denver, I knew that the stories you shared and the photos you posted were even more curated than we could imagine. Thinking about you alone for Christmas, for ten Christmases, broke my heart."

These words are breaking mine and sewing it back together in the process.

"I'm sitting here because I deserve this, not you. I should have stopped you. Called him out for being a moron. Maybe it's wrong of me, but I'm really fucking glad he's such an asshat. It means he wasn't smart enough to really see you." His gaze intensifies and he leans in close. "He's missed out on dozens of moments that I wouldn't trade for anything."

Trying to deflect the heaviness of this moment with teasing, I ask, "Not even in return for Jonathan's stamp of approval?"

He doesn't blink. "Not for a million of them. I wouldn't trade sitting with you, here, for any *damn thing*."

His hand tightens on mine, like he needs me as much as I need him in this moment.

Exhaling, I hold on tighter. "I-I… I'm not good at talking when it's like this. So big and important. There isn't anything that would make me doubt you. I need you to know that. I was trying to make a joke to lighten the mood because I don't want anyone to see me cry."

He tugs me closer and kisses my cheek chastely.

I breathe deep a few more times and let my words fall out in their typical rambling waves. "I can't believe you are sitting here. I can't believe that I am sitting here. It's not so much that I doubted you; I doubted me. I doubted that I was worth the hassle. Even I exhaust myself sometimes. I'm tired of moving all the time. I'm tired of missing out on important milestones and wondering what I could have done differently. Before Atlantic City, I kept thinking about the idea of ten years from now…"

I tilt my head up, though I can't quite meet his eyes. I get as far as his chin, because looking at someone in such an emotionally charged moment is a struggle.

"I considered whether I could picture a future here, with our friends, with their future families. Could I be there, wearing your ring, watching Pete steal snacks from kids playing nearby?"

Struggling to breathe a little, I look straight ahead and survey the Featherweight, garnering the strength to answer honestly, like he asked.

"It scares, but I think maybe we could get there. I don't know if I'll want a wedding, but a life with you? A partnership, traveling, maybe taking over for Miss Nicole when she's ready to retire? Yeah." My breath comes out easy now, my chest loosening, my shoulders lowering. "Yeah, I think I would like that a whole lot, darling."

———

WE'RE QUIET FOR A WHILE, but when Landan's silhouette appears behind sheer curtains in what was Grant's office when I lived there, I can't help but scoff.

"Are you fucking kidding me?" *What is this chick's problem?*

Nessa pops up across the wooden boards, between our feet, her smile impish.

"Don't worry about that C U Next Tuesday," Nessa adds, popping up beside her. Rumor is that she's about to deal with karma." With a wink, she heads off.

"That what?" River asks me.

"I think it's from an old TV show. C U Next Tuesday is a euphemism for cunt."

Our friend group congregates in front of Pages, each bringing a seat along with them. Seth doesn't even seem mad about it, which may be the most surprising thing at this moment.

Before we know it, the mail carrier is doing the usual loop of the square. He finishes at the set of mailboxes for Grant's condo and the apartments he owns above the rest of the buildings on the block, then heads off.

Nessa whistles, snagging my attention and makes a V with her index and middle fingers, pointing at her eyes and then the mailboxes.

The condo door opens, causing a summery wreath to bounce and the nautical door knocker to clunk. Then Landan makes her way gracefully down the steps. Her long brown hair is flawlessly straight, not a single flyaway or strand out of place. She's in her usual all-black outfit. Wearing a smug, tight expression, she glances at us, though she quickly looks away. It's funny that she could miss how her actions made her the villain in my story for so long.

With a key, she unlocks their mailbox. She takes out a gift box and immediately rips open the perforated strip. As if controlled by a spring-loaded device, the top flies away. Then it's raining glitter and confetti. I can't contain my laughter as the cloud of glitter smacks her in the face.

The wind sends the confetti flying, and then tiny multicolored penises are fluttering around us.

She yanks a bag from the box, and in red letters large enough to read from here, it says *Eat A Dick*. Shrieking, she drops the box and the bag and darts into the house. A second scream follows shortly thereafter, and Nessa whistles again to get my attention and winks.

Prudence arrives with an old iron key, large and heavy. "Get out of here now," she says, eyeing Nessa. "And do not tell me how you managed that, you hear? Let Elizabeth and me handle the committee. As far as we're concerned, you did the hard thing. You talked it out. So welcome home, Lily. I missed you."

The lock pops open, and then Lee and Seth are there, lifting the board.

Slowly, we stand. It takes a minute to find our bearings. It's like stepping onto solid ground after a long boating trip. When we're steady, we run toward the Featherweight, shrieking with laughter.

Once inside, Delia heads behind the bar. Her shirt is tied up into a knot over high-waisted jeans, and she's wearing a pinup headband. She's clearly been preparing, as there is a full spread of the best bar snacks laid out.

Seth joins her and uncaps bottles for us all.

"Stef, you're on music," Delia orders. "It's time to celebrate the official return of Peacock Springs, New Jersey's number one firecracker. The girl who has a heart almost as big as her hair, Miss Lily Jayne Long."

Cheers bounce off the walls, and I bask in the warmth of my friends' affection. All the years of stress and worry that had begun to melt now evaporate completely. The love these people have for me fills me to the brim. There is a rush of footsteps, and then I'm crushed from all sides.

Delia and Seth pass out drinks as a familiar drum beat pumps through the speakers, and the joy in the room swells greater than before. In a rare moment of boisterousness from Lee and Seth, they belt out the lyrics from our teenage anthem. The introductory bars shift into the pre-chorus lines about bars closing and carrying each other home. Home.

I am finally home.

Glasses are lifted, and the room bursts as the chorus begins and we sing about setting the world on fire.

The irony is not lost on any of us. I dissolve into hysterical giggles as we make toasts and clink bottles.

This is not the kind of evening that'll lead to hangovers. Our first round is followed by water and snacks. We sing along to song after song as we each take control of the music, mixing songs from our three decades of life. When the snacks are depleted and the plates are loaded into the dishwasher, Stef yawns and tells Lee she can't stay awake another minute.

Nessa looks at her phone and rolls her eyes, heading for the exit. Delia ropes Seth into taking out the trash with her and shoos us out the back door.

"Boss," she says, "go home. We got this." As she shuts the door on us, she says, "I don't want to see you here before noon, River. I will lock you out of your own place."

fifty-three
River

"YOU GOT IT." I shout to the already closed door.

Having her to lean on these last months has been huge. I won't look the gift horse in the mouth. The only mouth I want to be focused on is Lily's.

Placing my palm on her cheek, I tilt her head until our eyes meet. Her lips are plump, the familiar freckles visible in the moonlight. I press a gentle kiss on the middle of her forehead, then another on the tip of her nose.

"Thank you for staying. If I'd lost you again, I don't think I could have survived. Can I take you home, please?"

With a gentle nod, she kisses me.

Rather than take her home, I pin her against the side of the bar and capture her lips again.

Breaking our kiss, she places a palm on my chest. "Home," she breathes. "Take me home."

With a boyish grin, I tease, "Are you admitting that you *like me*, Lily?"

"I've already told you: I love you, you goofball," she chides.

"Yes, but you *like* me. You want to spend your time with me. You want to be on that picnic blanket with me in ten years. So does that mean you're mine?"

Determination flashes in her eyes. This woman is strong, like I always knew she could be. "No, it means that I'm *mine*." Gaze softening, she adds, "Just like you are yours. But when the two of us are together, life is better. It means that this team we started in elementary school is in it for the long haul. That when one of us struggles, the other will step up and give gentle support. So, no. I'm not yours, but this right here is ours." With another soft kiss, she says, "Let's go home."

Halfway to the cottage, she barks out a laugh.

"Hey. Maybe I'll finally buy myself a hamper."

———

AS WE TUMBLE INSIDE, all I can think about is how badly I need to get this woman naked.

She unzips her hoodie, and as she steps out of her shoes, she frowns at me. "Why are you staring?"

"I just really like this view. You, comfortable in our home." I shrug. "I also really want to get you out of all of these clothes and make up for all the time we lost."

With a wicked smile, she pushes her leggings and socks off, leaving them on the floor. It's like that first night all over again, with another T-shirt draped across her thighs and swimming over her, hiding all the places I've come to know so well. My patience tonight is nonexistent, and we don't make it beyond the staircase.

Hands on her hips, I guide her to sit a few steps up. Then I spread her legs wide, exposing the thin strip of material between me and her soft, warm pussy. Clutching the armholes of her ridiculous top, I pull it up, exposing her stomach and then the tattoo on her ribs.

She's seated before me in nothing more than a set of comfortable yet incredibly sexy lingerie. The mesh bralette and thong are a shade of midnight blue that matches the wall to my left perfectly.

Sighing, she caresses the growing bulge at the front of my jeans. The touch reminds me that because I dressed so quickly, I'm at risk of finding myself in a very uncomfortable position with my zipper, so I pop the button. But I wait for her to drag my zipper down, aching for her to free me from this denim prison.

She skillfully lowers the fly, then slips her hand beneath my waistband.

She hisses my name as she realizes that there isn't a second layer there keeping me from her. Gently, she eases my pants down my thighs. With much rougher movements, I yank my T-shirt off.

Dropping her elbows to the step, she falls back on an angle. She looks commanding. She's still in the thin layer, and as much as I want to rip the fabric off her body, I want to worship at her feet more.

Kneeling at the bottom of the stairs, I dip my head to her bent knees.

With her left foot lifted, I kiss her ankle, then her calf and behind her knee. Then I start over on the other side. When I sink my teeth into the inside of her thigh, I'm rewarded with a soft whimper, and her knees fall open farther.

"Stop teasing me," she growls. "The last few nights without you were torture enough."

Standing, I give myself a slow, lazy stroke. Teasing her without touching her. Fully taking charge like this is freeing. With each pump of my shaft, the damp spot on her panties grows. It's clear that despite her bratty words, this is working for her too. Angling in, I drag my hands across the soft skin of her stomach and around her ribs, stopping to trace the tattoo, the reminder of how she carried our home with her all along.

"I fucking love this," I grit out.

Her only response is a low groan.

Plucking at one taut nipple, I kneel and lick the other, nipping and laving it through the thin mesh.

Kissing lower, I draw a line down her stomach to her core. As I lap at the material, I dip my fingers into the elastic at her hips and pull the panties away. Her flavor bursts on my tongue as I lick her button of nerves. It's intoxicating. She's intoxicating. She moans in appreciation, unwinding slightly below me.

"I need to be inside you," I admit, despite the way I've been drawing things out.

"Thank fucking god," she laughs.

Grasping her rib cage, I flip her over, and when she's got her elbows planted on one step and her knees on the one closest to the floor, I stand behind her and fist her wild waves.

I gently guide her head back, looming over her. "If you tell me no more, I'll stop immediately."

She nods, though she quickly grits out, "Don't you fucking stop."

I yank lightly on her hair and smack her ass, eliciting a gasp from her.

She shudders, her pussy absolutely soaked. "Fuck, darling. You like that, huh?"

She's barely coherent, but she moans as I slide home hard and fast. I've never felt so right. Her warmth is welcoming, her muscles contracting, encouraging me more with each thrust.

"Fucking incredible," I say, mindless as I increase the pace. "So fucking wet for me. You like that, huh? You like to give up control? You like to be fucked until you can't move? Until you become a little rag doll?" I yank on her hair, noting the way her eyes have glazed over.

Her walls tense around me, and my balls follow suit. My leg muscles clench, and a tingly sensation builds at the base of my spine.

I yank her hair again, and she screams my name.

"Don't you fucking dare stop. I'm right there." She presses her forehead to the step and shifts her hips back, taking me deeper.

I release her hair and slip my hand around her hip, searching for that tiny button between her legs. When I find it, I add pressure, sending her soaring higher. The two of us are panting, sweating, and screaming before long, and then she's shaking around me. Falling forward, she practically pulls me by my dick on top of her. There's no moving, no talking, just this moment of being fully sated.

Grabbing a discarded shirt, I pull myself free and wipe her off, then myself.

Leaning forward, I whisper, "Wait right here."

I pop into the bathroom to run warm water over a washcloth for her, but before I can dart back to her, she appears in the mirror behind me.

"Sorry." She blushes. "Can I…" She ducks her head. "Um, I need to pee." After a beat she adds, "I realize we went from friends to cohabiting quickly, but I'd like to pee alone if that's okay with you."

Laughing, I shake my head and smile. I leave the washcloth on the edge of the sink, then step out and shut the door.

I owe this girl a lot. Including a little more romance. A lot more. It's time I make a plan, just for Lily.

epilogue
River

LILY COLLECTS her things and gives me a kiss, then she's out the door, headed to have her hair and makeup done with the girls.

The guys are headed out to play nine holes on the venue golf course, so I hop in the shower. As I'm drying off, my phone dings.

LILY:

Hey! Nessa isn't here. She's probably getting coffee or a mimosa, but if you bump into her, will you tell her that Stef is starting to worry?

RIVER:

No problem. I'll keep my eyes peeled

BEFORE I CAN LOCK my phone, another message appears. This time it's from Seth.

I CHUCKLE. Guess that makes my next stop Mateo's room. I knock, and when he doesn't answer right away, I assume he's still passed out, so I use his second key. He gave it to me last night so I could drop things off after dinner.

The last time I saw him, he and Nessa and Delia were playing a drinking game that seemed to consist mostly of Delia handing them tequila shots and making them confess things.

The keypad beeps, the light flickers green, and the gears turn, the door unlocking. As I push the door open, I'm met with a little resistance. His pants. Looks like he left them lying just inside the room. I stick my arm around the door and pick them up. Then I step inside. A few feet in, I discover a silk dress on the floor. Scrubbing my hand over my face, I call out so Mateo and his bedmate have time to cover up. I'd rather not see anyone naked today but Lily.

"Hey, co-best man, we can't be late for golf with your sister's father-in-law. Lee doesn't have brothers, so it's a big deal for you to show up and be your usual charming self." As I fumble for the light switch to wake him, a woman shrieks. Looks like his friend from last night is awake. That is good. Gotta get her out of here first, I suppose.

"Don't." she yells, but it's too late. The overhead light flips on, and I come face-to-face with Nessa Rabin. Wide-eyed, frozen with the sheet over her chest, messy hair and melted makeup on her face, an angry Nessa stares like a bull about to charge.

"Fuck, River. No. Please. You can't tell anyone. This was a one-time thing," she swears. "It won't happen again."

She shoves Mateo, and he startles. As he tumbles off the side of the bed, I catch a glimpse of a lot more of him than I bargained for.

Grabbing a pillow to cover his junk, he grins up at me. "What's up, dude? Can we get a little privacy?"

Nessa groans while I try to hold back my laughter.

"Morning. I'd love to give you time to go again, but Mr. Carter expects us downstairs in ten. I'd hop in the shower. Nessa, Lily said Stef is looking for you in the bridal suite. Should I tell her I found you?"

Simultaneously, they shout, "No."

They talk over each other, begging me to keep this to myself.

Overwhelmed by their ranting, I toss my hands in the air.

"Fuck this. Not again. I'm not the group's secret keeper. Also, I'm in a relationship, so loophole." I leave the room, letting the door slam loudly behind me.

the end

fighting
chapter one

nessa
Present | Labor Day Weekend

"People, people," Jim Kelly, mayor of Peacock Springs and town veterinarian, calls from the makeshift dais in front of the floor-to-ceiling mirrors in the dance studio. He runs his hands through his wiry hair and adjusts his tortoise-shell glasses. He's wearing charcoal-gray scrubs covered in tufts of pet hair, clearly having come straight from work. Unceremoniously flipping a binder open, he tries again to quiet the room.

This school year, meetings moved from the local bar and restaurant, The Featherweight, to Lily Long's dance studio. Like most changes in a tiny town, it has taken some getting used to.

Now that Lily is seated in her new place up front, I can't join her, so I crane my neck, searching for another friend to sit with. My roommate, Delia, is in the back of the room, looking two seconds away from falling asleep after a long weekend tending bar. She gives a quick wave, but I know she's not moving.

Where is everyone? I check again, finding my dad and brother Shua, but neither of my other two siblings are anywhere in sight.

"We'll start with last week's business," Jim says. "Then we'll move into establishing committee leads for the upcoming Sunflower Festival. From there, we'll discuss the upcoming sale of the Morgans' full real estate portfolio, including the undeveloped lands on the north side of town." Clearing his throat, he peers at someone at the back of the room, though I can't tell who it is from this angle. "Once we're finished, we'll open the floor to new business."

Beside me, a warm, solid body slides into the open seat, and a knee knocks mine. Without turning my head, I can make out a pair of cognac loafers and a large, well-manicured hand splayed over a thigh clad in black jeans.

It must be my lucky night. I groan internally and shift away from the man I haven't been able to avoid in the months since his sister's wedding.

Though I attempt to put space between us, the irritatingly attractive man I do not want to want leans closer.

"Quit it," I hiss when Mateo spreads his legs a bit wider, causing his thigh to graze mine.

With a fake yawn, he stretches his left arm out and drapes it over my chair. Now that he's exposed his ribs, I jab an elbow into his side, eliciting a yelp.

Don't laugh, don't laugh, don't laugh, I repeat to myself while trying to muffle the sound with my palm.

"Excuse me, Miss Rabin. Would you like to share what you find so funny?" Jim chides from the dais.

"It's Doctor Rabin," Mateo says before I can respond.

Well, damn.

"Sorry." I half-heartedly apologize.

"Don't be like that, Ivy," Mateo whispers. "I hoped I'd see you tonight. Can we talk after the meeting?"

While Jim moves on to the plans for this fall's Sunflower Fest, I try to tune out the electricity that prickles my skin because of the man at my side.

Clearly ignoring the vibes I'm giving off, Mateo rests his arm across my chair again, distracting me enough to cause me to miss which committee Jim is filling. I put my hand up, intending to ask him to repeat himself.

Rather than call on me, he grins and jots a note in his notebook. "Wonderful. Nessa Rabin will lead the volunteer teams this year. Who is willing to co-chair with her?"

I stare hard at Lily, begging her with my eyes to say yes. Come on, come on, don't let me get stuck with someone who has gross breath or is going to try to set me up with their grandson.

"Perfect. She'll be paired with Mateo Santos-Manolo," Jim announces, banging the gavel on the podium.

Oh no.

"Looks like I've got time to grow on you, Ivy," Mateo teases, giving me the boyish grin that did me in the one and only time we slept together. The grin that's a little lopsided and makes his deep dimples pop.

"Quit calling me that," I snap.

"You called yourself that." Chin lifted, he faces the front of the room again.

"Last order of business is the Morgan property divestment," Jim says from the podium.

"Good riddance," I grumble under my breath.

Beside me, Mateo snickers.

As Jim titters with excitement, he glances at the dark corner again.

Interesting. Do we have a surprise guest?

"In the coming weeks, Caleb Reynolds will be in town. He plans to present his development plans for the north side once he's gathered the necessary information. Please be kind and keep your gawking to a minimum while he's in town."

"Un-fucking-believable. Is this a Dickens novel?" I grumble. Apparently the ghosts of past mistakes have come to haunt me. This one in the form of my ex.

Is it just me, or is it getting harder to breathe?

"Fuck that guy." Mateo leans closer. "Not happening." He leaves tiny puffs of air on my neck. His lips nearly skim my ear, stirring feelings I'm not interested in revisiting.

"What do you have in mind—"

Before I can finish the question, he jumps to his feet.

"Mr. Santos-Manolo, can we help with something?" Jim asks, his tone stodgy.

Mateo adjusts the leather band of his wristwatch and clears his throat. "Yes, Jim. In fact, you can. As you know, I am a developer myself, and I'm familiar with the work the Reynolds Group does."

Jim continues to glance at that darker corner.

"They're from the city. Are we sure they're really the right group for a town like ours?" He lifts both brows. "I'd appreciate the opportunity to provide my own proposal. As a lifelong resident of this town, I want to ensure we keep the integrity and history of this place intact."

The room breaks into a round of applause, and on the other side of the room, his parents, Susan and Eddie, nod in approval.

"Call my office and schedule an appointment. We can talk about it then," Jim hollers over the din of the crowd.

Movement in my periphery catches my attention, and I turn in time to see Caleb step out from the dark corner. With Caleb "Satan's Bikini Waxer" Reynolds the Third lurking nearby, suddenly being this close to Mateo is a comfort. Not that I'd tell him that.

This is the first time I've seen him in years. Standing at six feet tall, with thick blond hair and wearing a navy suit, he looks every bit as devilish as my name for him.

He still looks like the boy I met at the Skull and Cross fraternity party, where he played up his family's rumored billions and their key place in society.

We dated through graduate school and while I completed a doctoral program in psychology. The longer we were together, the more dysfunctional, selfish, and possessive he proved himself to be. I squirm in my seat; my head drops and my muscles tense at the shameful memory. The old urge to withdraw from confronting the irony returns. I am a fraud. Despite focusing my academics and career on supporting healthy intimate relationships, I lingered in a toxic relationship out of convenience.

Standing in my hometown, Caleb looks equally out of place as I felt with him.

His family regularly made comments about my parents' background that left me uneasy. They'd toss in what they deemed compliments about my blond hair and tiny nose. The underlying meaning? In their eyes, I don't look Jewish. And they assumed that because my family is secular, it shouldn't be a big deal to give up our holidays. Couldn't I get on board with things like being married in their church, no rabbi needed? Couldn't I pretend my last name meant that I'm distantly related to a former prime minister? Because a connection like that would elevate my status for their optics.

The worst part was that Caleb didn't have any issue with any of it at all.

The Reynoldses wanted me to give up my identity and become a trophy on his arm. I had worked too hard to agree to that and slowly distanced myself. Eventually blocking his number and breaking all contact. Not that it stopped him from getting a new phone number and trying again. Ignoring him had worked for a bit, but somehow, he's back like the cold sore he is.

The meeting wraps in a blur and people file out.

I grab my purse from under the seat and glare at my festival co-chair. "Why would you do that?"

He's co-chairing a town event with me and trying to outbid the most narcissistic group of gentrifiers in the country? What is his goal here?

His wide smile only highlights his beautiful bone structure and makes that damn dimple pop. His brown eyes glimmer, and his thick jet-black hair hangs just long enough to be unruly in a '90s teen heartthrob kind of way.

I clench my fist to stop myself from brushing it away from his eyes.

Mateo chuckles, the low rumble vibrating through me. "There's your pal..."

"Satan's Bikini Waxer," I bite out.

Just the sound of Caleb's smarmy voice over the crowd makes my hackles rise. I need a shower. I feel dirty breathing the same air as him.

"Bikini Waxes? I thought you were vehemently against those. Did you have a change of heart? I would love to see that," Caleb says as he appears at the end of the aisle, wearing an oily smile.

Pulling me close, Mateo holds out a hand. "Mateo Santos-Manolo. We were supposed to meet for drinks this summer when I was representing Merrick Paul on the Park Ave project. It's nice to finally meet you." His tone is terse, belying his words. "However, I'd prefer if you didn't talk about my girlfriend's pubes. Seems a little inappropriate, my dude."

Rankled by what looks like the start of a pissing contest, I try to step away. But he squeezes me closer to his side.

I bite my tongue. *Girlfriend? What the hell?* Sexist Satan here, though, will probably respect the request coming from him, since a woman equates to property in his mind.

I thought we didn't believe in hell. How am I already here?

As if sent by God himself, my brother walks by, giving me an excuse to free myself from Mateo's grasp.

"Joshua, wait up!" I yell, but my brain is shouting *oh-em-gee, kill me now.*

I follow Shua to where Aba—Dad—and Tal are standing close, talking. Aba pulls me into a bear hug. "Motek! Do my ears deceive me, sweetie? Or did Mateo just call you his girlfriend while speaking to... the one you call, em"—he arches his brows—"Ha'Sah'tahn?"

My dad has been in the states for over thirty-five years, but he often slips between languages when he's emotional or confused.

Laughing, I nod and hug him tighter. "I'll walk you all home. I can explain." I link arms with him and peer over my shoulder to where Grant, Jim, Caleb, and Mateo are still talking. "I'll explain what I know, at least."

As we head out into the cool night air, I pull out my phone and send a quick text.

———

NESSA:

I am NOT pretending to be your girlfriend.

BAD IDEA:

Who said anything about pretending?

———

Keep reading Nessa and Mateo's story now
Fighting

before you go:

Thank you so much to every reader for giving me your time. If you enjoyed this book, please consider rating and reviewing it online.

My books would not exist without the support of a group of truly amazing people.

Lyle, loving you is the easiest thing I've ever decided to do. I will continue to choose you every damn day. Love Bug & Wildflower: Thank you for being the reason I've slowly gone crazy and put myself back together. Read these books & my journals at your own risk.

My own "fr-amily" whose traits provided bits of the PS NJ crew: thank you for being my family when blood was not thickest of all. You are my maple syrup – thicker than blood and the sweetest parts of life. No character is one person, but pieces of you are here, thank you for inspiring me. Stephanie & Leighanne, you made me feel at home when I was losing mine. Ashley, Elaine, Lindsay, and Deirdre: you are the best ever. Sara, thank you for introducing me to Altius Farms and suggesting honoring Rami Rank when I reached out about creating a similar spot in my fictional world. May his memory forever be a blessing.

The 2018 Maybies, Bridgette, Jenny Adams, and the Taylor Swift Eras Tour: you provided the forum for entering motherhood and a drunk conversation about writing. This book you are holding today is because of you.

My team of alpha/betas, ADHD Bookish Girls, and the Neurospicy Book Babes: thank you for walking this road with me. Particularly to anyone who slogged through reading the very messy draft I thought I was ready for betas.

The list of authors I want to thank is too long: so if you ever answered a random question from me, this includes you. However, I need to give extra gratitude to Kayla Martin, Valerie Pepper, and The Writing Cave.

Chloe Liese: thank you so much for creating Ren & Frankie. Without you being brave enough to write an Own Voices story, I may have never done the same. I am so inspired by you, and I hope that I did the community of fiercely human women justice with Lily.

Last, but not least: the original Lily Blake, I hope you know how deeply you've been missed. This may not be my first baby, but my first book baby was named for you.

about the author

Jordana is a textbook Millennial: she has a Master's Degree in Social Work she'll be paying off in the nursing home, a history of changing careers, and obsession with 90s nostalgia, and cannot talk before coffee.